Available
LIGHT

Phillip Gardner

AVAILABLE LIGHT

PHILLIP GARDNER

Published by Boson Books
An imprint of Bitingduck Press
Formerly an imprint of C&M Online Media, Inc.

ISBN 978-1-938463-15-0

For information contact
Bitingduck Press, LLC
Montreal • Altadena
notifications@bitingduckpress.com
http://www.bitingduckpress.com

Cover design by Greg Fry
Cover photo, Rick Cary

The words to Emily Dickinson's poem, "The Chariot," were reproduced from the public domain edition of her collected poems, *Project Gutenberg's Poems: Three Series, Complete, by Emily Dickinson* (Release date: May 3, 2004 [EBook #12242]).

Your beliefs will be the light by which you see, but they will not be what you see and they will not be a substitute for seeing — Flannery O'Connor, Mystery and Manners.

For Tressa

Contents

Get Drunk and Screw

M Y WIFE WENDY AND I devoted our weekend mornings to yoga, to breathing and stretching and finding a place where we heard the flow of a soft current and felt the touch of a fresh breeze. From about eleven until one, we watched the war on CNN. We drank from one until I'm not sure when.

Our dream had been to move to Costa Rica one day because it's so beautiful there, so resplendent with life. We couldn't imagine a place more ideal for yoga and meditation. You can still get war news on CNN. The last time we were there we saw a special on Chet Atkins, who had recently died. Just for the record, you get Braves baseball, too.

You don't have to worry about freezing to death in Costa Rica. That had been another attraction for us. It's true that you don't have to worry about freezing in Florida. But in Florida there are the Republicans. Costa Rica had been our dream.

Jimmy Buffet is from Florida. Jimmy was singing on the radio. The song was "I Wish I Had a Pencil Thin Moustache." I'm not a Buffet fan, and now I loathe that particular song. I think that Buffet-the-man is probably a good guy. And he can't be held responsible for all those seventies fraternity boys who took his advice, got drunk and screwed and had frat children who became Buffet fans. Can't fault him for all those Republicans. The point is, Wendy and I weren't parrotheads, so I took notice when she turned up the volume and sang along, only she changed the lyrics.

"I wish I had some silicone implants," she sang, looking down at her crossword puzzle. At first I let it slide, but then every time the chorus repeated itself she sang, "I wish I had some silicone implants." She was still humming the melody after the song faded.

"They're dangerous," I said.

"Every woman with beautiful breasts is dangerous," she said, reaching for the gin.

"I mean the silicone."

"Not anymore," she said. "New studies show they're safe. *I wish I had some silicone implants.* I saw it on CNN."

❦ ❦ ❦

THE NEXT DAY, I called. She didn't answer. I tried again. For three hours.

"How was your day?" I said. She was making drinks.

"Okay, I guess." She looked away with that blank stare I associate with people watching television.

"What did you do this afternoon?"

She spoke as if she'd not heard the question. "Nothing much."

"I called. I left messages. Where were you?"

"Shopping."

"What did you buy?"

"Nothing. I was running errands." She lifted her glass, held it suspended before her like a crystal ball. "What's for dinner?" she whispered to the glass. "I thought we'd go out."

The restaurant, which was painted in soiled parrot colors—murky reds, yellows, blues, and orange—was crowded and deafening. Its walls smelled of hamburger grease. Cheap, shrill speakers piped in Jimmy Buffet non-stop. The hostess seated us beside a long table of twelve softball players still in uniform, each ripe with spent chewing tobacco and sweat.

"Why this place?" I said.

"Because we've never been here," she said from behind her menu. "Let's have a margarita, a giant one."

Before we'd finished our drinks, I ordered. Wendy laid down her menu. "I don't think I'm hungry. I'll have another one of these," she said lifting the goblet.

My food was slow to arrive. I ate quickly, but not quickly enough. "Do you want dessert?" I said. Wendy looked from her empty glass to the men seated at the long table. She smiled but didn't answer. Waiting for our bill suddenly seemed a bad idea. "I'll go up front and pay," I said.

I stuffed the receipt into my pocket and looked back for my wife. She was standing behind one of the seated ball players. His cap was on the floor. She held his head back against her breast and ran her fingers through his hair.

"Look what I found," she called to me. The men were taking it as good fun. "I found Yoga Berra, at least one of them."

"Wendy—"

"'Which one of you is Yoga Berra,' I said, didn't I, guys? Isn't that what I said?" She was holding his cheek against her, combing her fingers through the young guy's black hair. "'Yoga,' I said, 'he's my *favorite*. When you come to the fork in the road, take it. It's not over till the dead woman croaks,' that's what Yoga says. Now they're all Yogas. Aren't you? I'm a hit," she said smiling brightly. "Get it? Tit's a hit."

The men were polite, I have to give them that much. The one bent down then looked up apologetically as he retrieved his cap. I gripped Wendy's hand and started for the door. Behind us a table in back sang Buffet loud and out of tune. Gawking parrotheads looked up from slogging back their beers and gnawing their cheeseburgers. Suddenly she stopped and took my face into her hands. "His last name, Buffet, it has a meaning," she said to me. "Guess what it means, I dare you." Looking away, I again reached for Wendy's hand, but she pulled away, turned and called out to the ball players. "Hey, Yoga, watch this!" She formed the perfect Warrior III and held it flawlessly. Then relaxing from the yoga pose, she lifted her chin and crossed her arms against her chest. Smiling, she majestically bowed then curtsied grandly.

In the car I was too angry to talk. She wouldn't look at me. When she reached for the radio, I pushed her hand away.

"I'm getting some new tits," she said. "Maybe I'll get just one and see how I like it. Or maybe I'll go the whole hog. We'll have to wait and see."

❦ ❦ ❦

THROUGHOUT OUR MARRIED LIFE, fifteen years, I was absolutely faithful. Wendy had been married before, in her early twenties, to her college flame. But that didn't last long. I, meanwhile, traveled, made work my life, earned good money, and slept with lots and lots of women. But not after I fell in love with Wendy. Even now my erotic fantasies converge upon my wife. I can't imagine another woman. I believed that our having both been around the block was a good thing, that we had explored and satisfied the doubts and curiosities that threaten others. Our carnal past might promise a greater degree of conjugal safety, I'd thought.

It was our practice not to go out during the week and rarely so during Charleston's peak tourist season. But when I walked in from work, Wendy stood near the door waiting, purse in hand.

"Let's get out of here," she said.

"What's up?" I said.

"Stir crazy," she said. She gave me a drive-by kiss on the cheek. I smelled the gin.

"Where were you this afternoon? I tried to call."

"Stir crazy," she said. "I had lunch at Magnolias. Alone. Come on, I'll tell you about a conversation I overheard at the table beside me."

The telephone rang. "Don't answer that," she said. "They were a lovely bouquet of lesbians, at the table I mean. They were so, so beautiful, I can't tell you. Hilarious, too. Don't answer. Let's just go, I'm famished."

The old market is the center of Charleston's tourist trade. O'Henry's is one of its tourist bars. That's where we were headed.

The clamoring mass of vacationers spilled from the sidewalks onto Market Street and advanced with the velocity of cooling lava. Upon the eastern horizon, a full moon hung like a white shadow. From the west, yellow beams of dying sunlight penetrated her thin white blouse, exposing the pink flesh of her shoulders.

"Because we won't run in to anybody we know there," Wendy shouted. "We'll pretend we're tourists. Maybe we'll be outrageous." Then she spoke in an exaggerated Brooklyn accent with a little extra nasal thrown in, "Maybeee we'll shoow our aasses," she said.

The only open table was near the restrooms. Wendy ordered a double. She sat with her back to the room but turned to look around as I spoke.

"Who was on the phone?"

"I'm thinking about going into business for myself."

"Is that what the call was about?"

"How should I know? No, the concept just now came to me. Look at those guys."

The three were middle-aged. One wore a vintage Braves baseball cap, plaid shirt, and cheap tennis shoes. Another wore a reversed fishing cap to cover his baldness and a wife-beater tank top. The third clawed his scabby cheek for sand fleas.

"Give me six months, and even old Yoga Berra in the Braves cap would leave this bar with a woman's number," Wendy said. "I'm calling my service Losers to Choosers."

The music was too loud to carry on a conversation, the service slow. By the time we'd finished our second drink, the room was writhing with tourists and fogged with cigarette smoke. Wendy stood. "I'll be right back," she announced. I watched as she vanished into the crowd. She was there. Then she wasn't. I watched and waited. After a time, I signaled for the hostess to hold our table while I looked for my wife. Just as our young server spotted me, I saw Wendy, working her way back. She had a fresh drink and held up a lighted cigarette like a trophy. She glided into her seat.

"Where have you been?" I shouted over the music.

"Talking to the DJ," she said. "He's a hoot." She pulled awkwardly on the cigarette and glanced back over her shoulder. "I made a request. Some Buffet."

"You've taken up smoking?"

"A young guy at the bar offered. I just couldn't resist."

The waitress was at our table now. "Oh, good," Wendy said in a spirited, overly animated voice. "Let's go ahead and order another drink. It's sooo crowded." Averting my look, she tilted her head slightly and appraised the waitress head to foot. "Two," she said, raising two fingers then looking from the buxom young server to me. "My, my," she said. The woman turned.

"Wait!" Wendy called over the roar. "I have to tell you the funniest thing." The young waitress, a coed, rested her elbows on the table, bent her ear, and closed her eyes to listen. Wendy's eyes widened cartoonlike at the serving of abundant cleavage before her, then turned and mouthed the word, "WOW!" She laid her hand over the server's, intertwining their fingers. "You'll want to hear this," she said smiling up at the young woman, who smiled back. Wendy lifted her glass, then drew in a deep breath. "At Magnolias today, I sat beside a table of lesbians; you're not a lesbian, are you?" The waitress was being a sport. "And they were talking about sex, about the benefits of girl sex, and one of them—they were all lovely, not butch at all—and the one who was really gorgeous, I mean drop-dead, said in a voice like this, 'As long as we've got two of these,' Wendy pointed at her breasts, 'we can *always* get one of those!'" She pointed toward my crotch. Wendy and the waitress laughed.

The server reached for our dirty glasses. Wendy held her arm. "If you were a lesbian, you could say so," Wendy said to her. The woman looked to me for help. My wife stroked her arm. "You could tell me. You're so beautiful. You ought to live."

"Yes, ma'am," she said, pulling her hand away. "I'll get your drinks."

"We're all bi," Wendy called after her. "Curious anyway."

The drive home was silent until my wife said she wanted to stop at the Holiday Inn.

"I have to work in the morning," I said.

"I didn't mean to spend the night. I just wanted to pee in the ice machine. I never peed in an ice machine."

"Not tonight," I said.

"Buffet" she said. "Warren Buffet, that is. I'll bet that guy pees wherever he wants."

❦ ❦ ❦

THE NEXT DAY WHEN I walked in from work, I asked Wendy again where she'd been.

"Nowhere," she said. "It's just been me, my crossword puzzles, and the war here, all alone together all day."

"Why won't you answer the phone? Tell me."

"Oh, I did run over to Lowe's." She was taking a towel and a bath cloth from the hall closet.

"What for?"

"They were having a special. I bought a stud finder." She closed the closet door. "To hang the Costa Rica pictures, you know. I have to bathe now." She locked the bathroom door behind her.

❦ ❦ ❦

AT THREE O'CLOCK THE next afternoon, I sat alone in my office staring down at the phone. I wasn't thinking about calling Wendy. I was considering calling my lawyer for advice. Before I dialed, the phone rang. The speaker said she was calling for a Dr. Sloan. She said the man had been trying to reach Wendy.

"You his secretary or his wife?"

"No, I—"

"Who is this Sloan character? What is his connection to Wendy?" The woman wouldn't answer. "Listen lady," I said, "you called me. I'm her husband, and I want to know what's going on."

"All I can tell you, sir, is that it's very important that your wife call the doctor immediately. She has the number."

"Who is this really?" I demanded. Then the line went dead.

I didn't get an answer at home.

There is a kind of sadness that literally hurts your heart. That sadness is not a figure of speech. It's the opposite of a metaphor. The metaphor becomes the thing itself. That was my feeling as I drove home. I didn't know if Wendy would be there, or what shape she might be in if she was—or who might be with her. I only knew that there wasn't enough air to breathe.

Not even enough to stir the flames of anger or jealousy. Only enough to experience the sort of love you only come to know when you feel it leaving you.

Wendy sat on the sofa in front of the muted television, her back to me. She didn't turn when I walked into the living room. She didn't question my coming home in the middle of the afternoon.

"Wendy," I said, "we have to talk."

"The war is going badly," she said. "I don't want to hear any more about it. Badly. I'm thinking that tonight's dinner should be a Chinese buffet, or maybe a Jimmy Buffet buffet, what do you think? Do you know what his name means, Buffet?" She was still facing the screen. "It means like a battle."

I saw the full glass on the coffee table. Our photographs from Costa Rica covered the carpet at her feet. She patted the sofa cushion beside her. "Sit, sit," she said. Her eyes veered to the photos. "I'm planning our next vacation."

I didn't sit. I stood looking down at her. "We have to talk, Wendy." She wouldn't look up at me. I couldn't see her face, but I heard the shift in her voice. "Okay, okay," she said. She selected a snapshot, studied it, and laid it in her lap. "We'll talk." She reached for another photo. "But not now." The air left her voice. "First, we'll do some yoga. Then we'll have a drink and watch the war. Then we'll have a Jimmy Buffet buffet, and then we'll come home and watch the end of the Braves game, and we'll take a warm shower together and then we'll talk, okay?" I knelt in front of her, but she bowed her head denying me her face. Faintly she said, "And then, I promise we'll talk, about anything you want." She turned her face away and touched my hand. "We'll even talk about mammograms if you want. But then you have to promise that we will get drunk and screw."

"Okay," I said, taking her into my arms.

"Say it," she said. "Promise."

"I promise," I whispered into her ear.

"Okay," she said. "Okay."

Brother

WHEN I WAS NINE years old, my mother woke me and Jim in the middle of the night. Jim was sixteen. Our tiny room was winter dark and hard cold. Her voice filled it up. "Help me get him out of the wagon," she said.

Outside, our mule blew vanishing white puffs. At the rear of the wagon, my father, a tall, thin man, lay on his back upon the gray wooden planks, the span of his arms open as if to welcome us. Mama, Jim and I stood in the silence of the black winter night, the aching cold from the frozen clay biting through my bare feet and cuffing my ankles. Mama turned, gathered the quilt to her throat and walked to the porch. "At least the mule knows his way home," she said. Jim hoisted father's shoulders and I clasped his muddy brogans. "Leave him by the bed, on the floor," Mama said. "That's what he gets."

We didn't know he wasn't drunk, that instead he'd suffered a stroke, or that my mute father would spend the next three years staring at the ceiling, shrinking, dying.

❦❦❦

As I DRESSED FOR his funeral, the Japanese assaulted Pearl Harbor. At twelve years old, I was growing too fast for the clothes Mama made me, not fast enough for what Jim had outgrown. My shoes didn't fit. While machine gun blasts of Zeros, the Japanese fighter planes, tore through the flesh of sailors and civilians and their bombs penetrated the steel decks of American war ships, Mama pinned up my sleeves, the shirt, too, a thread-bare hand-me-down from Jim.

I remember nothing of the church service or of the tears I may have cried, or should have if I didn't. At the graveside, we all sang "Will the Circle Be Unbroken?" Afterwards, Jim stood apart from everyone, his back to us. Staring out across the barren cotton fields, he smoked alone. Mama's eyes were fixed on me, her face lean, austere. Neighbors, kin, and Mrs. Wills clustered around her speaking in somber, muted whispers, but I could see that she'd had a bate of well-intended store-bought grief instruction. She called to Jim, then to me. Mr. Wills offered to drive us from the cemetery. She refused. In silence, we walked the two miles home, Jim, Mama, and me. Both my heels flared with blisters.

The house was brittle cold and I fetched firewood. Inside, Jim hunched over the radio. Ernest Tubb was his favorite singer, "Walking the Floor Over You" his favorite song. But this December seventh was a day without music.

Jim was soon drafted and fought in the Pacific where the Japanese burrowed in caves and bunkers. My brother carried a flamethrower.

Two years after Jim left, the war came to us. This was early March 1943. That Saturday morning, Mama sent me to inspect the progress of Mr. Wills' tobacco beds. Mr. Wills owned the farm we sharecropped. He sometimes drank. A bad tobacco crop meant debt for Wills. It meant the end of us. The early morning sky was crimson, the sun a giant red smear. Weeks earlier, I'd burned a strip of land to purify the ground and make ash to enrich the seed bed soil. Now I carefully folded back the thin white linen that protected the tender plants from frost.

I looked up. From the river bottom echoed a low consumptive rumble. The ground beneath me trembled. Against the fiery sky a convoy of earthmovers slowly ascended from the dark horizon like a caravan of prehistoric beasts. For more than an hour I stood upon the quivering earth and watched their slow progress.

Over the weeks and months that followed, an ominous grey cloud appeared above the three thousand acres that would become Seymour Johnson Air Base. We paused from plowing, planting, and hoeing, looked up at the gathering storm of dust and smoke, sopped our sweaty brow, and then turned back to our labor. Before we finished topping and suckering in July, the facility was operational.

In most ways, the air base was a world apart from ours, living as we did within the confines of the farmland we did not own. We had a cow, pigs, and chickens. Mama made everything we wore except our shoes. Without money for extras, we had little reason to go into Goldsboro, where we'd be reminded of our conditions and subject to want, and where the recent arrivals, faceless young men in crisp blue uniforms, paraded about the hotel, honkytonks and movie theater. We rarely saw them. But their presence bore down upon us. Their flight maneuvers turned our days into lightning, our nights into thunder. We lived beneath a roaring hive of giant piston-pounding steel bees. For a time the cow stopped giving milk and the hens quit laying as they should. We were robbed of good sleep, our dreams splintered. Our tempers became tender to the touch, our words in that house bundles of kindling. It seemed that a huge bite had been taken from the world we knew and in its place there festered a black asphalt scab.

✤ ✤ ✤

LATE THE NEXT WINTER, the P-47 Thunderbolts arrived and with them a different kind of airman, replacement pilots in training, young, arrogant city boys with last names you couldn't pronounce and dispositions that attracted blowflies.

Hoeing cotton that spring, we'd hear them come shrieking toward us just above the tree line. "Don't you look up," Mama said, pressing the blade of her hoe deep into the black soil, holding it there. "Don't you give them the satisfaction." But sometimes I did look. They'd slash in so low you could see the eight .50-caliber machine guns, four on each wing. If the sun was right, you'd catch a glimpse of their ravenous smiling faces when they spotted the stooped white sharecroppers and black field hands. They were practicing strafing the enemy. We were their practice enemy.

The following winter, Jim's letters stopped arriving.

There was little work for Mr. Wills, and in January the side meat ran out. Mama and I ate sweet potatoes and dried butterbeans. Bill Patterson, a drinking buddy of Wills, ran a crossroads country store before the war. But with the base came a fluster of traffic, enough for him to bury a fuel tank. He needed a boy to pump gas, and we needed the five dollars a week. Bill gave me a job. I manned the pumps, cleaned windshields, and quickly worked my way up to oil changes. I washed the cars of the newly moneyed town merchants.

Gasoline was rationed of course and at that time reduced even more. All pleasure driving was outlawed, and the speed limit was set at 35. But laws and limits meant nothing to the Thunderbolt cadets. Or to Bill. Inside the station, he sold bootleg whiskey. His place was the nearest one to the back gate of the base, and carloads of airmen headed to or from Morehead City or Wrightsville Beach stopped for gas and liquor and to hopefully catch a glimpse of Jen.

✤ ✤ ✤

BILL HAD A WIFE and then he didn't. Then he had Jen, his new wife, who was half his age, seventeen, only three years older than me. Bill's new wife was one way when Bill was around and another way when he wasn't. She rarely spoke in Bill's presence, assuming a stately school teacher manner, chin up, shoulders back, hands clasped before her as if she were awaiting the class's complete attention. Jen was reliable and responsible. She kept the books balanced and the coffee fresh and could read Bill's moods. She baked him pies and knew the game of baseball. She provided Bill a timely formal kiss when a kiss was in order.

But when Bill was away she was more of a girl. While we loaded the drink boxes with Coca-Colas, Pepsis, and Orange Crush, she described to me the latest gossip surrounding Ava Gardner, who had grown up only twenty miles from us and whose folks still lived near Brogden. In wide-eyed excitement, Jen whispered the lurid details of Miss Gardner's most recent and tempestuous sins. When I feigned disbelief, she'd raise one finger as a place holder, then dash off to their apartment at the back of the station. Her limbs were long, her hips still narrow. In motion, other girls of similar shape and design were gangly and clumsy, but Jen's movements were harmonious and graceful, her arms and wrists and fingers gliding as if under water. She'd return smiling victoriously and brandishing a movie magazine, from which she recited Ava's scandals in low, breathy whispers of collusion. I watched her lips form the words. She had the face of a girl, narrow and long. But the flush lips of a woman, large and plump, always a little swollen. Thick brown hair danced upon her animated shoulders, and her index finger moved in and out of the ringlet she wound round it as she read to me. When she looked up from her magazine, her titillated eyes were as black and soft as a doe's.

Most evenings Bill drove me home after closing time, which varied depending upon pay days and liquor traffic. But on Thursday nights, Bill made midnight trips to his bootlegger, a man named Lancaster who lived near Saulston and made whiskey in one of his tobacco barns. I'd lie awake on a cot in the dark storage room. The station and the apartment had running water, and I'd listen to Jen bathing on the other side of the cinderblock wall that separated us. Eyes closed, I listened. When Bill returned, I'd help unload the whiskey.

❧❧❧

AT HOME, I'D BEGUN sleeping in Jim's bed. I don't know why.

Mama woke me. "Bill's come for you," she said.

"But it's Sunday," I said.

"There's a warm biscuit on the stove."

My room was cold and I dressed quickly. From the kitchen window, I saw Bill's black Ford, its chugging exhaust puffing smoke signals into the frigid morning air. Mama stood at the sink, her apron knotted in her hands, eyeing me as I ate the biscuit. "You be partic'lar," Mama said. "You best be partic'lar."

Bill didn't look at me, didn't speak, just shifted into gear. As we lurched forward, I heard a clanging and turned to see a shovel in the back foot.

I tried to read him. His body was thick, his sinuous arms muscled, his fingers thick and blunt as pork sausages. He hadn't shaved and flecks of white beard shone in the bright morning sunlight. Dark half-moons sagged below his severe blue eyes as we jolted over the rutted dirt road. He had installed heavy truck springs at the rear of his car on account of the weight of the whiskey he hauled and the sharp eye of the Wayne County law. When his trunk was empty, the car rode with the jarring discomfort of an old tractor. "Do something about that shovel," Bill said. "Make it shut up." When we turned onto the smooth pavement of New Hope Road toward the Beston Stretch, I spoke.

"Where we goin'?"

"To the station. Then you and Jen are going to the movies," he said.

He backed the Ford to the side door that connected the station and their apartment. "You haul it out," he said. "I'll watch the road." He handed me the key to the storeroom. As I passed the open door to their apartment, I saw Jen sitting at the small kitchen table wearing only a loose housecoat. She was drinking coffee. Her hair was up in a towel.

The gallon jugs of whiskey were packed inside motor oil boxes. I stacked the boxes on the two-wheel dolly and rolled them back to Bill, who filled the boot of the Ford. "One more load will do it," he said, his anxious eyes fixed upon the road that led into town. "I got help on the other end. You stay here with Jen. If you see the law, lock the doors and y'all climb down into the changing bay," he said. "Stay there until I get back." I watched as he drove away.

Jen called to me from the apartment. "You want a cup of coffee, David? I made a whole pot."

From the doorway I saw her standing with her back to me, her long fingers kneading the towel that cocooned her hair. I'd never seen her sleek, bare shoulders. In one long smooth motion she pulled the towel away, allowing the dark wet hair to cascade to her shoulders. She turned and smiled. "Want some?" she said, indicating the pot on the stove.

Looking away, I said, "I'd better get up front."

"If the law comes, they'll come from town, silly, right past this window." She smiled. "Sit. I'll tell you the latest Ava news. You know she's only three years older than me? Imagine."

"What's happening?" I said.

"She's divorcing Mickey Rooney."

"I mean here."

She poured. Her naked legs were too long for the housecoat, her feet bare, her toenails bright red. "I don't know what's happening," she said over her shoulder. "I only know what I don't know."

"That's funny," I said. She handed me the steaming cup.

"That's Ava. She's something, ain't she? That's what she said to the magazine writer about her and Mickey. Or that's what the writer wrote that she said." We sat at the small table.

"So, what don't you know?" Above the pleasant aroma of coffee I smelled the scent of Jen's shampoo.

"I don't know that the phone rang about five this morning. And I don't know that the man on the other end said Bill's bootlegger shot an airman during a poker game last night. I don't know that when that airman don't show up today that the law might come around. And if they do, I don't even know what I don't know." She smiled as she brought the cup to her lips and winked at me.

It was almost noon when Bill returned for the second load. In a matter of minutes, the Ford's trunk was again packed full. Jen sat up front, I in the backseat. Bill reached for his key, paused, then looked up into his mirror at me. "Go back inside and bring me a pair of coveralls," he said. "And my boots." On the way into Goldsboro, I held the shovel handle on my lap.

Bill parked on Center Street in front of the Paramount Theater. I checked the show times. "Don't start until two," I said at Bill's window. He opened his wallet and handed some folding money to Jen. "Get yourselves some hamburgers. Take a walk. See the picture." He turned to me. "When the show's over, you come to the lobby. If I ain't parked where you can see me, y'all sit through the picture again, understand?" He turned back to Jen. He handed her more money. "If I ain't here by then, call a taxi." He said to me, "Open up the station. Everybody knows we open on Sunday night for the airmen returning to base. Tonight's no different. But if the law shows up, you don't know where I am. They want to look for liquor? You let 'em 'cause there ain't none. I'll call you." He looked at Jen. "You be safe." He looked at me. "Keep her out of this."

Jen waited at the candy counter while the usher drew fountain Coca-Colas. A few people still in their church clothes dawdled about the lobby waiting for the show to begin. Jen handed me a foamy cup and tucked the box of popcorn under her slender arm.

"What do we say if somebody sees us together?" I said.

"What are you talking about?" she said. I felt my face redden. She stepped closer and spoke in a whisper. "We can sit in the back of the balcony with the colored people if you want. Might be just the two of us." She smiled. "Come on, you," she said, taking my arm. The theater was dark and quiet. We sat close to the screen and shared popcorn. Our shoulders sometimes touched. I closed my eyes. The scent of shampoo was in the air. My hands felt foreign to me.

The entertainment began with newsreel footage from Point Cruz, where the Japanese had dug in, and we watched as our boys heaved hand grenades to loosen up the embedded enemy. Streams of flaming petroleum incinerated their bunkers. Popeye and Mickey Mouse cartoons came next, followed by coming attractions, then the feature, *So Proudly We Hail!* When the picture was done and its credits began to roll, I stood in the lobby. Bill's black Ford wasn't outside.

During the repeat of the newsreels, I studied the faces of the soldiers. The face of the man with the flamethrower was hidden from view.

❦❦❦

"It got dark," Jen said when we stepped outside. The usher had called a taxi. I'd never been inside a taxi. We sat together in the dark backseat. My hands felt foreign to me.

"I couldn't do what those women did," she said, speaking of the movie. "I could never be a nurse. The sight of blood makes me woozy."

"But you could be an actress and play one in a movie." I could say that only because the taxi was dark. "Like Ava."

She turned to face me, opened her arms and looked down at her slight bosom. "Ava?" she said. "Maybe Olive Oyl."

I unlocked the station, shut on the solitary light outside the door and hit the power switch for the gas pumps, then changed into my soiled work clothes. From seven until ten I pumped gas. Jen made change. The cars carried four or five airmen, and most often one opened his door and started inside. "He ain't here," I said. "Won't be back before closing." The cars drove away. I sat on the stoop beneath the hooded light, my mind adrift, and studied my shadow as I smoked. Fighter planes came in so low a hint of spent petroleum wafted upon the crisp breeze. Then all was quiet. The cold was like a heavy weight settling in for the night. After a time, I went inside. Jen sat reading a magazine at a small table where old men sometimes played checkers and young men poker.

"You got some paper, a pencil?" I said. "I want to write a letter. To my brother."

She twisted her hair around her finger and slowly turned a page of the magazine. "Where is he?" she said into the magazine.

"I don't know."

"What are you going to tell him about?"

"I don't know."

Not looking up from her reading, she raised her arm and pointed. "There's stationery in the nightstand beside the bed. In the drawer."

The bedcovers were in a heap. There, splayed upon the white sheet, were Jen's black silk panties. My fingers felt foreign to me. Jen called.

"David? David. There's a man here."

The man stood framed by the open doorway, head down, swaying slightly from side to side. The outside light above and behind cast his face in black shadow. He was a slight man, not much bigger than me.

"You want gas?" I said.

"Walkin'," he said. He looked up at me. "Youse open for business, right?"

"He ain't here," I said. "Won't be back till after closing."

The man sauntered unsteadily into the room. He looked at Jen as if she'd suddenly materialized before him. "Jeeze, kid," he said. "She your girlfriend?"

"I said he ain't here."

"Ain't that a shame." He looked at Jen. Smiled.

"Ain't no liquor here neither," I said.

"You're wrong about that, kiddo." He reached inside his coat pocket. Brought out a small silver-plated revolver. "Let's sit down. I'm tired and thirsty." He pointed the gun at me and spoke to Jen. "That means you, doll." As she rounded the counter and crossed to the small table, he performed a mocking little shuffle, his wolfish eyes bright with whiskey. "Damn. Look at that mouth, kid. You can't buy lips like that in Jersey." Jen wouldn't look at the man. He affected a southern drawl. "Now don't y'all fret. I don't mean no harm. I'm just in need of a little hospitality, that's all. We're all friends here." He returned to his own voice. "You," he said to me, "bring the lady and me a bottle of that bootleg booze, the good stuff."

"Ain't got none, I told you."

A look of contemptuous surprise flashed across his face. "No booze? Well, well, well. Let me just see what we can do about that." He gently rested the pistol on the table, lifted a pint bottle from inside his jacket then ceremoniously offered it to Jen. "Help yourself daaalin'." Jen wouldn't look at him. "Name's Rico," he said offering his hand. Jen didn't take it. I eyed the pistol on the table. "And you and me, we're gonna be friends." He laid his hand over Jen's and spoke in a lyrical childlike voice: "Now. I. Said. Have. A. Drink. Of. That. Whiskey."

Jen unscrewed the cap and tilted the bottle up to her lips. When he reached to force the bottle higher, I went for the gun. His right elbow harpooned my left eye. Jen screamed. I floated upon the cold cement floor feeling blood swell my cheek. When my vision cleared I saw the pistol only inches from my face. "Sit," he said. He pushed the chair out with his foot. "That's a good boy."

He pointed at the bottle. Jen took a pull, her face contorting then retching. Looking over at me, he reached and drank in three short jerky hits. He turned the pistol on me. "This one," he said to Jen, "he's a regular hero, ain't he? Yes, I do believe he is. Your little bumpkin in shining armor, he deserves something special, don't you think, sugar lips?" He looked at me and smiled, his yellow teeth spanning the width of his face. He pressed his hand to my shoulder. "Don't we all, brother, don't we all. History of war? Man goes off to fight, leaves his girl to cheat. The bitch. He comes home a regular hero. Comes back to get some of that candy he's been missing, been fightin' for. Ain't that right, sugar? Now this regular hero, the one here with the swollen up eye, he deserves something special. And what would that be?" He drank, this time slow and long. With mechanical deliberateness, he set the bottle before him and brought down his eyes upon Jen. "Unbutton that blouse for your hero lover."

Jen looked at me. Disbelief begat terror begat pleading.

"Now would be good," he said. The man sat at attention, pressing his rigid back against the wooden chair and slowly folded his arms across his chest, the pistol leveled at my eye. He looked from Jen to me, then back at Jen. "Wellll?" He drew in a deep labored breath, nodded in apparent disbelief, and slowly released the breath with a deep sigh. Then he slammed the pistol butt against my ear.

For a few seconds, I was out. He fisted my collar. "You're missing it, kid," he said, heaving me up into my chair. I sat head down, both palms on the table to steady myself, feeling that I might fall left or right. "Yummy, yummy," he said.

"David?" Jen said. I looked up at her. She had loosened the first button. Her fingers rested on the second one. "Look at me David, like he ain't here. If you don't, I'll cry. Don't make me cry, David."

The smiling man drank as Jen opened her blouse. In a limp-wristed cranking motion he rotated the gun. "Now, get rid of that little white bra, sweetheart." Again, he laid his free hand on my shoulder. "What's hidden under those little white ice cream cones? You've never seen this before, have you, kiddo? But you want to, don't you? You do. I know you do. Me, too. I want to. You and me boy, we're gonna see what candy's on this stick."

Jen spoke in a whisper as the bra fell away. "I'm looking at you, David, only at you. I ain't giving him the satisfaction. You are all I see."

"Ahhh," the man said. That's so sweet." He tilted his head to one side. Conducted his extended inspection. "Well, now. That's more like it, ain't it squirt? If them puppies are for sale, I'll take the ones with the brown nose." He turned to me. "Damn, hero. I always said everything over a mouthful is wasted. But one of them little things could put your eye out, don't you think?"

My fist caught him square in the mouth, and he fell straight back in his chair. He lay on his back, still in the chair. But he didn't let go the revolver. He pulled back its hammer and slowly rose to his feet. "You know the last words of a dead hero?" He ran the back of his hand over his bleeding lip and pressed his face close to mine. "I'll tell you what he says!" He held the gun in his right hand, punched my swollen eye with his left fist. I fell back but I did not fall. "I'll tell you what he says!" I went down with the second punch. My face was on fire. My arms and legs were not my own. "Nothin'. That's what the dead hero says."

The sound of a car horn drifted in from the gas pumps. Then blew a second time. A blurred ghostly image of the man backed toward the door. "Don't you move," he said, waving the pistol at me. "Don't you fuckin' move. I ain't done with you." He shouted out the door, signaling to the driver to shove off. "Get outta here, you bum!" Somewhere a telephone rang. And rang again. Outside someone shouted a curse at the man. When the man glanced back at the driver, Jen made for the phone. The man pointed the gun at her, "You!" he shouted then looked outside, then back at Jen. "You bastard!" she screamed. She lifted the phone. The man jammed the pistol into his pocket and ran out into the night.

❦❦❦

I SAT ON THE stoop smoking. Sounds that entered my left ear seemed to come from under water. My eye was nearly swollen shut, but the bleeding from my mouth and nose had stopped. From way off, I saw headlights. Bill skidded into the station lot, flung open his door and ran toward me. He didn't speak as he rushed past calling to her. Jen answered from their apartment. In less than a minute, he was back, something heavy and L-shaped in the brown paper bag he held.

"Here," he said, handing me the keys to the Ford. I was too young for a license, but I'd been driving Mr. Wills' truck for two years. When I opened the driver's side door, I saw the shovel, its face and handle stained with red river clay, the soiled coveralls and the muddy boots in the back. "Jen said he was on foot," Bill said.

"That's right," I said.

"You know where we're headed, don't you?" Bill said.

"Yes," I said. The man had only one place to go, the base, and there was only one road to get him there. Bill lit a cigarette. I watched the road but could feel his eyes moving over my battered face.

"You pull up beside him, slow, like you're offering him a ride. You understand? Till then, keep your speed at 35. Look out for the law."

The road was dark. The night cold. The shovel in the back trembled like a divining rod. "You're gonna kill him, ain't you, Bill?"

"Yes. Yes, I most certainly am."

"Good," I said.

I was not angry, and I was not afraid. Instead I felt a great emptiness was about to be filled, that somehow what was to happen had been waiting for me all of my short life. For three years I'd stood alone at my father's bedside daring myself not to look away from his shrinking, fading figure, arms like the limbs of a sapling, fingers as thin as chicken's feet, eyes receding a little slower than the sockets that held them; I alone there looking upon him, grieving, my heart spilling over with repentance and terror, thinking of the sweating and crying at brush revivals, the wailing in foreign tongues, then seeing before me as I stood at his bedside his sheets erupt into the flames of Hell, aching most for what I did not possess, a voice to pray to God to wash away my father's sins and my own, certain only that God looked down upon me there, alone at my father's side, God Above waiting, waiting as I stood watching my father die. And all that was given to me, all that I had to take away with me was the hot blood of my father's pride, hard fierce pride. And now pride rushed in to fill that empty place inside of me.

"You need to say what you're going to do when this is over, David. When you get back to your mama's. I've got to know. And what you tell me is what you've got to do. You understand?" Bill looked at me. He wasn't talking to a boy now.

"I'm writin' a letter."

"I mean as soon as you get home."

"I'm writin' a letter to my brother."

"Where is he now?"

"I don't know."

"Are you going to tell him about everything?"

"Yes."

In the mirror, a speeding car closed in on us. "That the law?" I said. Bill didn't answer. Seconds later, painfully bright, predatory headlights filled the inside of the Ford as the car lurched near our bumper then fell back as if readying to strike again. "Steady," Bill said. "If they ain't too drunk they'll pass us." The driver laid heavy on his horn, producing a long-sustained blast. In the mirror I saw the distorted face of a shouting passenger leaning outside his window. Then the bright lights shifted to the other lane. A chorus of slurred curses roared past. As the car rounded the curve ahead it swung fully into the left lane and disappeared.

"We're close now," Bill said.

We crossed Neuse River and began to climb. When we topped the hill, I saw the headlights of the speeding car in the distance. In the spread of those headlights stood the silhouette of a man on the side of the road holding out his thumb. The red brake lights of the car flickered, then lit up. The car slid to a stop. The man leaned into the window of the passenger's side.

"Slow down," Bill said. "They ain't giving him a ride. They ain't got room. They're all drunk. They're just fuckin' with him. Slow way down. They're gonna leave him for us." Bill pulled the long-barreled pistol from the brown bag. "Go on, you bastards," he murmured. "Git." He looked over at me. "When I crank down the window, you look away. Understand? Don't look."

Ahead, the car's rear door swung open. "No," Bill whispered. The man climbed into the back seat.

"What do we do?" I said.

"Son of a bitch," Bill said. The car ahead threw gravel and burned rubber as it fishtailed onto the highway. "Damn it to hell," he said, slowly squeezing and releasing the handle of the pistol. I thought, We could kill 'em all, Bill. Soak the car with gasoline and send them all to hell. Bill set the gun on the seat beside him. "Ain't nothing to do. Pull over," he said. "I'll drive."

❦ ❦ ❦

Our tenant house was dark. Bill shut out the headlights but left the engine idling.

"What are you going to tell your mama about that eye?" He touched his finger to my chin. I tilted away as he examined my face.

"Won't be the first time," I said.

He offered me a cigarette and I took it. "I 'preciate what you done for Jen." He didn't know and I never told him. "What's he like, your brother?"

"I don't know."

"What you done for Jen—"

"I'll take that shovel, your boots, and them coveralls," I said. "They'll be under Wills' packhouse when you want them, when the law's done."

Bill pressed out his cigarette butt in the ashtray. He looked away, out into no man's land. Slowly, he ran his thick fingers through his hair then reached for the pack in his shirt pocket. He bowed his head against the window and spoke to the out yonder. "Don't even know his name."

"Jim."

"Where you going to mail it, that letter?"

"I ain't. I don't know where he is. I'll hold on to it till he gets home."

"Good." Bill turned and looked at me. "Maybe that will bring him good luck, give him a good reason to get back in one piece."

"Maybe."

Bill retrieved a bottle from under the front seat. He took a pull and offered it to me. I declined.

"If I ever see that guy again," I said, "I'll know him. We'll finish this."

"You won't see him again. He won't be back. What's done is done. Ain't no satisfaction comes for some things, David." He offered another cigarette. I declined. A light appeared in the kitchen. "What are you going to tell your brother?"

"That I love him and miss him."

"He'll need to hear that," Bill said.

"No more than I'll need to say it," I said.

What We Talk About When We Talk About Dean Martin

MY BOYFRIEND HAS THIS woozy Dean Martin voice that really works on me. I think about it on purpose sometimes when I'm on the road. It's like my own version of aerobics music as I practice my Kegels. I'm a cosmetics rep and in the car a lot. Nick, that's my guy, is crazy about me. He'll do special requests.

So it's a Friday, and it's been four days and Nick's goodnight phone conversations have made the hours in the car so intense that by the time I reach the city limits I'm squirming in my seat. Out of nowhere I'm envisioning those machines that check your blood pressure at CVS Drugs.

Which reminds me that I have to make a purchase.

I've forgotten that Marshall Blackmon, who had this giant crush on me in high school, works at the drug store, and I'm not hearing much of what he says about whether or not he'll be going to our ten-year class reunion, when we both look down at the items he's ringing up: a stack of two-for-one tampons.

"Got any film for developing?" he says, giving me that goofy smile I remember from his butt-trance days in school. I say no and he stacks everything up and hands the bag to me, holding it with only his thumb and pointer. As I'm unlocking the car, I remember the photos I once left for processing, the ones Nick and I took that New Year's Eve. Yeah, those.

By the time I negotiate the cell phone appendages and the vibrating rap speakers that double as automobiles and make it out of the lot, Dino's voice has drifted away a little.

Then I turn into the drive. I see Nick sitting on the front steps waiting for me. Tuxedo jacket and pants, no shirt, no shoes, no problem. Parts of me suddenly pump up the volume.

I offer my backside to him as I step out of the car. Then in slow motion, I turn, drop the keys into my new Coach purse, recline against the warm Mustang, toss my long brown hair, and slowly finger down my sunglasses, giving my guy an eyeful, an appetizer. I put a little deliberate extra into it coming up the sidewalk.

I can tell by his smile, even before I see the highball glass in his hand, that he's gotten a Friday night head start on me. Turns out he's already done several laps. I bend, giving him a little kiss, but one full of promise. The taste of bourbon on his mouth reminds all of me that we're home.

Nick leans back on the step and looks away. His manner suddenly takes a turn. "I couldn't take it anymore," he says, lowering his head like he's got Oprah-quality bad news. "I had to put some hope in the woman's life." He lifts his hand and points like a sage, and I follow his eyes to the Winnie the Pooh flag hanging outside my neighbor, Sue Anne's, front door. The flag hasn't come down—not once—since I bought the house. With a black marker and the less than steady hand of my Nick, Winnie has acquired an impressive penis, as firm and curved as a rhino's horn sporting a chef's hat.

"Somebody had to do it," Nick says. "The woman's in need." He takes my hand, kisses it, then rises ceremoniously to open the door for me. Despite the build-up, I think about having to deal with Sue Anne, and the urgent desire to do my guy is gone. The chorus to "Everybody Loves Somebody Sometime" couldn't bring it back.

Inside, Nick reaches across the bar for the drink he's made for me.

"It may be a little flat," he says, kissing me again, then handing me the glass. "You're later than I hoped you'd be."

"You've got to get that flag down before Sue Anne sees it," I say. Sue Anne is a nice person if you go down deep, really deep. She recycles. She's into bird watching. When she bikes, which is about as close as she gets to a sexual experience, she wears a helmet and mouth piece. She teaches high school Civics. But most of the time she's just so awful.

"I don't know why I did it," Nick says. "I just snapped."

"Get it down. Now, please."

"For you, darling," he says, lifting his highball glass and opening up his bare, brown chest to me, "anything."

He knocks off his drink and starts for the door, then turns and sort of skates backward, doing Dean Martin at perfect pitch: "In Arizona—Mona Lisa—feeds a truffle—to a parrot—that imitates—a troubadour—she laid."

"What?" I say, smiling.

"I made it up. For you. There'd be more, but when I turned and saw Weenie-with-no-wiener, well, like I said, I just snapped." He stops at the door. "I ran you a hot bath," he says. That's my Nicky, I'm thinking. "If you hear a crash, don't worry. It's only me, not the ladder," he says.

I step into warm bubbles and bath beads, and when I lie back and feel the lightness of my body, the blood rushes to the playground areas. I close my eyes and take the first sip of my gin and tonic. Twist of lime. It's Friday. I think of Dean Martin.

I hear the door close and Nick making his way up the hall, singing: "On the mantle—in a photo—in a prom dress—in Pamplona—she holds the hand of blond-haired smiling—Denny Laine." I turn when he opens the bathroom door. He is naked, except for the Pooh flag, which he wears like a Superman cape. "In Sarasota—ten years later—" he stepped into the tub, still wearing the Caped Crusader gear, "—she's getting loaded—with her girlfriends—when she sees his face—but simply can't recall his name." Nick leaned forward, cupped my hips, pulled me to him and kissed me. Yeah, like that.

The doorbell rings. "Ignore her," Nick says, kissing me again. I feel that electric circuit kick in, the one that runs from up here to down there. Meanwhile Sue Anne is pounding at the door.

"I'll get it," Nick says. Standing, his erection rivals Pooh's, and now I'm losing patience. I rise and snatch my robe.

"Put that thing away," I say, pulling on the wrap. The pounding has taken on this John Philip Sousa effect: Oomph...Oomph...Oomph... Oomph. I glance back at Nick, who is proudly displaying the empire.

"Zzall right?" he asks in a squeaky voice and looking down at our buddy. "Zzall *right*," he answers like a ventriloquist. As the pounding up front drones on, he smiles at me, lifts the rest of his body to military atten-tion, salutes, tosses back the soaking Pooh flag, and then glides down into the water. Nick owns a string of tanning salons. He carries gold-embossed business cards that say, "I don't work."

When I open the door, Sue Anne looks up at me through thick gray glasses framed by a dirty blond retro bowl cut. I'm thinking she's added some number 30 red dye to her eye drops and applied a fingernail file to her flared nostrils just to add a little dramatic effect. Behind her, the afternoon shadows are like a heavy hand pressing her toward me.

"That man stole it," says Sue Anne, pointing toward her house, not taking her suffering eyes from me.

"I don't know what you're talking about, Sue Anne." Me, innocently.

"I've come for my Pooh," she says with the indignation of a jilted divorcee. "I'm not leaving without my *Pooh.*" I think I smell Scotch.

I lift my hands to my hips in a kind of cop pose and give her a look. My hair is dripping and I'm starting to puddle. Behind me I hear Nick begin the chorus of "Mack the Knife."

Sue Anne oh-so-slowly turns and points like the Grim Reaper she is. "He left your ladder leaning against my house."

"I'll replace the flag, Sue Anne," I say.

She thrusts her bubbled lower lip up at me and waddles in place. "To-mor-row," I say slowly, giving every syllable a beat.

Sue Anne tilts in close, rolls her head back then over onto her shoulder, and does this lizard thing where one eye becomes a slit while the other becomes a bowling ball. "I'm not leaving without my Poooooh," she snarls.

Behind me, Nick calls from the bath. "I'll name the title, you name the artist, okay? Here goes. 'Love is a Long and Slender Thing.' What's your answer?"

Sue Anne folds her arms and snorts like an angry bull.

"In that case," I say, stepping to the side, "please come in. Let's all have a drink."

"I don't drink." She does that bobble head thing.

I turn and leave her standing there.

"Scotch," she shouts to my back as I enter the kitchen. "Single malt."

As I pour her a double, Nick splashes and sings. "You gotta know the answer to this one," he calls. "Who sang 'I Left My Hard in San Francisco'?"

"How do you put up with that?" Her tone of voice is like a guilty verdict.

I don't begin my sentence with the word Bitch, but the thought does cross my mind.

"Pretty well," I say. "Every night when I'm at home." Sue Anne just gives me the fish eye again and drains her drink. She doesn't even ask. She just shoves the glass toward me for a refill, then turns and glares at the hallway door, as if she holds the power to vaporize Nick when he enters the room. I pour myself another gin-tonic, squeeze a wedge of lime, and take a long sip just to make her wait, just to send the message that she's in my house, not some sophomore classroom, just to give her a moment to wipe that sanctimonious schoolteacher look off her face.

She's thirsty. It doesn't take long for her to get the message.

"Thanks," she says, reaching for her fresh Scotch. "If he's hiding, you can tell him I'm not leaving till he comes out, not without my Pooh. You can call the cops if you want." She tilts up her glass and closes her eyes. "I'll make a scene. That, I promise you."

The chorus to Dean Martin's "Promise Her Anything" echoes down the hall.

Nick isn't a mean guy. Strays come up to him from nowhere, and small children take his hand at the mall. But he's not the kind of guy you want to push around. Last summer on our anniversary—we celebrate the night we met five years ago—we were at Myrtle Beach, and a drunk, a big burly guy, the type with thick black fur covering his back, made an uncouth remark about the size of my breasts to the dude beside him. I wasn't supposed to hear. Yeah, right.

When Mr. Burley passed out on his beach chair, Nick went up to our hotel room and returned with a couple of those Crest Strips, you know, those peroxide things for bleaching your teeth white? Nick pasted them on the guy's eyebrows. That night we went dancing in the hotel bar, a club filled with black lights. Mr. Guess Who is there. You should'a seen the guy. Spook-E. People were pointing and calling him Headlights. Before we left, Nick asked the guy to bow his head so that he could find his car keys.

I'm not looking forward to what's going to happen next, but I don't have long to wait. I'm studying my drink when I hear this in-suck of air from across the table. Sue Anne has the eyes of a Chihuahua.

Nick stands, framed by the doorway. Wet black hair. Broad shoulders. Chiseled, brown chest. That sharp arrow of hair pointing down—below the towel. Nick holds the Pooh flag like a matador's cape, hands at his hip. He assumes position, bending forward slightly, then shakes the Pooh cape at Sue Anne a couple of times, rousing her to charge.

"Give me it," Sue Anne says, slurring her words. She teeters a little when she tries to stand up, and Nick glides, pirouetting with the cape at his side. My Nick has some very graceful moves. Refusing the bait, Sue Anne just sits, and then holds out her limp hand for the Pooh. Nick inches in, cautiously extends his sculptured leg like a dancer and slaps the floor a couple of times with his right foot. Deadpan Sue Anne knocks off the rest of her single malt, then turns away from Nick and speaks to me.

"I know it was him that put that porno movie in my mailbox. Inside the plastic case that said *Bird Watcher's Guide to South Carolina*? I've never looked at it, I don't even know what's on that tape, but I'm sure as shit it was him."

My guy inches in, slaps his foot a couple more times on the floor in front of her. The towel falls a few inches below his navel, low on his hips. It's been four days.

Nick turns with a perplexed look and lifts his shoulders, dropping the matador pose. "How can I say I'm sorry?" he says. Sue Anne stands and struts like a cowpoke toward the bar, zigzagging over the strips of yellow light and shadow that steam in through the kitchen window.

"Do I have to beg and plead?" he calls to her. Sue Anne refuses to answer. "How about I do tricks for you?" She reaches for the bottle and begins pouring. The Pooh flag falls, and suddenly Nick is up on his hands, his heels resting high up against the wall.

His tan lines are something. Upside down like that? The way his testicles hang down alongside his penis? His stuff looks like an elephant's head instead of his stuff. Mr. Upside Down Elephant Head smiles. "The Artist is Elton John. Can you name the title? Hurry, all the blood—as you can see, it's rushing to my head."

It's just about the funniest thing I've ever seen.

"No answer? Title: 'Sorry Seems to Be the Hardest Word.'"

Sue Anne's shoulders shudder a little, and I know she's crying. Nick inches down from his handstand and picks up the flag. We exchange a look. The shadows have made their way to her face. She won't look at either of us.

"I hate you," she says. "I hate you both."

"It's impolite to drink the whiskey of people you dislike," Nick says. "Bad form." And now she's really crying, doing that slurping thing drunks sometimes do when they lose it.

"Gee," says Nick, "Now I need a drink." At the bar, he presents the Pooh flag to Sue Anne, but she crosses her arms and refuses to budge. She's making these snorting sounds and Nick gives me a look that says, What's she gonna do with all that snot? When he begins to fold Pooh like a flag at a veteran's funeral, she whacks it from his hands and huffs over to the table, nearly missing her chair when she sits. Nick makes drinks all around.

As he pours, the remaining light slowly drains from the kitchen. I watch him in black and white.

"You two wouldn't know," Sue Anne says, dragging her glass in front of her. "You two don't have a clue. You, the both of you, you two have something. If you didn't, you'd have to have something. You can bet your ass on that. Without something, you'd have nothing. But not you two. You've got something. You two don't know shit." She looks from Nick to me, me to Nick, nodding a big uh-huh. "You can't even spell l-o-n-l-e-y. *Spellllll check!*"

Nick reaches over and gently pushes a knot of hair from Sue Anne's eye. I put my hand on his thigh. The towel is warm and damp.

"In that video," she whispers, "the 'birdwatcher' one, their breasts aren't even real except, you know, in that looong scene at the beach? Jenna Jameson?" She tosses up her wrist dismissively. "Whuuu! No way! And the men. Whuuu-*wee!* The men, the men are—un*natural.*" She lifts her glass, and then sets it back on the table. Looks at Nick, then at me. "They all have something. But they all, you know, lack—feeling. You two, you got feeling." Nick takes my hand. "But, then, sometimes," she whispers, turning that look into a mischievous grin, "what you want isn't feeling, if you know what I mean. Where is my Pooh?" We all raise our glass to that.

Nick steps over to retrieve Pooh. Like an offering he gently lowers the flag onto the table in front of her. She takes a drink, looks calmly from Nick to me and then rests her elbows on Pooh's high cheeks. She bows to her glass. All that schoolteacher stuff is gone out of her.

She says, "Can I tell you a story?" The three of us lift our glasses for an awkward toast. "I refuse to be looking for a man," she says, "because when Christy wished for patience? What she got was Mama? So I will wish for other things but I will not wish for a man. And I'll learn that I was right: that by not asking for what I need most, maybe I'll get it. Life works in mysterious ways?" She lifts her hands, touches them in the form of prayer, closes her eyes then sort of withers, face-down onto Pooh's cheek. The snoring is not pleasant.

Nick takes down the ladder from Sue Anne's front porch and brings in the two-wheel dolly from the garage. He slides the lip of the dolly under the back legs of the kitchen chair, pulls Sue Anne's shoulders toward him, tilts her back like an astronaut awaiting liftoff then rolls her into the living room. I lay out sheets and a pillow on the sofa. Nick goes back to the dryer for the flag and sets the laundry room trashcan within her reach. Before turning off the coffee table lamp, he drapes Pooh over Sue Anne so that the two are sleeping cheek to cheek and so that the other parts, including

Pooh's mighty penis, fit where they should. My Nick is a detail-oriented sort of guy.

"You want another drink?" he whispers.

"Nah."

"Me neither."

We have this love ritual, where I sometimes spend an extra couple of minutes in the bathroom while Nick waits for me in bed. He says he likes the way I look with the light to my back when I walk out and pause as if I don't know he's watching before making my way to our bed. So I glance at the mirror and then reach for the door. He has remembered to turn the air conditioning up to cool the sheets, then down again before I come out.

Lying awake in hotel rooms alone, I sometimes can't sleep, the room so dark, the bed so empty. I think of him. And I think of our cool, crisp sheets. Sometimes I can even smell them. I sleep holding the other pillow.

Nick lifts the covers and I slide in close, flesh upon flesh. He shuts out the light and the room is suddenly black. I don't know where the moon went. I can't see a thing. I rest my head on Nick's chest and listen to his heart and his breathing in the dark. "Sing to me," I say.

He purrs a melody in that Dean Martin way: "In Monte-Carlo— Leonardo—lifts an infant from a carriage—and whispers that he'll love her till he dies. And at that very moment—there's a killer in Manila—who checks his watch—and wets his lips—then shuts his eyes."

"I don't like that last part," I say, touching his nipple in the dark. "I like the way it starts, but not the way it ends."

"I don't either," he says. He presses his fingers lightly to my lips. "I don't know where that one came from. I wish I hadn't said it. That ending won't do. I'm sorry. I won't sing that one again."

Kids Rule

For Mikee and me, our last family vacation began in the middle of the night with a zombie walk down the dark hallway to the brightly lit bathroom to pee, followed by Dad's strong hands lifting us onto the backseat. Then we were moving through the darkness, traveling from Dayton to Myrtle Beach. Dad was driving. This was before he moved out. Mom had insisted that Uncle Archie come along, and the smell of smoky old dirt, garbage dump dirt—which was the smell of Uncle Archie—filled the inside of the minivan.

When we woke, the sun was bright. The old man was telling family stories. Mom didn't seem to be listening. She stared off into some imaginary world and twisted her hair and stopped him every couple of minutes to ask a question about something he'd already said.

You'd think Archie had been born during pioneer days. He told Mom about when he was a boy, "No bigger than this one," he said, giving Mikee a pat on the knee. He was telling about when his baby brother died. "My Aunt Ava came over and built a little box to bury him in," he said, "then bathed and wrapped him in a square of linen. She put pennies on his eyes." Mom looked over at Dad, who was watching the highway, I guess. She looked at him as though there was a question hanging in the air. You could tell he felt her looking. He sat stiffly, hands like fists on the wheel, eyes straight ahead.

"Sometime during the night," Archie said as matter-a-fact as anything, "somebody, one of my brothers or sisters, stole those pennies." When Mom's eyes began to water up, Mikee and I glared over at Uncle Archie, then exchanged the look we shared the first night Dad made her cry. The look of two gang members. Old dirt bag Archie just kept looking out the window into

La-La Land and talking to himself. "Aunt Mae brought cheese," he said, "and we got to eat all we wanted." Mom was boo-hooing. Her sad eyes were still on Dad.

As we sped along, a sign said we had entered South Carolina, but we could see in the mirror that Dad hadn't noticed. His eyes had the look of someone searching for a lost memory.

We were up early and on the beach by eight. Mom and the old guy and Dad had sat up late drinking fizzy water with green slices of lime in it and laughing at Uncle Archie's stupid stories, ones that Mikee and I knew were sex jokes. He smoked his stinking cigar and Mom laughed like a yapping puppy until late in the night.

Because Uncle Archie got the other bed, Mikee and I had to sleep on cots. But as soon as the sun came up, we carried out our revenge, shaking their covers and whining through our nose, "We're on vacaaaation," over and over, demanding that they take us to the beach. The elevator smelled like cigars and green pine needles. On the ride down, Mikee looked up at Archie, then over at me. He mouthed the new words we'd heard Dad shout, "Son of a bitch."

Our group settled just behind the line that divided the dark hard wet sand from the dry white sand. Mom and Dad held their arms out and the giant new brightly colored beach towels fluttered like a parrot's wings in the wind. Then together they lowered the towels to the soft sand. Mom spread one for Uncle Archie.

The sun was already like a warm hand on my face, and Dad covered us with lotion that smelled like coconut. He said to raise our arms as he lathered us. Then he held us tight and tickled Mikee and me until we shrieked and darted from his reach.

"Boys?" he shouted against the wind and surf. There was something in his voice. When we looked back, he was still on his knees with his arms open wide. There was something about his brown eyes. Maybe it was the bright sun that made them the color of dark, wet copper. "Boys?" he said again, arms wide.

"Ahhhh!" Mikee shrieked. We raced for the surf.

By the time we'd dug a moat for our sandcastle, the three of them were asleep. My brother was the first to toss a toy shovel of sand onto Uncle Archie's bone-thin calves. Mikee didn't look at me when he did it. But I knew. Before breakfast, Mom had changed the channel from the Nickelodeon Network to TV Poker for Uncle Archie to watch. "No fair,"

Mikee had said. "Kids rule!" Uncle Archie said nothing. He just lit another cigar. "Ma-maaa," Mikee begged.

"That's enough," Dad said, exactly as he'd said it to our mom the night he dropped a photograph on the table in front of her, pointed, and said the name of some guy we didn't know. The first night he made her cry.

Mikee and I dug faster and faster, and in no time Uncle Archie's legs disappeared. We took turns dumping beach sand onto his butt. After a few minutes, we struck water. We staggered the few steps with our small shovels and dripped the soupy sand like hot wax over his shoulders. Then we lost interest.

Though we had been threatened with death if we entered the water without an adult, we went in anyway. "Don't you go and drown on me," I shouted. Mikee dropped his head to one side, over his shoulder, and puffed out his chest like a little bird. "Sweetheart, I'll never leave you," he said in a little girl's voice. He wiped the imaginary tears from his cheeks, pinched his nose and fell back into the water.

The surf was rough and the undertow was really fast, and when I looked up, I thought the earth must have tilted. Mom and Uncle Archie and Dad had slid far down the beach to our left. They were as small as our plastic toy soldiers. I didn't see my brother.

"Mikee," I shouted. "Mikee!" Then he surfaced about thirty feet away, pressed his palms against his ruddy cheeks and wiped the salt water from his red eyes. I pointed. We could just about make out Mom's screams. Her arms were flying up and down and in and out and around.

Mikee spit water like a fountain. "Looks like a cheerleader," he said.

People were beginning to circle up around her. "She thinks we drowned," I said.

"Or that we cut off Uncle Archie's head."

She was still going at it, like a cheerleader on a pogo stick.

We ran in to catch the action.

Uncle Archie was dead from a heart attack. That night we reclaimed our bed.

We rode back to Dayton with the smell of suntan lotion filling the space where the landfill had been and cursed Uncle Archie for ending our vacation after only two days.

"Son of a bitch, son of a bitch," Mikee and I whispered over and over. We were in the very back of the minivan watching the shimmering black highway stretch out behind us, and these were the only curse words we knew. Up front, Mom and Dad spoke in a shadowy language we couldn't understand. When we heard Mom say she loved the guy, Mikee puckered his lips. "Son of a bitch," he whispered in a little girl's voice.

The flat land became hills, then mountains. In a Donald Duck voice, I whispered the punch line of one of Uncle Archie's sex jokes—something about the smell of fish—and Mikee doubled up. His face was the color of a strawberry. He couldn't stop laughing and neither could I. Until we heard Dad say, "That's enough." We turned. He was looking at Mom, who blew her nose into a Kleenex. Then she turned to him and said to be quiet. To please be quiet.

Before leaving our house for Archie's funeral, Mom put in an old movie called *Home Alone*. It was Mikee's favorite. Every time the kid in the movie threw his hands up to his face, Mikee did the same and shouted, "Ahhhhh," like he had that day at the beach. After that, when their shrieking voices woke us in the middle of the night, Mikee would look at me as he covered his ears and whisper, "Ahhhhh!"

For a long time, Dad called almost every night, but Mom said we didn't have to talk with him if we didn't want to.

After his bath, Mikee sat about a foot from the screen and watched cartoons. His eyes didn't move. Nothing moved.

From where I sat on the sofa, I looked down the dark hall into Mom's dimly lit bedroom where she was having a long conversation on her cell phone. She wore a shiny red bathrobe and moved around the room like she was slow dancing, playing with her hair, smiling from time to time into the new mirror that hung beside the bed. When she was like that, I'd sometimes slip into the living room and listen to the messages he left on the machine. He'd say, "Boys?" And in the silence while he waited for Mikee or me to pick up, I could see him as I had that day on the beach, on his knees, arms wide, his eyes like wet copper.

But later I'd just sit with Mikee and eat giant cheese pizzas and watch TV. And at some point and for a long time we didn't even hear the phone ring.

You Can Laugh If You Want To

THIS WAS EARLY ON a Friday morning. My wife Linda and I were having breakfast. Eggs, scrambled. Link sausage. I looked up from my newspaper. Her eyes were shut tight. She held her fork suspended over her soft egg like a Geiger counter.

"You okay?" I said.

"I think I'm going to be sick," she said.

"What is it this time?"

"I just remembered," she said. Her eyes rolled beneath the twitching lids. "My dream. A woman, a stranger...she was a candy striper. She was wearing the outfit. She was giving birth in the backseat of my car."

"What?"

"I was pumping gas at the Sav-Way. After filling up, I opened my car door and there she was, in the backseat of the Honda, her knees tucked up and wide apart, her sex looking back at me like the opening of a cannon barrel. The red nursing stripes didn't help." Linda paused as if she were awaiting incoming footage. Then, "Her face was all swollen and screwed up, tight as a dried prune and purple as an eggplant."

I didn't know if I should whisk Linda's plate away or leave it there just in case.

"Are you going to eat that sausage?" I asked. Sometimes I have a snack on the loading dock at the ten o'clock break.

"You can have it," she said, eyes still shut. "I'm done."

We recycle Ziploc sandwich baggies, keep them in the drawer beside our cigarettes. So I put the sausage and a slice of toast in the used baggie and filled my thermos with sweet tea. Linda sat still as a statue at the kitchen table, eyes wide now, like she was seeing past where she could see.

"There's meaning there," she whispered.

"Meaning what?" I said. I looked at the clock.

"Meaning meaning," she said.

"Are you going to be sick?" I asked.

"I'm already sick."

"How?"

"Of *what* is the question."

"What?"

"Yes," she said.

"Can I get you something, Linda?"

"You've already given me something," she said. Her far away eyes slowly turned, then suddenly zoomed in on me.

"I'm late for work," I said. "What can I do for you?"

"I think I'm going to be sick," she said. She pressed her palms into the table top and stood very slowly. Taking my face into her hands, she kissed me. I wanted to kiss her back, to really kiss her, but I was afraid of what might happen. So I gave her a little smack on the lips. She turned without speaking. The bathroom door closed behind her.

Driving to work, I read the new Easter message on the sign in front of the Pentecostal church: Christ Is Aloose and Alive, it said.

I work in a hospital supply warehouse. I used to be a forklift driver, but something happened, and so now I'm a picker. I started out as a picker ten years ago. I pick up orders and fill small plastic crates with everything from enema solution to forceps. First I look at the order and then organize my picking route. Dallas Haze, the big boss, has a term for what I do: economy of movement. He nods a big uh-huh when he says things that please him.

Unless somebody screws up majorly, we have only two warehouse meetings with Mr. Haze each year, one in July when we do inventory and one at Christmas. But sometimes someone screws up majorly. My buddy Scottie and I always have a bet on the table going into these meetings. I pick "economy" and he picks "efficiency" and we count the number of times Mr. Haze uses those words. The winner takes five bucks from the other. At home I pick my fights, the ones Linda sometimes wants to have. Usually, though, I pick up the remote and pick a channel.

After two hours picking beakers and bedpans, I suddenly think about my wife and about kissing her. In the men's room I shut the stall door and unroll some tissue on account of what's about to happen. Whenever I think too much about how deeply I love Linda, I cry. I wish I knew why. It hasn't always been like this. But some things happened. When my love for her rises inside me, it just keeps going up and up like the mercury in a thermometer, and it doesn't stop until it gets to my eyes and then just floods out. I really don't understand this. I should be happy. I love my wife so much that my love makes me cry. Nobody knows this. I'm a man, after all. Who could I tell?

It's not always been like this. Sometimes, although she's never said it, I know Linda wonders if she made a bad pick. So I have no choice but to love her more, to hold her tighter, and even as I do it, I know I'm making myself harder to love. I'm a failure at economy of movement.

My face is in a ball of tissue and I'm blowing my nose when I walk out into the warehouse, almost colliding with Mr. Haze. He sometimes spot-checks the men's room for guys taking an extra break in there.

"What's with the red eyes?" he says.

"Pine pollen," I say.

I'm not allowed to work in the chemical room anymore. Some of the chemicals in there are so toxic your eyes water and the labels on the brown glass jugs disintegrate and flake off. Even the bottles' extra-thick brown glass won't contain what's inside. Their corrugated shipping boxes turn to thick brown crusty chips. There was an accident in there once. Lois, who was my friend when she worked here, learned a few years later that she couldn't have children.

"You sure?" Mr. Haze says, glancing toward the chemical room entrance. "Vomiting? Dizziness?"

"I've got to pick these," I say pulling the orders from my shirt pocket. As I'm walking away, I say in a voice he can hear, "I haven't been on a forklift in years."

❦❦❦

MY FRIEND SCOTTIE LIKES to talk about buying stock in the company. He's a forklift operator. He hopes to retire in ten years when he hits six-ty-five. He says the future is in bedpans. For the past fifteen years, Scottie has kept a graph in black Magic Marker on the cement wall outside the chemical room. He coughs a lot. We both do. Mr. Haze approves of the bedpan graph.

Scottie and I sit on the edge of the loading dock. He smokes while I eat my sausage sandwich. Then I smoke.

"The future is in old people," he says.

"The future's in the young," I say. "Always."

"Les," he says, offering me a second cigarette, "You don't know shit. Look at my graph. Bedpans are at an all-time high. No end in sight. The old keep living longer and longer. Consider the modern advances in health care."

I pretend to consider.

It's only ten-fifteen in the morning, and already the windshield of every car in the warehouse lot is a hazy yellow color. Pine pollen. "Can't stop sickness," I say, looking out at the lot. "Some things are just wired to die."

"Eventually," he says, "yeah." We smoke. I count the wooden pallets stacked on the dock.

"What do the really old do with all their memories?" I say. "Those stacks and stacks of memories from so many years?"

"That explains why their memory goes, to make room."

"What if they can't forget?" I say.

"Then if you're lucky the good ones outnumber the bad ones, I reckon." I play a tic-tac-toe game in the pine dust on the cement loading dock. "If you're not lucky," Scottie pulls hard on his cigarette, "you're screwed," he says, just as the warehouse buzzer signals that break is over.

I fold a one-inch stack of orders into my shirt pocket. I walk past the shipping clerk and down the long conveyor where the women packers listen to 103X and sing along. The place smells of spent propane that powers the forklifts. Is this what the end of the world looks like? Towering racks of hospital supplies beneath a giant grid of fluorescent light tubes, like we are all living underground in a secret military installation.

My wife says she can't keep a secret. She says that a lot. I begin counting the sprinkler heads that hang from the steel beams high above. There is nothing flammable about bedpans. The chemical room could blow, maybe any minute. I count sprinklers as I pick. Economy of movement. Soon after we met, Linda recited a list of former relationships. This was a time of love chemistry. A time when you can't imagine that you could love the other person more. When all you do is laugh and read each other's mind, and make love like in the movies. I couldn't have believed then that my love would grow and rise up over time until it flooded from my eyes like water from fire sprinklers. I'm sure Linda thinks about her list sometimes, especially now. Thinks about it like it's a pick order from a long time ago and wonders if she screwed up majorly with the man she picked. My wife has a secret life.

I can list every hospital, complete with addresses, every hospital in South Carolina. Sometimes I help the guys in shipping and receiving make labels for the cartons. Sometimes I help load the trucks that deliver to Rock Hill, to Beaufort.

Once Lois, my friend, found a dead possum in the back corner of the chemical room.

❧❧❧

AFTER THE FIVE O'CLOCK buzzer, I call Linda while walking to my truck. I can't wait to get home. I've loved the life out of her. I didn't know it at the time, but that's what I've done: a sort of no-fault death. I just couldn't shut up. I couldn't foresee the consequences. Over and over I said to her, I never dreamed I could love anybody as much as I love you. I love you more than I ever have. Blah, blah, blah until she wants me to just shut up. What choice did you give her, you silly willy? Twilly-willy wit boom-boom. Just shut up, she thinks. She thinks she's going to be sick. I am Doctor Iron Beard. I've never learned what I needed to know about the economy of love.

Linda doesn't answer until after I leave the message that I'm coming home. Then she picks up.

She doesn't say hello. "You have to clean up the Honda," she says.

"It won't do any good," I say. By this time, I'm standing at my truck, playing tic-tac-toe on the pollen-yellow windshield. There is a long pause on the other end.

A song my mother sang when I was a baby, maybe even before I was born, suddenly comes into my head: I am Doctor Iron Beard.

"Are you sick?" I say.

"I was wrong," she says. "About my dream. After you left this morning I remembered that the stranger in the backseat of the Honda wasn't giving birth. She'd had an abortion. I don't know what to do."

"On first impression—"

"I don't want to be a part of anybody's first impression. You can't trust them," she says.

"What exactly does that mean?"

"Exactly," she says.

"First impressions. Forget them."

"Because nobody knows," she says. "You only think you do because you have an impression."

"Like speed dating."

"I'm not telling," she says.

"Right," I say.

"You have to clean up the backseat of the Honda," my wife says. "It's a mess."

I shut off my phone and when I look up I see Dallas Haze standing on the dock with his arms hugging his chest. He's giving me the fish eye as I slowly drive past. I raise my hand and provide him a soft, economical wave. When he sees my lips move, he thinks I'm saying, Good evening Mr. Haze, see you Monday morning. But I'm not.

When I pull into our drive, I spot a white envelope taped to the front door. Fear hits me like a flash fire. I park and sit for a long time looking at the envelope.

I have no choice. The envelope says I've given my wife no choice, that's what I'm thinking. The door is coming at me. Picture yourself standing in one place and seeing the door come at you until your nose is right there in front of it. Invisible tape holds the envelope in place. Invisible—like a secret. I'm relieved to find there's no letter inside. Even before I get it open I know it's a key. The weight, the shape. For a second, my fear turns to joy.

Once, Linda left a key for the door. And when I entered, I saw she'd left another key that unlocked our bedroom door. Behind that door stood Linda in her wedding dress. This was years after we'd married. You need to know this about my wife. But that was a long time ago and this is the ignition key to the Honda. I'd give anything for the key to her secret life.

Inside, I call for her but she's not there. We only have my truck and the Honda. When I call her cell she doesn't answer.

I can't explain, but sometimes I have these strange thoughts. Outside, as I'm nearing the Honda, I'm overcome with the certainty that I'm going to find Linda in the backseat, sick—or worse. The red afternoon sunlight is mirrored in the car's yellow windows. I can't see inside. I know the name and address of every hospital in South Carolina. I pull the handle. The door is locked—she never locks the car doors. Darlington is a small town in South Carolina, not a town where strange women give birth or have abortions in the backseat of your 1998 Honda. We don't even live within the city limits. We live three miles out in the country. Three miles in the country outside a small town. Some things, you should be able to count on them.

I've lost count, but there are more than five hundred sprinkler heads in the warehouse where I work. In case of fire. She's not really lying in the backseat, I say to myself. Linda is coming home to me. Otherwise she would have left the house keys too, not just the one key. Or else she would have taken all of them and driven off in the Honda. I turn the key in the lock and take a small step back before I pull the handle.

The backseat looks as new as the day we bought the car. Linda and I have no children. The chemical that illuminates blood that the eye can't see is called Luminol. It may go by another name, a scientific name. It may be stored in the chemical room where I once worked.

Before I shift into reverse, I light up. I play it safe. I don't smoke while I'm pumping gas. Linda's dream—that she gassed up the Honda—was just that; the needle is to the left of empty. I'm not much of a risk taker. I make mistakes, sometimes bad ones. Some things have happened. But my mistakes, the awful ones, the ones I'd do anything to undo, were never the result of foolish risks. Love is always a risk. Three miles. Six minutes. No major risk to assume that I'll not make it to the Sav-Way on the gas left in the tank. You can't measure love in miles or minutes. You can't always tell when the tank will run over. Or run dry.

❧❧❧

THERE IS A CARWASH at the Sav-Way. A tide of happiness waters my eyes. I'll fill the car with gas and get a discount for the carwash drive-thru. Then I'll vacuum. I'll buy one of those green Christmas tree-shaped deodorizers that hangs from the rearview on account of the cigarette smell. And I'll buy a lottery ticket, maybe two, because you never can tell. Sometimes you just can't tell. In twenty minutes I'll be home with a clean car, no trace of a crime anywhere, not even a dusting of pine pollen, and Linda will be there waiting for me. I am Doctor Iron Beard.

❧❧❧

THIS IS LATE ON a Friday afternoon. The sky is going from pink to purple, the time when wild animals stir, those that take cover at night, those that come out only at night. There must be at least a moment when the two feel a sort of disorientation. This is South Carolina. And a country road that takes me to the Sav-Way on the edge of town.

On its way to the paper mill, a pulpwood rig with shimmering head-lights blows past me at eighty miles an hour. Wood chips float out the back of the open trailer like brown corrugated flakes. Eighty miles an hour equals road kill at any hospital in South Carolina. I can't see the driver. The trailer has a South Carolina tag. I think the state's plate should say, South Carolina, Nation's First in Road Kill. But that's just me.

AT THE SAV-WAY, I stand looking into the backseat of the Honda as I pump a highly flammable chemical into my wife's car. Accidents can happen. If my friend Lois were still alive, she'd tell you so. The drive-thru carwash, which is about the size of the chemical room, is dark and empty. The green Christmas tree-shaped car deodorizers near the cash register are packaged in thick clear plastic so that the chemicals remain intact. The pine smell is artificial. I choose one, hold up two fingers and nod toward the Power Ball lottery tickets.

"And a car wash," I say. The large black woman inks her scalp with a ballpoint pen and punches numbers with her free hand. When the register drawer opens, I say, "Four quarters, please." Then I think about Linda, about the vacuuming job I want to do. "Make that eight, please."

The fake stoplight changes from green to red inside the dark carwash. I shift into park. The storm begins. I feel I'm at the bottom of the sea, with the tentacles of some giant spider monster sucking the life from me. The backseat is empty. After a storm like this, the highways are cluttered with road kill. So are the emergency rooms.

I open my eyes. A dim green light trembles behind the water and steam. I flip on the wipers and pull ahead. The engine hums as I park beside the tall chrome car vac. Economy of movement, I think. Preparations begin. First, I rip the cellophane, which is made from chemicals, from the cardboard, which is soaked in pine-scented chemicals after the cardboard leaves the paper mill. I hang it from the rear view. The scent is authentically pine. I feel happy. A clean car seems to run better. The smell inside is a clean smell. Next I prepare to vacuum. Switch off the engine and open the car door. That annoying buzzing sound fills the car. The mats come out first. The car is a four-door, which makes for easier, more thorough and economical vacuuming. We bought the Honda used. Believe it or not, the four-door is cheaper than the two-door. This flies in the face of economy. Four doors are necessary for some but Linda and I have no children.

The buzzing reminds me of the warehouse. I place the mats outside on the asphalt near the vacuum pump. The ashtray, which is never empty, comes next. I dump its contents into the large plastic garbage can provided. Because I want to do something special for my wife, I will also vacuum the ashtray, remove any hint of ash, every sign of trouble. I am Doctor Iron

Beard. For another second I feel a rush of happiness. But that feeling is doused by the buzzing inside the car. I reach for the ignition key to stop the Japanese noise torture, but then think better of removing the key.

Clean as a whistle, I think. Then to take my mind from the buzzing, I whistle I Am Doctor Iron Beard. I open the glove box, the pocket. Why not? I have eight quarters. I feel for the plastic sleeve that holds the insurance card and registration.

There is a small cloth bag on top. Inside the bag is a pair of new red panties and travel-size containers of deodorant and hair mousse. One blue earring. I hold these in my hands, then place them and their bag on the dash above the steering wheel. The buzzing fills my head. I remove the ignition key and lay it on the console between the two front seats. Linda's. Mine.

The vacuum hose has the diameter of an industrial strength fire hose. Vandals have cut off its head. I stretch the hose to the extreme right rear of the backseat, drop in the four quarters and begin. The hose is the size of a bazooka. I force its barrel into the dark hidden spaces under the seats, where no one can see. The secret areas. My fingers part the folds of the backseat. Forced entry. Every movement is efficient. I have four more quarters but I know that time is running out.

Up front, I begin on the passenger's side. I'm no longer whistling. I consider vacuuming up the bag that holds the panties, deodorant, and mousse. One earring, the color of a blue eye. I've been part of a cover-up before. The machine makes an odd sound when it sucks debris from inside the pocket. I look over at the bag again, lean forward and reach for it. From the corner of my eye, I spot something near the mouth of the hose: The ignition key appears to levitate from the console. The key sort of waves bye-bye—then it's gone.

I sit looking at the console, where the key used to be.

The vacuum is still running when I enter the convenience store, but when I walk out with a twelve-pack under my arm, the vac shuts off. I set the beer in the passenger seat, open one then dial Linda's number. She doesn't pick up. I finish the beer. After pushing the Honda away from the vacuum island I open another one. Press redial and drink. Drink and redial, holding the red panties in my hand. Open a beer and redial, holding the red panties and the deodorant. Open a beer and mousse my hair. Open a beer and empty the whole container of mousse in my hair. Then I remember the remaining four quarters in my pocket and drop them into the vacuum machine. It's that time of night when I feel disoriented and confused. With my eyes closed, I hold the vacuum a few inches above my wet, moussed head and feel a tugging at the roots of my hair follicles. When I open my eyes I see people pumping gas. They stare.

THE LIGHTS OF THE Sav-Way have disappeared behind me. It's only three miles, I think. In the warehouse, I walk more than three miles every day. Three miles is nothing. Scottie, my friend, is disoriented and confused about the future, I think as I walk. He doesn't know his Xs from his Os. My friend Lois was very disoriented and confused, especially near the end. She was a definite X. But her eyes were very, very blue. I feel for the lottery tickets in my pocket. The odds are against the South Carolina possum, which is wired for road kill and carries its babies in a pocket on its stomach.

The night is dark now, not a star, no moon. Rain maybe. The worst thing you can do is throw water on some kinds of fires. A dry powder, another chemical, is the proper response. If you're there when it happens, does that make you a First Responder? Sometimes you don't even want to know. Linda has a secret life. If I were there and saw her secret life with my own eyes, I can't say what kind of First Responder I might be.

I would leave me if I had the chance.

A slight breeze comes up, a promise of rain. I feel it most in my hair, which stands up like iron quills. I touch them and think of Linda. "You can laugh if you want to," I say aloud as I negotiate the dark country road. "I wish you would." I've said nothing of my wife's laugh. Yes, I've lost the key to the Honda and must walk, but only three miles. I still have my truck and another key to the Honda. I'm a porcupine walking home like a drunk to the woman I love. I know that Linda is there waiting for me. Otherwise she would have picked up when I hit redial.

I can't stop pressing the button, and I know the more I press it the more impossible I make everything. So now she's at home waiting, probably in the recliner watching TV. And when she sees me, my spiked head like a floating contact mine, she'll laugh until her eyes water. Breathless, she will point, her pained face gone purple, and say, "No more, No more," as she clutches her stomach and raises her knees to her chest.

Before I hear the sound of the semi, I see the yellow line of center-lane reflectors brighten into the distance. Then I hear it and turn. The shimmering headlights appear to be two stories above me. The horn blast sends me sideways. Something happens inside my head. A buzzing. I perform a classy crossover step, like placing an X in the center of a tic-tac-toe game. Small chips of pine rain down on me. I think I hear my phone. Soon I see a speck of light, but I don't hear anything now. The tiny light grows and I feel that something I've been trying to remember is on its way, that it's just a matter of time. Suddenly the light is blinding. I sing: "I am Doctor Iron Beard, twilly-willy wit boom-boom. I'll cure your ills with healing art, twilly-willy wit boom-boom. I can make the dumb to walk, twilly-willy wit boom-boom, boom-boom. The lame to see, the blind to talk, twilly-willy wit boom-boom."

"Get in," says Linda, pushing open the passenger door to my truck. She wears a red and white dress and the remains of red lipstick on her mouth. When I close the door, I can smell her, the deodorant. The cab is dark now. "What happened to your head?" She touches one of the spikes. "My phone was off," she says. Now she touches my face, cupping my cheek in her palm. Her hand smells of soap. "What happened?" she asks again.

"You first." I say. She doesn't answer. Above the dark trees, distant lightning turns the thick clouds the color of Linda's lips. She is driving us home.

"I saw someone this afternoon," she says.

"Sick?"

"Not now."

"Feeling better?"

"For now."

"How long will it last?"

"Which part?"

"This part," I say, reaching for a cigarette.

"Don't smoke," she says.

"Since when?" I say.

"Since it makes me feel sick," she says.

In five minutes, we will be at home, where we live together, where once I had a key and my wife stood waiting for me behind our bedroom door in her wedding dress. You must know this about my wife.

Linda looks straight ahead now as she speaks. "There's something I haven't told you," she says. Her face gives away nothing.

"Good or bad?" I say.

"Not sure yet," she says.

Beyond the soft folds, a cloud slowly rolls and turns in the red light.

"Could go either way?" I say.

"Too soon to tell," she says.

"Give me the odds," I say.

"Don't have them to give."

"What do you have?"

"When I know, you'll know."

The clock on the dash has stopped. The LED is all zeros. I remember the lottery tickets and pull them from my pocket. "Anything is possible," I say. But it comes out sounding like a question.

"What happened to your head?" she says.

"I wish I knew," I say. "I really do." My wife smiles, I think.

"It looks funny," she says. She doesn't look at me, but I think she's smiling.

"You can laugh if you want to," I say. "If it would help." The horizon is a deep fiery red now, the color of the first days on earth. Or the last. "You can laugh if you want to," I whisper. "If it would make a difference, I wish you would."

Like a Little White Chapel on the Beach

EYES PINCHED SHUT, LAUREN bowed her head and pressed a damp palm against the window to steady herself. The stench of spent diesel fuel and the bus's relentless swaying produced a gnarly knot in her stomach and the scent of bile on her breath. But as the hours passed, the Cumberland Mountains faded into the Blue Ridge, which unfolded into rolling hills and finally into gentle, dazzling waves of wide, green country. The dark tide of nausea slowly receded. And only cloudless sunlight stretched between Lauren and the glittering Atlantic.

As her finger slowly traced the pocket of her jeans and the folded curve of the two hundred dollars Drew had given her, she saw the Welcome to South Carolina sign. Her blue eyes brimmed with tears. "Bye," she whispered, looking back over her shoulder.

Lauren felt inside the plastic bag on the window seat for the sandwich and warm soda Drew had packed for her. She ate quickly. South Carolina was Myrtle Beach. Then hovering from her seat like a hummingbird, her keen, expectant face at the window, her heart certain, she held her breath knowing that the blue line of surf would rise up before her at any second. But it did not. And after a time, the gentle rocking of the bus lulled her into tender reverie. She pictured Drew, and beyond the girl's drowsy smile there awaited the promise of clean, salty air and the dream of a blue-bright endless horizon of good fortune.

∵∵∵

THE GREYHOUND STOPPED AT the depot in Columbia, just as it had in Knoxville, Asheville, and Spartanburg. Fearing the bus would suddenly vanish and leave her forever stranded in wide, naked country, Lauren hadn't left her seat. Exiting the bus, she reminded herself, was not a part of Drew's simple plan.

She waited for the other passengers to disembark, then she set her small canvas University of Kentucky bag in her seat to hold it and entered the stinking hot toilet. When she stepped out, the boarding passengers filled the narrow aisle. The seats were nearly full, the people mostly old, mostly black. Lauren had never been in close company with so many black people. Their numbers were few in the Cumberland Mountains, fewer still in the hills overlooking the Powell Valley. Rising to her tiptoes, she scanned the empty seats for the blue bag. She didn't see it. Tiny fissures of fear seized her. Suddenly the bus engine growled and the floor trembled as if it might crumble or, worse, swallow her.

Ahead a very old and large lumbering woman panted toward her, beads of sweat streaking her coal black furrowed brow. Lauren spotted the blue bag. Mopping her dark, hollow eyes, the woman paused to steady herself and Lauren lurched forward, nearly colliding into the woman before collapsing into the aisle seat, her hand securing the bag. As she waddled past, the old black woman slowly lowered her cavernous eyes, forcing Lauren to look away.

Just as the bus driver set down his clipboard and glanced up into his mirror, a white man wearing a starched shirt stepped up onto the bus. He stopped in the aisle. His eyes swept the coach from side to side. Swaying toward her, he smiled and nodded at nobody in particular. When Lauren felt him towering at her shoulder, she did not look up but set the blue canvas bag on the floor and slid into the window seat. Her fingers searched inside the plastic grocery bag for her white-framed sunglasses. Turning to the window she slid them on.

"Thank you, miss," the man in the nice shirt said. She smelled his aftershave, his sweat. She didn't answer. When a man sat beside her, even in church, he always took a snapshot first thing. She could feel their picture-taking, even when she looked away. "Whew!" she heard him say, and a cold pang of fear shot through her.

❧❧❧

EARLIER, IN THE CAB of his truck at the Tazewell bus stop, Drew pressed the ticket and the two hundred dollars into her palm, then gathered her tender face in his hands and kissed her. If he was not at the Myrtle Beach terminal to meet her, she would take a taxi to the Raintree Inn Motel in North Myrtle Beach where he had called in their reservation. "You have the address on that scrap of notebook paper?" he said. Lauren pressed a hand against her pocket. He smiled. "Just follow the simple plan," he said. "It's gonna work. Baby? Look at me. It's gonna work." He kissed her again. "Don't forget the sunglasses when you check in." He rested his cheek against hers and whispered, "In those sunglasses," he touched her hair, "with this wavy blond hair, you'll look just like a movie actress. They can't say no to a movie actress." Drew kissed her cheek and looked into her eyes. "You are *my* movie star."

❦❦❦

LAUREN'S EYES REMAINED FIXED upon the distant flat squares of tall corn, lush green soybeans, and cotton outside the bus window. The murmur of the engine lay like a quilt over the conversations surrounding her. Beside her the man wiped his face with a handkerchief, wafting a light cloud of aftershave around them. His cologne reminded Lauren of the five nights with Drew at the Oak Ridge Motor Inn. "Hot, ain't it?" the man said to nobody. Then he turned and spoke to Lauren in such a way that she had to look at him. "You know how they make cars with brains in them?" he said to her. She slowly pressed her shoulders into the window. "You know what I mean?" She could smell beer on his breath. "Some cars are smarter than some people. They can even talk to you, tell you when to change their oil and stuff like that? Give directions? You can say to the car, 'Tell me where in the *hell* I'm at,' and the car will do it." He smiled, and Lauren smiled back. "Well, I think me and my car are getting a divorce."

The man was at least as old as her daddy. She liked his smile, the way he smelled and that he looked only at her face when he talked to her. The hint of beer reminded her of Drew. "Whuuut?" Lauren said.

"You know your car hates you when it breaks down on a day as hot as this one. They do it on purpose, you know. To send a message." He nodded. She nodded back.

"I got an idear you did something to that car to make it like 'at. I'll bet your car has a girl's name, like Mustang Sally, don't it? You didn't treat her right."

"*Whuuut?*" he said, watching her face light up with a smile. "What's your theory?"

"My idear is that you drove her too hard, didn't take care of her like you promised her you would. A woman never forgets a broken promise."

"I loved her, treated her like a queen, kept her spotless for a hundred thousand miles."

"Maybe she was just a no-good."

"You can't talk that way about my car," the man said. Now they were both laughing.

"You know her better than I do," Lauren said. "I never even met the girl."

"That's good for you," the man said. "She threw a timing belt."

"At you?" Lauren had never heard of a timing belt.

"And that was that."

"Left you high and dry."

"Last I saw, she had hooked up with a tow truck. Didn't even wave bye."

"Hooked up. That's funny," Lauren said.

The man reached for his handkerchief, swabbed his face then adjusted his seat. Lauren liked the conversation, liked that she'd forgotten about things for a minute.

"Florence?" he said.

"Sir?"

"*Sir?*" the man said. "You sound like my car talking, only I guess she ain't mine anymore. She, you know, hooked up with another guy. You headed for Florence?"

"Myrtle Beach."

"I should'a known. No pretty young girls stop in Florence. They all go to Myrtle Beach. All the women in Florence are ugly. Except my wife. My wife is the most gorgeous woman in Florence. I thank God her sense of direction is so bad. If not for her poor navigational abilities, she would have married some Myrtle Beach lifeguard. I wouldn't have my three girls. I wouldn't be on this bus." He rolled his eyes. "One of my girls has a softball game tonight. I promised I'd be there. A man's gotta keep his promise."

"I'm gonna have two girls," Lauren said. "And two boys. I have their names picked out."

"Does the lifeguard know this already?"

"I ain't marrying no lifeguard. I'm marrying Drew, at a little white chapel right on the beach. If Drew gets to Myrtle Beach like we planned, could be tomorrow. Next day for sure."

"Oooh," the man said softly. His face had taken a turn, away from funny. "Oh," he said again. "You got family in Myrtle Beach? Friends?"

"No," Lauren said. "Never been there. I can't wait."

The man was looking down at his hands. For a second he glanced up at her with words on his lips, but then he looked back down at his folded hands.

"Right after we're married," Lauren said in a rush, "we're gettin' a tattoo. I forgot to tell you that part."

❦❦❦

"Puck-it," the cop said.

He wasn't dressed like a cop. He was dressed like an insurance man. Drew wished he *was* an insurance salesman. He'd buy some. "Something Puck-it," the cop said again, circling the bare table with one hand in his pants pocket, the other against the side of his thick face, shoring up his jaw like he was studying the ceiling. "You know, the singer. What was the name of that band? From the sixties. On the oldies station." Drew didn't know what any of this had to do with him and Lauren.

"Is this a test?" Drew said.

The cop dropped his hand and slowly tilted his meaty face down on Drew, who sat in the wooden chair at the table. "No," the cop said. "The test is happening down there." He pointed as though he could see through the cement wall, to the lab. "We'll know about all that blood, Drew, where it came from, whose it is. I'm talkin' here about that Puck-it song, 'cause there's a message there for you, in the words to the song."

"I wasn't born then," Drew said. "I'm only twenty-four."

The cop patted his open mouth like he was stopping a surprise from flying out. "That's *good*, Drew. Now we're getting someplace. Now we're getting to the facts of the case. So you're good at arithmetic, huh?"

"Not too good," Drew said. "I dropped out on my sixteenth birthday." He thought of Lauren, who was fourteen.

"But you might be good at *Name-That-Tune*, Drew. Might 'en you? Everybody's got some hidden talent, don't they?"

"I reckon," he said.

"Maybe yours is disposing of bodies?"

Drew didn't answer. Then: "I reckon you didn't drop out. You wouldn't be a cop if you'd dropped out, would you?" he said, but what Drew was thinking was, *You ain't as smart as you think you are.*

"I've got it now," the cop said in a fake funny voice. He assumed vulture mode, looming so close Drew couldn't look up at him. "I've put it together: Gary Puckett and the Union Gap. If you don't go to the electric chair, that's the song you'll be singing for the next ninety years."

"I don't know that title," Drew said, leaning away and looking up.

"That's the band, Drew, the name of the band. The title is something like, 'Girl, You'll be a Woman Soon'. No, that's not it. It's 'Boy, You'll be a Woman Soon'." The cop slowly sauntered to the other side of the table then turned, twisting his fists inside his pockets, striking that school principal pose. "The blood will tell the story, Drew. Then you'll say where you hid her body." Drew gave him the look he'd given principals for ten years, that blank I'm-watching-TV look. But what he was thinking was, *Man, you're dumber than a post.* "Where you're going, Drew? Boy, you'll be a *woman* soon." He placed both hands on the table and bore down on Drew. "A good lookin' boy like you? A year from now, boy, you won't be able to shit in a foot tub."

"I know what you're talking about," Drew said. "But I never liked that song." He wanted to say to the cop, *Neil Diamond*—his mother had all of Neil Diamond's records—but he didn't.

Back in his cell, Drew thought, *For a cop, you're dumber than dirt. You might know cop stuff,* he wanted to say to him. *But you don't know nothin' about love.*

❦❦❦

THE BUS LEFT FLORENCE at ten o'clock. Inside the coach all was dark and quiet. Lauren closed her eyes and rested her head on the blue University of Kentucky bag on her lap. For the next two hours, she slept.

❦❦❦

WHILE THEY'D WAITED FOR the bus in Tazewell, Drew said, "I'll stick around just long enough to check ever thing out, pack our stuff, and make me an alibi. Then I'm gone. Hell, I might even get to Myrtle Beach before you do." He patted the truck dash like it was a puppy's head, then his look turned serious. "But you can't count on that. Just follow the simple plan."

❦❦❦

THE BUS DRIVER PARKED and switched on the dim yellow interior lights. Lauren woke slowly, then at once. Knots tangled in her stomach. She stood unsteadily and lifted her bag. Her insides felt as if she were reeling upon an unsteady boat, and swaying up the aisle, she reached for each headrest for balance.

When she stepped off the bus, the air smelled sweet, not salty. She said to the driver, "Where's Myrtle Beach?" He smiled and said, "This is it." But Lauren didn't see any beach, any ocean.

Drew's truck was not waiting.

In the lobby of the bus station, she stood holding her bag with both hands gazing out the terminal window as the other passengers trickled away. After a time, she settled into a teal plastic chair on the first row. The station was nearly empty. Through the hazy window, the doughnut shop across the street was brightly lit. There were empty booths at the restaurant window, and at the counter farther back, men sat drinking coffee and smoking cigarettes at stools like red-capped mushrooms.

When the bus station door opened, the aroma of fresh warm doughnuts flooded in. She thought: Drew's truck will pull up at any second and before we go to our motel room, we'll have us some doughnuts. Then she thought, Maybe we'll buy the doughnuts and eat them in Drew's truck on the way to the Raintree. Then she thought, We'll save some doughnuts for after we're done in bed, and we'll watch TV naked and eat some of them and drink a cold Mountain Dew from the motel machine. She imagined Drew's arriving the way she'd imagined the appearance of Myrtle Beach, like a perfect thing one minute away. Like a little white chapel on the beach.

Lauren checked the station's big clock above the door. Any minute, she thought. Any minute now. Then: *We might have just missed one another. He might be someplace in the station, waiting for me.* Canvas bag in hand, she circled the seating area twice looking for Drew before taking a chair in view of the men's room, just in case. Thirty minutes passed.

Standing at the curb outside the station, Lauren heaved a pensive sigh and searched the empty street for Drew. Mountain air was all she'd ever breathed, and the thick dark August ocean wind, thicker still with fog and mist and the heavy, sweet scent of doughnuts weighed upon her chest. She closed her eyes when—

—the piercing shriek of metal on metal, a blur of yellow.

Falling back, she dropped the bag. The yellow box-shaped car squealed to a convulsive halt. The bag lay on the sidewalk between Lauren and the yellow cab.

The music churning inside the car sounded like the rattling of so many tin cans accompanied by a banjo without tuning. Her blue bag lay on its side. The instant she looked from the bag to the driver, his eyes darted to hers as if she'd screamed his name. He was a white man charred almost black, his brows like thick black caterpillars, his penetrating white eyes bright and steady as searchlights. A paralyzing charge passed through her, cinching her breath, jolting her balance. For a long moment his luminous eyes consumed her.

Lauren fell to her knees, reaching for her suitcase as if it teetered on the edge of a giant cliff. Her small fingers hooked its cloth handle. She fled like a flushed bird.

"Hey," the dark man called to her. She did not answer.

She careened into the station, a panicked stuttering recitation spilling from her lips. "Take a taxi," she whispered, collapsing into the plastic teal chair. "Hand over the address, put on my sunglasses, say we have a reservation, Raintree Inn Motel, North Myrtle Beach. Hand over cash, count the change." Then she began again. "Take a taxi." But she had never been inside a taxi. Lauren couldn't get into that yellow car with the charred man.

She would wait for Drew.

Across the street, people came and went. She might sit in the doughnut shop, she thought, in a lighted booth at the window. She could see Drew's truck as well from there as from here. By the time she ate a doughnut he'd be waiting outside. He'd be smiling.

She locked the stall door behind her, raised her head and listened. The reeking toilet was silent. Her fingers clawed inside her jeans pocket, then pinched the folded money. Whispering the numbers, she counted the twenties, then counted again. Near the station entrance, she made one final slow turn, just in case Drew had entered through some hidden door. When she'd come full circle, she reached for her bag.

Something caught her eye: In a booth in the doughnut shop across the street. A lean, angular man with a narrow, pointed face wearing a faded black tank top over skin the color and texture of deer hide. His sun-bleached hair was cut in that shaggy way, like Drew's, and he held his cigarette so that his wrist arched, like Drew's did, but the man's smile was not Drew's smile, for it was extra wide and not so sweet. With a twitch of his shoulder, the man thumped his cigarette into the ashtray in front of him and looked away.

The instant Lauren stepped outside, the world came down around her like a rockslide, the smell of doughnuts, the rattle and twang of strange foreign music, the dense, stiff ocean wind, the flat, naked openness of the landscape. The white eyes of the driver.

The man in the tank top wasn't looking in her direction as Lauren paused for the traffic before fluttering across the street. He just sat at his window seat, profiled and limp-wristed.

Entering the restaurant, she lowered her eyes and veered right. She sat at the window of the third booth staring across the street into the bus station, at the empty teal chair she'd occupied for the past two hours. She pictured herself sitting there.

The smell inside the shop cramped her insides with hunger. She looked all around. No waitresses. She'd have to walk past the leather-skinned man. Lauren reached for her white-framed sunglasses and made for the counter, angling her body away from him. Still, as she waited to pay, she felt his eyes working her over like fingers black with coal dust. Behind the counter, an old man wearing a white paper hat smiled as he counted back change for the twenty. When she turned, the leather skinned man glanced down into his ashtray and squashed out the last of his smoke then examined the coffee cup in front of him as she passed.

She pulled the warm doughnuts into finger-sized morsels and ate slowly, sipping just enough of her cold soda to get the food down, saving the rest. The taxi with the dark man and the foreign music sat across the street in its space at the curb. The driver's free hand reached up, and a small, bright light suddenly illuminated the book he held. Slowly, machine-like, he turned and looked at her. Despite the shield of her sunglasses, she felt their eyes meet. Lauren looked away.

A squeaking voice at her shoulder sent a violent stab through her. "Why, yes I am, and what about you?" Lauren recoiled from the singsong Carney-like talk. He was a wiry man made of beef jerky and dressed in a faded black tank top and ragged cut-off jeans. The scabby bleached arrowhead beard on his chin gave his long hollow face the look of a mountain goat. Lauren's fingers knotted under her chin. "I thank you so much for asking." Whiskey shellacked his breath. He lifted his limp wrist and pointed down at her. She pressed her back against the glass. He nodded toward the light blue suitcase. And in that freak show voice he said, "It says U. o. K.? And thank you very much, I am. I'm fine. Got a cigarette?"

"No," Lauren said, looking down at her fingers.

"Then have one of mine," he said, flashing that too-wide smile and extending the pack. He scratched at his neck and shifted his weight from one foot to the other, then shifted again.

"I don't smoke 'em." She pushed the white sunglasses tight against her face.

"Don't mind if I do," he said lighting up. He used his cigarette like a pointer as he spoke. "Why don't you take off them glasses? Too bright in here for you? Let me see them pretty doe eyes up close," he said. He touched his finger to his own eye, then took a half step back, tilted his head sideways and tugged at the tuft on his chin. He pointed again before speaking. "Or are you . . . a movie star?" He scratched his thin brown thigh just below the rag of his cutoff jeans and then fingered his navel. "I ain't kidding. Keep your eyes open, you'll see movie stars all over Myrtle Beach. I been watching you the whole time." He nodded toward the plastic teal chair across the street. Then, holding his pistol-shaped hand before him, he rotated on his bare heels until he was pointing into the bright glass at the far end of the restaurant. Lauren saw his reflection pointing back at her. "Seen your every move." He made a quick sidestep. His eyes flashed on her: "You-know-that-ZZ-Top-song-'Cheap-Sunglasses'?" He began humming the melody.

Her heart contracted with such force she thought she might retch, but Lauren didn't let on. She'd been propositioned by grown men but never so alone, never in a foreign land, never a man like this one. And she'd never used the words f— off, but she'd heard them used and she knew the look that accompanied those words. She gave him that look.

"My, my," he said. "You are one pretty thing."

"Tell it to my husband," Lauren said, reaching now for her soda.

"I'll do it," he said. "Where is he?" The goat man did a little disco spin, a three-sixty. "I'll do it. Let me guess." He looked up as if he were seeing a vision. "Your *husband's* at home looking for that *wedding* ring you lost somewhere." He did that know-it-all smile again. Lauren looked down at her doughnut remains. "I'm just kidding around," he said. He gave his cigarette a hard pull, tossed his head to the side, knifed one hand into his hip, and blew the smoke in a thin string over his shoulder. "I'm just naturally a easygoing guy." He pointed the cigarette down at her and whispered. "I do evera'thing easy. You can call me Mr. Easy if you want." Lauren turned away from him. Inside the yellow car across the street, the charred taxi driver hovered over his brightly lit book as if he were praying into it. His eyes turned up, found the goat man, then darted to meet Lauren's eyes. He lowered the book.

"I got this brand new tattoo?" Mr. Easy said. He turned his shoulder and pulled the tank top to the side, revealing the tattoo above his left nipple. A white lightning bolt divided a red and blue heart, its fresh colors like neon on his hide. "My girlfriend got one too just like it right here." He pointed to the other breast. "When we lay together just right and line up them lightning strikes? Whew!" he said, "We got some electricity happening, know-what-I-mean?"

She thought of her and Drew, their tattoos kissing as the two of them lay in their honeymoon bed. The colors and the design were just right. "Where'd you two get 'em?" Lauren said.

"Can't remember the name of the place," he said. He glanced back at the old man in the paper hat, then coiled down into the booth across from her and leaned in confidentially, studying his fingertips. "The guy who did it, he was bald and had a big ol' open eye—tattooed on his scalp." He tilted down his face and pointed to his crown. "Right there."

"Was it near the wedding chapel by the sea?"

"What?"

"The wedding chapel—"

"I know the one. On the north end. Know it well."

"My husband and I are getting tattoos while we're on vacation. We're staying near there."

"Near there, you say. No kidding. How 'bout that?" His lips parted. He looked away. "That's funny," he said, reaching for his cigarette. He wasn't smiling now.

"*You* got one," Lauren said.

"I got more 'en one tattoo, baby doll," he whispered with a thin, wide-lipped grin and a wink. "But that ain't the funny part. The *husband* is the funny part. Ain't it?"

Lauren heard a voice inside, the one she'd begun hearing two years ago, the summer she turned twelve and her breasts grew so fast and large they hurt, that voice that said *Run Like Hell.* She reached for her blue suitcase.

"Where you going, Sweet Pea?" he said, rising from the booth as she did.

"I gotta git," she said. The old man behind the counter turned.

"Shhh," Mr. Easy whispered. "Shhh. Was it something Mr. Easy said?"

She raised her arm and skirted around him. The old man, who was drawing himself a cup of coffee, stopped, looked Mr. Easy up and down, set down his cup and pulled off his white paper hat. "Well, let me at least get the door for you," Mr. Easy said, giving a slight bow to the other man.

The moment Lauren stepped outside she felt panic like a snakebite. She rushed to the sidewalk, her fledgling eyes bright with terror. Across the street in the taxi, the eyes of the dark hunkered driver fixed upon her.

"I was just being friendly. I'm Mr. Easy," the man said, trailing a step behind, his erratic hands flickering like a bat's wings.

❦❦❦

COPS WAS DREW'S FAVORITE TV show, and so he was pretty sure he was under videotaped surveillance. You can't be too careful, he thought. The authorities can read blinks of the eye like Morse code. He stretched out on the narrow cot, turned facing the cell wall and closed his eyes. Thinking of tomorrow, he pictured Lauren drenched in shiny coconut oil, lying on a giant rainbow towel in her white two-piece, surrounded by sparkling sand, her body glistening in the brilliant eye-aching sunlight. Above the sound of crashing waves, he'd call out to her and she'd turn, smiling up at him from behind the white sunglasses, then rise, spreading her arms as he ran to meet her. Nothing but blue water and blue sky above and beyond.

The languor of the moment settled upon him.

On the drive to the Tazewell bus station, he'd rested his hand on her knee. "If you want to make God laugh," he said, "just tell Him *your* plans." He held his smile until she returned it. Then he gave her knee a soft squeeze. "It's gonna work, Baby. This is God's plan for us. It's gonna work."

The cell lights suddenly dimmed, the spell was broken and the muddled disembodied voices of other inmates floated in from the long hallway. Drew's eyes shot open.

Late one afternoon when he was fourteen, he fell asleep in his deer stand. Hours later, the predatory sounds of the deep woods night startled him awake. Darkness swallowed him. He lay trembling until fear forced him down from the stand. Hour after hour he wandered aimlessly through the jagged blackness and brush, afraid to call out, afraid to remain silent, the weight of the mountain's darkness like a giant devil-cat sucking the air from his chest; blindly afraid to pause, blindly afraid that with his every step there awaited an immense precipice, afraid that his fall would be eternal and that he would remain forever lost in the black belly of the mountain. Even now, ten years later, he sometimes relived that night in dreams, and lying on a small cot in a Middlesboro jail, he sensed that nightmare fear working its venom into Lauren, and his heart fell and then fell farther. He said a prayer for her.

Drew told himself the lie he had to tell: In the next hour or two, at most, the cops would know the blood was deer blood, and that's all they'd have to know. No crime had been committed. He'd even volunteered to come in. They'd have to release him. His truck sat parked outside, their wedding rings in its glove box. Nine hours from now, he'd be at the Raintree Inn Motel, in time to wake Lauren from her sleep. When you think of the rest of your life with the one you love, nine hours is nothing.

Drew sat up on the cot and covered his face with his hands, lest the enemy see. He had spent his life negotiating things not going as planned. But this time everything would be okay. All was going to be fine, he told himself. Everything according to plan. Because on the other side of all this was Lauren, who would be waiting for him, waiting with open arms and a loving heart. And before the earth turned again on its axis, he'd be lying with her on the sands of Myrtle Beach, where the blue sky and the blue water came together like a kiss that lasted forever.

When he dropped his hands from his face, Drew saw the crude etchings of naked women scrawled on the cell wall a few inches in front of him. Monster breasts and burly vaginas. Drawings a boy would make. The childish work of boy criminals, he thought. Not like him. He wasn't a boy. He was a grown man who had committed no crime. Real love was no crime. Those drawings were the work of someone not like him, he thought, someone who had never felt love, never made plans for keeping it.

❦❦❦

"PLANS ARE LIKE CAR engines," he'd told Lauren as he fired up his truck that first night outside The Oak Ridge Motor Inn. He and Lauren had tried without success to keep their love a secret. "The simpler they are, the fewer things can go wrong with them. The easier they are to fix." He took her face into his hands and kissed her. "I'll make us a simple plan," Drew said.

The Powell Valley authorities claimed the ten years between fourteen and twenty-four made their love unlawful. But even at fourteen some girls know that all the love they're likely to get might all come at one time, and that one time might be now. And a man might see that look in a girl's eyes and know that all the love he was ever likely to see had all but passed him by. Both parties can believe in a miracle. Can feel it like a covenant.

But there were two things Drew hadn't counted on when he devised their simple escape: the Oak Ridge Motel room key Lauren had saved as a token of their first night together and Lauren's daddy's dogs.

This was the first plan, the simple one. A few days before their getaway, Lauren would leave her house each morning carrying an article of clothing in her pocketbook. Then, before the school bus came, she'd pull the blue University of Kentucky bag from inside the wrecked Ford at the end of the drive and store the neatly folded piece there. In the beginning, the simple plan was to just run off. But then there was the problem of the law and of Lauren's daddy, too.

"Don't ask me how, but he knows something's up. He won't give us a minute's peace," she'd said. "He won't stop looking, and he'll get the law into it."

"Then we'll just give him a reason to stop looking, and the law something to find," Drew said with a wink and a smile.

From that came Drew's bigger plan. He'd soak some of Lauren's old clothes with deer blood and bury them behind Lauren's house, on the bank of the Powell River. After they were married and Drew got a roofing job in Myrtle Beach, they would cut words and letters from old newspapers and magazines that would tell where the clothes were buried, and everybody would think that Lauren had come to some tragic end at the hands of a traveling serial killer, the kind that's never caught, and that would be that. Lauren cried when she pictured her mama and daddy reading that letter. But it had to be done. Because from now on it was her and Drew. No matter what. Scripture said she must leave her parents and cling to Drew. That was a marriage.

Yesterday afternoon, Drew had parked out of sight, buried the panties, bra, and dress, and then waited for her school bus. By dawn the next day they'd be gone, their simple plan complete. But late into the night after she'd not come home, Lauren's mother riffled through her jewelry box searching for clues. She found a key belonging to a motel located outside Oak Ridge. Drew had signed in under his own name. At five o'clock the following morning the two lovers woke to the threatening message Lauren's daddy was laying down on Drew's machine.

These events produced a bigger plan.

Drew stopped at the Middlesboro bank machine for cash then drove over the mountain, through Cumberland Gap and Harrogate to Tazewell. Between sobs at the Tazewell bus stop, Lauren confessed, saying the motel room key had been a memento of their love. She just couldn't part with it after that first night, she told Drew. "I never thought Mama would go snooping," she said. He wiped away her tears and kissed her gently and told her it was all right, that everything was all right, that their love was greater than all that opposed them.

Three hours later, when the Sheriff's car pulled up to his trailer, Drew wasn't surprised. But when the cop showed him the plastic bag with the bloody panties inside and asked Drew where they'd come from, he said, "Hell, I got *no* idear." And he was right. He was befuddled by how the cops could have found those panties. He hadn't thought about Lauren's daddy's dogs, that they might pick up a scent and bring home their find.

❦❦❦

THE CELL DOOR OPENED behind Drew, but he thought it best to feign sleep.

"I got some good news for you, Drew." The voice belonged to Mr. Fathead Allstate. "You'll wanna hear this. It's amusing."

Drew turned but didn't sit up.

"What's the difference between d-e-e-r and d-e-a-r?"

"Is this a test?"

"Know what a punch line is? Sit up, asshole." Drew dropped his elbows to his knees and looked down at his shoes. "You are dumber than dog shit, boy. That blood, you know, it was deer blood. Ha. Ha." Drew glanced up, blank-faced. He waited for the cop to go on. He just knew it wasn't over. But the cop was in combat mode, time was running out, and Drew was tired of the same old same old.

"I guess that settles our business then, don't it?" Drew said, extending his open palm. The cop leaned back against the wall and smiled. "Gimme back my truck keys."

"The bad news is we got us a missing little fourteen-year-old girl, and probably some foul play. I just hate it."

"You could always look for some other line of work," Drew said, standing now. "I don't know no fourteen-year-old girl."

The cop slowly turned and spoke to the ceiling. "Motel owner in Oak Ridge says different." He was facing Drew now, and for the first time his voice didn't sound like a cop's. "Fourteen-year-old," he said in a whisper. "And you ain't nothing but a ignorant twenty-four-year-old boy. But where you're going, boy, ignorant don't matter. A pretty boy like you? Where you're going you'll just be fresh meat. Fresh, ignorant boy meat."

Drew started for the door. The cop laid his hand on it. Drew stopped. "You arresting me?" Drew said.

"Not at the moment."

"Then get out of my way, 'cause you got to let me go."

"There is some middle ground here," the cop said, extending one arm like he was directing traffic. "We can question you." Drew gave him a look. "For seventy-two hours."

"I want a lawyer."

"But you're not under arrest—yet."

"I ain't answering another question until I have a court-appointed lawyer present."

"You watch too much TV, mister. But you're right. No questioning without an attorney. In the meantime, maybe you'd like to have a word with the girl's mama and daddy. The girl's mama, Drew, the woman's a mess. The old man would love to have a word with you. They're sitting in their truck outside. Been there all day. Bless their hearts, they won't believe the girl's dead. They think you're gonna tell them she's alive and where to find her. Say they're not leaving till they get an answer, till they get their little girl back. Pathetic," he said. "Pathetic."

Drew lay on the cot facing the wall. "We'll see if the State of Kentucky can get you a lawyer in the next seventy-two hours. We'll just see what turns up in the next seventy-two hours. Do you know how many days seventy-two hours is? Do the math." Drew heard the cell door shut behind him.

He had done the arithmetic, and he knew that one day had passed, and that it would be two more before he got to Myrtle Beach—that was if the law didn't work up charges to hold him longer. He told himself the necessary lies. That they'd have to release him, that the seventy-two hours was just a cop trick, that he'd wake in the morning and be on the road before Mr. Fat Ass finished his first cup of coffee. Lauren would be three nights alone in the dark woods. They had nothing to connect him to a crime that had not been committed. Time was not on his side, but for as long as he had time, he'd hold on. They'd have to let him make a call, he thought. He'd call the Raintree first thing in the morning. He'd have a plan by then. But maybe he'd be on the road instead of calling. The call would be traced. No doubt there. And the odds were against his avoiding Lauren's daddy, even if everything else fell into place. He'd make a quick and daring escape. Lauren's daddy would try to tail him, but Drew would lose him in the chase. Still, no matter what, they would have to allow him a call. One they'd trace. Two hundred dollars. The math said that was one night at the Raintree and money for food the day after. That night was already passing, and soon another would come. Seventy-two hours. Three days in the black wilderness. Three days alone. "She's just a fourteen-year-old girl," the cop had whispered. A woman never forgets a broken promise, Drew thought.

He extended his arms like a blind man, feeling for his balance as he knelt to the floor then gripped the edge of his bunk. His head fell forward in prayer. This was not a TV show. This was Middlesboro, Kentucky, a small town like a thousand other small towns. "Oh, God," he whispered. "Oh, please God."

❦ ❦ ❦

THE TAXI DRIVER SAW panic in the girl's face as she staggered from the doughnut shop. Runaways were a familiar sight here. This one glanced back then bolted toward him, hands up in surrender, eyes wide, like a trembling fawn's. Crossing the center line, she wedged one hand into the pocket of her tight jeans.

The driver recognized, too, the rat-faced man trotting to catch up.

Clutching a scrap of paper, Lauren stood panting at his window then extended her hand like an offering.

"We'll share," Mr. Easy called to the driver.

The driver read the address. "Okay," he said to Lauren.

"We'll split the fare," the leather man said, flashing a grin and reaching for the rear door handle.

"No way," the dark man said. He stepped out of the car and stood facing Mr. Easy, who tugged at his pointed beard and smiled, then glided back with a little bow. His eyes fixed on the other man, the driver opened the door for Lauren.

"Bye," Mr. Easy said, his smile like a painted circus clown's smile. "Be seein' you, darlin'. Soon." He tilted his face in mock deference and gave a little salute then backpedalled across the street as the taxi lurched from the curb.

The panting produced a buzzing in her ears, a charged tingling upon her flesh. She pressed the white sunglasses to her quivering lips and, heaving an exhausted sigh, laid back her head. Her dwindling strength flooded out. She turned, resting her head against the window and slowly opened her eyes. She expected to see the ocean, Myrtle Beach. It wasn't there.

After a few minutes, the driver spoke. "It's about a twenty-minute ride," he said. "Then we'll be at the motel. By two-thirty." The man's black finger touched the clock on the dash, and beside it Lauren saw the framed photograph of a woman in a long green silk dress standing between two teenage girls. The woman had a red dot, like blood, in the center of her forehead. "I know the owner," the driver said into the mirror. He saw Lauren's eyes. "My two girls," he said.

"Will we pass by the little white chapel?" Lauren said. The man's eyes flashed up again.

"What is that?" he said.

"Where I'm getting married tomorrow. Drew and me."

The man's eyes left the mirror. He didn't answer.

The sprawling landscape of tourist wreckage rushed past Lauren's window. When she was ten, her mother and father had taken her to Gatlinburg and Pigeon Forge. Lauren thought Myrtle Beach would look like Dollywood, only a city. Off in the distance, the dark silhouette of a rollercoaster track reminded her of a dinosaur's skeleton.

"Where's the beach?" she asked. The driver pointed. But she saw no ocean.

A deep current of exhaustion pulled her toward sleep, and the sway of the taxi triggered the memory of a Ferris wheel ride. As her lids gently descended, she felt the warm touch of her father's hand holding her steady. Below, she saw the bright carnival lights.

Then a snapshot of Mr. Easy's flickering hands flashed before her. Her eyes flew open. In the mirror, looking back, were the eyes of the charred man.

"There," the driver said with a nod.

The sign said Wedding Chapel, but the building was small, not much more than a playhouse shaped like a church. She thought of Drew.

"It ain't on the beach? Sure don't look like a church," Lauren said.

"It's not a church," the man said.

Lauren was looking out the rear window. "Then what, pray tell, is it?" The Wedding Chapel disappeared.

"A business. It's a business."

Outside the Raintree Inn, the driver reached for her bag. She let him take it. "The glasses," he said. "Remove them."

"I can't," Lauren said, remembering the simple plan.

"Yes," he said. "Or you'll not get a room. You wait here. And take off the glasses." The man started for the motel office door.

She smelled the current of salty air riding upon the black night. Lauren called to him. "Is this Myrtle Beach?" The man turned and paused, gesturing as if he were about to speak. Then he turned again and walked on.

Blue light from a television billowed from a small room off the motel office. After the driver pressed the doorbell, a short dark bald man with features like the driver's appeared rubbing the sleep from his eyes. He unlocked the door. As the driver spoke, the other man shifted in his sandals from side to side, then jammed his hands into his pockets. The smaller man looked out at Lauren. He scratched his bald head and talked down into the cheap burgundy carpet. The driver raised one finger like a candle before him. Neither man spoke. When the bald man lifted his face, the conversation was over. The driver looked at Lauren and nodded for her to come inside.

"She says she has a reservation," the driver said.

The older man looked at his computer screen. "I need some ID," he said.

Head down, Lauren turned the sunglasses in her hands. The driver cleared his throat.

"Money, then?" the clerk asked, but he was looking at the driver. Lauren dug out the folded bills and laid them in the man's hand. He spread the money on the countertop and then looked again at his computer screen.

"Who is this man?" He pointed at the name on the screen. "Is he coming here tonight?"

"My husband." Lauren's hand went up to her face as if she were still wearing the glasses. The two men exchanged a look. "He'll be here by mornin'," she said. Still the bald man did not look at her. Although his face was vacant, Lauren got the feeling that the two men were having a silent conversation. The older man set a key on the counter and, without looking up, pulled five of the twenties from the spread, pushed the rest back toward her. He showed her the money in his fist. "If your husband is not here by checkout, I'm keeping this. No discussion tomorrow," he said. "The money is now mine."

"Yes, sir," Lauren said, looking away. "He'll be here. I know he will."

"If he's not—" The motel owner looked again at the driver then pointed at the first room, beside the elevator. He laid his hand over the key and slid it across the counter. When she brought her eyes up to meet his, he spoke softly. "From here I can see your door," he said. "When your husband comes, I will see him. Goodnight." Lauren took the key.

Behind her, the two men talked in whispered broken English. She switched on the light and stood appraising the room before setting her bag inside. When she turned, the cab was driving away. The old bald man saw her. "He said you can pay me for the taxi ride when you check out."

Following the steps Drew had taught her, Lauren left the door open while she inspected the closet and bathroom. Thick brown drapes hid sliding glass doors. As instructed she stood in the doorway and studied the drapes for the shadowy figure of a man in hiding. Seeing none, she shut the door, turned the lock, set the chain and pushed the bolt.

Lauren sat at the foot of the bed, the soft lamp light behind her, facing the expressionless blond girl in the mirror.

She pictured herself on the school bus, her mind unmoored as the mountains floated by, wishing that she could see him, wishing like she was praying. Then the next second, it seemed, the bus stopped at the long steep drive that led to her house. Still thinking of Drew, she descended from the steps, still in that Drew dream, and before the bus was out of sight she'd hear a whisper and he'd be there, just on the other side of the road near the wrecked Ford, at the top of the ridge that runs down to the meadow. And for one or two delicious minutes he would hold her and kiss her, and just before it was over he would gently cup her face in his large hands and whisper that he loved her.

Lauren wanted to sleep now because only sleep would erase the time and distance between her and Drew. She opened the canvas bag and laid out the white two-piece bathing suit and a single change of clothes, the sundress with the white lace, her wedding dress.

Lifting her blouse over her head before stepping into the shower, Lauren smelled the acidic bus exhaust. She stripped off her panties and bra. As she waited for the water to warm, the fluorescent tube above the mirror began to flicker and hum. And in that stropping light the smiling face of Mr. Easy momentarily appeared, then vanished.

Lauren locked the bathroom door, turned and pressed her shoulder against it. With her arms bound to her like folded wings, she held her breath and pressed an ear against the cold metal door. She listened. She waited. Slowly she retreated to the shower. She didn't turn or close her eyes, not when she washed her face, not when she rinsed her hair.

❦❦❦

WRAPPED IN BLACKNESS, DREW lay curled upon his cot, sweating fear. Trying to believe. "It's gonna work, Baby," he whispered in prayer. "It's gonna work." And sometime during the night his praying conferred upon him sleep.

He dreamed of killing his first deer, seeing in the dream precisely what he had seen that day: his position high in the deer stand, the apparition of the buck, feeling his heart about to explode when the big buck turned and raised its head. Only now it was Drew in the cross hairs of the scope. Then

Drew and the deer became one, both sensing like a premonition the end, that moment of finality with blinding clarity.

He watched as his father dipped his hands, and the boy closed his eyes. The boy's face now bathed in warm blood. "This will make you a man," his father said. "This will make you a man." But as consciousness seized him, the voice Drew heard was not his father's but his own. And the blood on his face was not blood but hot tears. And as he sat alone in the blackness of his jail cell, Drew pressed his fingers into his sobbing eyes and whispered over and over, "No it won't. No it won't."

STANDING IN DARKNESS, LAUREN released the towel and it fell to her feet beside the bed. Her small white fingers gently stroked the crisp, cool sheets, then eased them back. Knowing beyond all certainty and conviction that she would wake to the sound of Drew's voice, she lay in the cool blackness, spooning his pillow, awaiting sleep. Her lips formed a dreamy smile. Drifting now, she felt the effusion of a levitating lightness, and in that space that is not space and time that is not time, she felt the touch of her mother's fingertips upon her young, tired brow and, from them, the soothing flow of warmth and love upon her tender cheek. The sound of her own breathing faded.

Then: something like a whisper from beyond the sliding glass door. "Shhh." Lauren thought: *You can call me Mr. Easy.*

Wide-eyed, she lay in a fetal knot panting like a breathless child. *"Shhh,"* the voice seemed to say, again. Again. And again. Trembling, she listened. A fist formed round her heart.

You have to look, she thought. You can't just lay here scared all night. You ain't a child no more. You've made your choice. You've got to do it. You've got to tend to what's out there.

She felt for the damp towel then eased stealthily from the bed. The thundering pulse in her ears beat time to the rhythmic breathy voice from beyond. Binding the towel round her, Lauren stared at the heavy drapes that covered the glass doors. She watched and waited. You ain't a child, she thought. Pressing her fists to her throat, she tiptoed toward the dark glass doors. At the edge of the thick drapes, she drew breath and held it fast. She closed her eyes. She listened.

She heard it, the slow in and out. Then, pressing her cheek to the wall, steadying one hand with the other, she brought a finger to the border of the curtain. With every heartbeat, she heard the blood rushing inside her ears. Her finger pressed the seam. The curtain inched open, allowing a thin blade of light. She turned her eyes.

Seizing breath, Lauren felt her heart give way to this: A full moon, suspended like a distant white beacon, divided the dark sky above from the dark sea below, and the moonlight's glow infused the billowing white clouds above with a soft luster while its gentle light fell upon the slate-colored sea below and sparkled atop its rolling whitecaps near shore's edge. Between sea and sky stretched a luminous glittering path that opened to forever. "Drew," she murmured, then whispered, "this is it."

A shallow frothy tide as white as lace unfolded and rushed toward her, then paused to reconsider: *Shhh,* it whispered, then scurried back to join its advancing mate. She pressed her palms together and listened. The soft unfolding waves were a summons and a reply, a tender voice that said, *Shhh.* Then: *Shhh.* Then: *Shhh,* like a soothing mother to her crying child. And in that moment, she felt her heart open wide. Wide enough, she thought, to embrace an endless tide of love. "Oh, Lord," she whispered. "God Almighty."

Everything I Needed to Know

THE TRASHCAN IN THE **toilet is where you discover the pregnancy test.**

"The only reason we fight is that we're not married," she says.

"Can I get you some toilet paper?" you say.

"You see? I bring up marriage and you change the subject."

"It's hard to talk to you with stuff hanging from your nose."

"You don't love me."

"By definition love is talking to somebody who has that stuff hanging from her nose."

"But you're never going to marry me."

"I'm going to the toilet for some tissue. Then we'll talk."

"No we won't, I just know we won't."

"Do you want to talk or not talk?"

"I want to get married."

"Not before you wipe that stuff from your nose, you don't."

"I want to get married and have a family."

"Not before you wipe that stuff from your nose, you don't."

She's talking to Ralph on the Big White Phone when you hear the voice of God.

YOU ARE DEEPLY ASLEEP when from your young daughter's bedroom comes a sound, a small sound—a sound without meaning, if she's not your child. Before you can get to her bed, you hear her vomiting in the darkness. Her eyes are closed but her arms are raised to you when you get there. She does not cry, but from inside her comes a whimpering melody, an innocent sadness, a lethargic lament. You feel the heat from her small limbs even before your hands touch her, and when you lift her thin gown, her body heaves again. "It's okay, baby," you say, holding her fiery skin against your comparative coolness. "It's okay."

You smell the bourbon on your breath when you kiss her soft shoulder. Leaning into the dim light of the doorway, your wife sways—a kind of balancing act—her right hand holding her head steady.

"I've got her," you say, and your wife turns, one hand extended near the wall, and feels her way back toward the bed you aren't sharing.

There is a Tinker Bell nightlight beside the toilet. You whisper that it's okay over and over as you wait, there on your knees, her tiny hot body against your bare chest, your hand holding her small round tummy with the tenderness once given her mother's breast. When you feel the cramping take shape in your hand, you guide your daughter over the toilet. She does not resist but instead gives herself to you as if this is a dance of love. When it begins, you press your hand against her fevered skin to help it along, to get it all out, and you hold her there. Just hold her.

Never allow your wife to watch you brush your teeth.
IN THE SPACE BETWEEN the intimate and the familiar, love dies. Today, the dying begins in the most wonderful way: with the touch of another woman's hand on your forearm during a conversation about policy that is never about policy, a drink after work to discuss a policy position, a promise to consider both policy and position privately.

Policy discussions go on for months.

But as you brush your teeth, you know that this is the day. This one. You two will finalize the new policy and put it into effect, this policy that is the first and final advance toward a newer death than the one you are living. Because once you know a thing you can't not know it. And already you know what you will do. You know that you have decided, that what you think you're deciding now as you bow before the mirror and brush your teeth is only a rehashing of what you've already decided. You know that you are living inside a conversation with yourself that is a lie. But at the same time, you know that you have not yet come to that point when there is only the now, the delicious now, the omnipresent now that is the union of two bodies, the slick hot now that is the sweet perfume of that death. But you know that you're close, and at some level, a part of you is praying for a miracle that will reverse the destiny you have already chosen. And it is at that moment that you hear your wife's voice. She's standing behind you at the bathroom door, head tilted, face smeared as if from an apparent stench, studying your frothy mouth.

"That's gross," she says.

The medicine cabinet is the worst place in the house for storing medicine.

CONSIDER THE CABINET'S LOCATION, above the sink and beside the toilet. It is a dark auspicious place where you go for relief and comfort from the fever that originated in that place, a site ripe with the seeds of your affliction: The heat and dampness, the fetid scent on your hands that doesn't go down the drain, the microbes that rise with the steam—the tepid sweat. At the office, you can't get enough of the cure, can't stop the illness, the accompanying aches and pains. You live for the little deaths, the moment when breath is gone, when breathing begins.

Her name is Cynthia, who, at your invitation, accepted the inoculation with elation and gratitude and whose gifts of breathlessness you wear after you've showered off her sex. Cynthia, who insisted upon paying for the hotel room because she knows you are married. The next day, Cynthia is standing in your office by the time your computer heats up. And it begins again, the ache, followed by its medicine. The two become indistinguishable.

The bathroom mirror is the only place to rehearse a lie.

THE PROBLEM IS THAT you can't see into it, can't really see yourself in it. This, you think, is the now, that omnipresent, radiant now. You tell yourself that because that empty place has been filled by Cynthia, that place that is always filling up, you will be a better husband and father because, after all, Cynthia knows you are married and when you are happy everybody's happier. All of this knowing brings a dark comfort to you, an illusory happiness that you are sure must translate to a better life for all. This is a good thing.

The good thing began with degrees of denial. Sometimes, you'd give anything to believe you love your wife. But there is nothing there in the interior negotiations to cling to. And so you begin with the premise that you do not love her. And in this way, the memory of loving her recedes until you take your stand before the bathroom mirror:

You do not love her.

Sometimes I do, I really do. I'm not making this up. I do. At times I feel this deep affection, compassion. Out of nowhere I feel it. She is bending, taking laundry from the dryer. She gently eases a strand of hair from her face. And I suddenly feel this tide of tenderness, and I want to take her into my arms. It comes out of nowhere.

But you don't act on that impulse.

I have. I have. Then she gives me a look that says, *What* are you doing? You may think this unrealized moment a scratch, a tiny cut, that it is nothing. Count the years. Do the multiplication. See the tiny scars, the slow bleeding. When that moment of desire arrives now, I say to myself, What are you doing?"

That's not what you say.

Yes.

No, now you say, I don't love her and I am biding my time. Now you fool yourself into believing you have nontoxic alternatives. You used to say, I know I am an unhappy man, but I have what I have and I don't want anything else.

Who told you that?

Then when that didn't work, you had to up the dosage. Okay, you said. I do want something else. I want it. But I don't need it. I have everything I need. After all, nobody has all he wants. That's childish. Grow up. Be a man.

I may have thought that. It's true. What you say, I mean. It's true.

You mean what you say.

You're putting words into my mouth.

If you weren't so pathetic, I'd be laughing.

Okay, so I said to myself, I don't want it. I don't need it.

No, what you said was, *Because* I don't want it, I don't need it.

This is exhausting.

True. For both of us.

There's nothing new here.

But that is not where it ends.

I know.

What comes next?

I say to myself, Okay. Okay. You do want it, that something else, that something that will take away that something that is nothing. And that feeling is a need. No denying that. Isn't that self-evident? So, okay. But—

We're not done here. Go ahead. Finish. Complete the circle.

I don't know what you mean.

It all begins with lying to yourself, doesn't it? At least give that lie a form: you know, words, a sentence. Go on now. Say it.

I can't have it.

That's right.

I don't want it. I don't need it. I can't have it. Okay. That's it. I've said it.

No, it's not. That is not it. Go ahead. You are so close. Go ahead. Say it for Christ's sake.

I don't want it. I don't need it. I can't have it. Therefore, I don't want it; therefore, I don't need it; therefore, I can't have it. Therefore, I don't want it. Therefore, Cynthia. I don't need it. Cynthia. I can't have it.

Cynthia.

Some things you can't wash off.

You come home late again.

You have spent the drive home inventing every minute of two fictional hours, and, expecting an ambush, you're trying to put that fiction into motion as you walk in, holding all of those created moments in your head, where you have arranged them like the tools hanging above your workbench outside in the garage.

Something lies on the bare kitchen table. For a second, the word on the outside of the small white envelope does not register. The three capital letters, two in green crayon, the other in blue, spell the name she calls you. One of the awkward Ds is backwards, but that doesn't change anything. You set your briefcase on the floor, rest your phone on the empty kitchen table and reach for the envelope. You hear a small voice:

"Find the magic dust, Daddy." The lilting voice comes from the hall behind you. "It's an *emergency*. Can you find it? Oh, Daddy, Daddy, Daddy. We must find the magic dust."

You see the tiny silver crown tilting from the black curls, and the one small blue eye hiding at the door. You smile at the envelope's seal, at the ounce of child saliva that has glued it fast. There is no place for even air to enter or escape. Your fingers can't break the seal without tearing something. You turn and see the red crinoline under the pink tutu, her face turned vertically now as she waits. Her mother has made up the child with patience and care: powder, a touch of mascara and a dab of rouge, pink lipstick. She points the magic wand. "Daaa-deee?" she says. "Hurry."

You pinch red and blue glitter from the corner of the envelope. "Come here my little princess, for you I have the magic dust."

"The dust is not for me, King Daddy."

"Sure it is, my little princess. All of the magic dust in my kingdom is yours for a kiss." You close your eyes, tilt back your head and purse your lips.

"Da-deee!"

When you look, she stands hands on hips. "This is not *your* story, Daddy." She points the magic wand at you like a saber. "She will die without the magic dust."

"Who?"

"Da-deee!"

You're still pinching the glitter between two fingers. Your daughter takes the hand and leads you down the hall toward your bedroom.

"Like this, Daddy," she says, looking down to see that you are walking in step with her. "Stop," she instructs at the bedroom door. Your wife lies on the bed, eyes closed, her hands folded across her stomach—wearing her faded wedding dress.

"See," your daughter says. "I told you. She's dead." She takes your hand and leads you to the bed.

"How did she die?"

"No pixie dust," your daughter says.

"This dress," your wife whispers, eyes still closed.

"Ma-maaaa!" your daughter says. "You are the princess. I am the Tinker Bell."

"I can't breathe in this dress. And that's with the back open."

"Okay, Daddy. Do it. Then kiss the sleeping princess."

You look at your daughter, who lifts her tiny hand and rubs her thumb and index finger together.

"Where?" you ask. And she guides your arm so that your hand is over your wife's heart.

"There," she says.

When your wife feels the glitter fall on her breast, she opens her eyes and smiles.

"I love you, Daddy," your daughter says. Your wife lifts her hand, takes yours.

Plastic flowers are always wrong.

YOU ARE A FAMILY that goes out for ice cream. Your daughter falls asleep in the car on the drive home. You have her in your arms. You lay her in her bed. Sleeping, she lifts her arms to you and you undress her.

When you come back to the kitchen, you see your cell phone vibrating on the bare kitchen table. See your wife reach, see her face when she decodes the illuminated numbers.

"Must be an emergency," she says, setting the phone back on the table. She turns and heads for the kitchen cabinet for glasses, fills them with ice, sets the gin and bourbon on the bar. When her back is turned, you put the phone inside a pocket of your briefcase. You stand with only the bare kitchen table there.

Looking up at the glasses, at the ice in the two glasses she holds up for inspection, she says, "I wouldn't do that if I were you." You can't bear to look at your wife. "Aren't you afraid you'll lose your charge?" She pours without measuring. You just stand there. She pours tonic into her glass. The bubbles spew over. "It's Friday night," she says looking up at you, the man in the lineup, there in the bright light that hangs over the empty table. "Let's play a drinking game."

"Okay," you say. "What will it be?"

"Truth or Dare," she says. "Like when we were in college." She sets the drinks on the kitchen table. She pulls out two chairs and you sit at an angle. Like people in a cafeteria. After some drinks, she tells you a funny story. Somehow the gin and the bourbon make their way to the kitchen table. Later, on the sofa, you try to take off her blouse and she tries to let you, and then you are both howling and making faces like lunatics. When you kick over your drink, you curse, but she laughs, red faced until her wet eyes glitter. She lies there half naked, her eyes closed, arms lifted up to you. At some point you know that you must get up and empty your bladder. You stumble into the bathroom and stand swaying at the toilet.

And somewhere in all of this you look down and see the Tinker Bell nightlight, the dim light that makes standing here possible.

Delivery Options

I T WAS A SHORT walk from the curb of Melody Street up the drive to Sissy Stuckey's front door, ten, maybe twelve, paces. Tim Walsh made it in six, seven max, vaulting forward, the steaming Dough-Dough's pizza cradled like an offering in his hands. At Sissy's doorstep, he inflated himself to an imagined height of six feet, filling his lungs with summer air and then blowing like an Olympic swimmer at the end of a heat, this an attempt to calm his palpitations. But he felt his face flush up the second he rang the doorbell. There Tim stood at the ready, eager as an Olympic sprinter awaiting the gun. When Sissy opened her front door, his gleaming eyes widened with want and lust. Taking a royal step forward, he announced the amount of her purchase. Sometimes it was pepperoni and cheese, sometimes a supreme.

Like most of his customers, Sissy never tipped, not even the spare silver from her order. She didn't know his name, never asked. Once, they passed in the Food Lion grocery aisle. She looked right at him. Didn't know him from Adam. But all summer, Tim lived for these fleeting seconds at Sissy Stuckey's front door.

His first delivery at the corner of Blue and Melody Streets began like any other. The pizza order received at ten o'clock, his delivery no later than ten-thirty. Sissy, who was at least ten years older than Tim, arrived at her door tightly wrapped in a thick, faded cotton housecoat that smelled of marijuana, her hair looking a little like a ragged hornet's nest, no makeup, cigarette hanging from her fingers.

"How much," she said, teetering, feeling for the doorframe. Tim smelled beer on her breath. He answered. She dug into her housecoat pocket and handed him a ten.

"You ordered the supreme, not the pepperoni," he said.

"Shit," she said. "I'll get the rest."

As he waited, Tim Walsh stood on the front steps looking down the hallway into Sissy Stuckey's small house. Something in the hall mirror caught his eye. He stepped to the side to get a better angle. From the TV in Sissy's bedroom, Tim saw the reflection of the adult movie she was watching. She had pressed pause, capturing a moment of intense anticipation on the part of both actor and actress.

"Here," Sissy said, veering around the dining room table, unfolding three singles. As he made change, Tim thought, Under her clothes she is naked. Inside her head are pornographic thoughts. It mattered not that Sissy Stuckey was plain, simple, that her dingy housecoat smelled of contraband and that her teeth bore a yellow tint, that she was ordinary in every way.

When Sissy shut the door, Tim dashed to his truck, snatched the lighted Dough-Dough's pyramid from the roof, switched off his headlights and wheeled around the corner onto Blue Street, where he shut off the engine. The curtains of Sissy's bedroom were pulled tight, but Tim could tell when Sissy hit the play button because of the flickering on the drapes. And watching the blinking rhythm of light and shadow and thinking of Sissy, love-struck Tim Walsh masturbated like an Olympic spider monkey. Then he continued his deliveries. This became the pattern.

On Sunday mornings, he always asked for forgiveness at The Swamp Fox Church of God, where he played the piano, and he prayed that God would grant him that forgiveness, for he knew in his heart of hearts that he lived for Friday nights.

❦❦❦

TURN BACK THE CLOCK eighteen months.

Denise Trotter was dyeing her hair, a necessary chore for the past two years, one that she postponed until her husband Trip Trotter attended his Moose Lodge meetings or his weekly poker games. He couldn't stand the smell of the chemicals, he said. He was allergic, he said. She'd sometimes do her nails while she waited for her hair to cook. So when the phone rang, she lifted it as if her fingers were pinchers and held the receiver an inch or so from her ear. She heard a strange man's voice say, "Mrs. Trotter?" She hung up, thinking it was a solicitation and that her nails were wet and that her hair was cooking. The phone rang again. She considered letting the machine get it, but after the third ring she felt so annoyed she picked up anyway. "Mrs. Trotter—" She hung up. When she picked up the third time she said, "The next voice you hear will be my husband's," and she'd already lowered the receiver when the man said, "I doubt that." She stared at the phone in her hand then slowly brought it to her ear. He must have heard her breathing, for he said, "Your husband is not at home, Mrs. Trotter."

A tide of paranoia swept over her and she spun her head like a wide-eyed possessed woman in need of an exorcist. Then she whispered, "How do you know that?"

The man said, "Because as we speak, Mrs. Trotter, he is screwing my wife."

❦ ❦ ❦

BACK TO NOW.

P.C. Hickman worked the drive-thru for almost two years before being assigned a teller's slot inside the bank. The move was treated by her boss, Ms. Grimes, as something of a promotion, although her pay remained the same. P.C., three years out of college, knew that the slow climb to branch manager meant taking all the baby steps—and maybe a few extra. Still she felt nostalgic when she thought of her days inside the little booth near the ATM machine, where she could look down into the front seat of people's lives as they waited for her to complete their transactions. And in those quiet minutes between customers, she was left with her own imaginings, her own dreams. Although her thoughts and fantasies could never be shared, she had been happy for the freedom to have them.

P.C. was counting out her drawer when she saw Gary Sheppard at the door.

"Hello!" she called. "Welcome."

He stopped at a tall glass-top table. "Hey, P.C.," he said. He smiled then reached into his shirt pocket for a pen. She watched as he filled out the bank form. He had been the point guard, the only white starter, on the university basketball team the year she was a freshman cheerleader. They sat together once on the bus for an away game. He was an Accounting major too, a senior, and he helped her with her homework. No, actually he had done it for her. After graduating, she had mustered the courage to ask to use him as a reference. "Only if you promise not to tell about—" he said, not finishing the sentence, and she knew that he was teasing her about their academic infidelity. In the past year he had begun to look his age, she thought, but she still liked the way he looked.

"Hey, Gary," she said as he approached her.

"Hey," he said.

She took his check and deposit slip. Lowering her voice and avoiding his eyes, she said, "Ahhh, putting money *in* this time." They exchanged a smile. When he'd discovered his wife was having an affair, he emptied their joint account. She knew that remarks of that nature were considered inappropriate, but the two were alone at the counter. These moments of light flirtation pleased her.

"Getting kind of personal there, aren't you?" He smiled.

"Never," she said. "I'm a regular vanguard of discretion."

"Right," he said.

"Go ahead," she said. "Ask me a personal question." Smiling, she slid the deposit receipt back to him. "Fire away."

Gary looked over at the Xerox machine, then panned back to her. "After hours," he said nodding toward the machine, "have you ever, you know, sat naked on the copy machine and—?"

She stepped back in mock horror, giving him a limp-wristed dismissive flutter. "That's not personal, Gary, that's *intimate*." They both laughed. "Besides, do you know how hot that thing gets?"

"I rest my case." Again they laughed. He nodded and waved, then turned back.

"One thing," he said. She tilted down her face and in that way that third grade teachers administer discipline, crossed her arms and tapped her foot. "No," he said, "really. What's your name? All these years, you've always been P.C. What do the initials stand for?"

"Politically correct," she said. "You should know that." She hoped that he would smile again and let it go. But he didn't. He waited.

She looked away. Then back at him. "Pepsi Cola," she said. "Pepsi Cola Hickman. My mamma said she didn't want to give me a name belonging to a white person, you know who oppressed us?" She swept her hand to indicate the bank. "Like corporations don't oppress us all, black and white."

"I'm sorry if I embarrassed you," Gary said. "I'll call you P.C."

"Whatever," she said.

Gary was sorry to have pressed for her name. He turned again for the door.

"You forgot something," P.C. called. She smiled and held up his deposit receipt.

When he passed through the glass door on his way out, she whispered, "You could call me darlin'."

❦❦❦

ON THE PHONE, GARY Sheppard asked Denise Trotter why it was necessary they meet in the Darlington Library. She said, "Because there I can't scream." There was a pause on the other end of the line. "Nobody cries in a public library," she said.

They'd met only once, at the office of the private investigator she'd hired, where they sat side by side on a fake leather sofa and watched the video of Gary's wife, Deidra, and Denise's husband, Trip, kissing outside the Fairfield Inn after having spent two hours inside soiling the sheets. The couple worked together at The Department of Social Services. Turns out they'd been servicing each other socially for almost a year.

Just behind a display for New Fiction, Gary spotted Denise thumbing through a magazine. "Hi," he said. "What's up?" She'd lost weight in the past year. Her hair was shorter, professionally colored and cut, her nails a work of art. She wore a stylish navy blue dress with a white collar.

"Thanks for coming," she said. They sat. Denise tossed the magazine, sending it sliding across the table. "They're getting married," she said.

"So I hear," he said.

"What do you think?"

"I think as little as possible," he said.

"You know that your wife, ex-wife, you know she wasn't Trip's first fling, probably not his last."

"We're all divorced now, Denise. Do you really want him back after all this?"

"No, never," she said.

"Me neither."

"But I do want something. I want it bad." Gary lifted his eyebrows. "I want to get even," she said. "I really, really do."

"Good luck," he said. He stood and offered his hand. "I'm trying to put it all behind me."

"In that case," she said. "We never had this conversation."

Outside in the library lot, Gary felt for his keys. Denise called to him. She handed him a business card. "If you change your mind," she said. Gary looked at the red embossed lettering. "I have my real estate license now," she said. "I'm trying to make a new life. I need your help." Gary dropped the card into his pocket.

❦❦❦

His TINY ONE-BEDROOM DUPLEX was dark. He switched on the end table lamp and emptied his pockets as he always did. The house he'd shared with Deidra had belonged to her parents. It didn't matter that he had doubled its value with his own sweat, transformed the attic space above the garage into a bedroom and bath, totally remodeled the two other baths and the kitchen, ripped up the carpet and installed hardwood floors throughout. His attorney insisted that he move out immediately, saying that Gary would fare better in the settlement if he did so. On such short notice, the duplex was the best he could do.

He was entitled to half of the house's contents, which he loaded into a U-Haul as his wife's lover, Trip Trotter, stood at the door with a pen and a Social Services clipboard, crossing through the property list. Two hours later, Gary unloaded almost everything at a storage bin in Florence, ten miles away. Six months later, he just wanted to get rid of everything that had been theirs. He'd sold it all for a fraction of its value. And now, looking down at Denise Trotter's real estate card, he again felt a rising contempt for his former wife. A fierce and violent impulse. One that he fought. "This is not me," he whispered. "This is not me." He opened a beer and reached for the remote.

It was almost eleven o'clock when he realized he'd not eaten. He ordered a pizza. He was still gathering beer cans when he saw the pick-up with the lighted Dough-Dough's sign pull to a stop outside.

♥♥♥

SISSY STUCKEY WAS EMPLOYED as a waitress at the Top of the Hill Truck Stop fifteen miles away, between Darlington and Cheraw, but she made her money selling dope there. On the graveyard shift, which was hers Monday through Thursday, the money was in green amps and black beauties. She only dealt in prescription varieties of amphetamines and stayed clear of meth. But she had connections for and samples of anything you'd want. She was well known and well liked by the truckers and was perfectly suited for graveyard shift. She could hold her own with the late-night clientele.

"Let me take you home with me," a driver would say. And she would say, "Only if you'll introduce me to your wife." And he might say, "Well, take me home with you." She'd reach into her waitress dress pocket and fist a small plastic bag of pills. "Don't live around here," she'd say, offering her hand. They'd do a little handshake, she a mock curtsey, and he'd receive the pills. She'd give him a big beige smile and say, "Besides, even a dog don't shit where he eats," and the trucker would smile back, thinking she was talking in code about selling drugs.

Once in a while, a drunk would try to feel her up. And when he did Sissy didn't flinch. She didn't even yell. In the same voice she used for, "You want them eggs fried or scrambled?" she'd say, "You want to take that greasy hand off my ass?" Then she'd go about her business. Her sassiness had a powerful erotic effect on men who otherwise wouldn't give her a first—let alone a second—look. Sissy Stuckey was just so slinky and cool. They'd nod and say, "She ain't much to look at, but I'll bet she's a bobcat in bed."

In truth, her apparent sexual ease with men was genuine disinterest. Although Sissy was easily aroused by all varieties of sex, her relations were exclusively with women, which is why she had moved to Darlington, only a little more than an hour from Myrtle Beach.

❦❦❦

AT BED, BATH & Beyond, Pepsi Cola Hickman purchased a special pillow for her bathtub and some half-price bath beads. She was of course good with her money. She knew the value of things, and she knew how to indulge herself in simple, inexpensive ways. On Friday nights in summer, she turned down the thermostat on the air conditioning until her apartment was crisp and bitingly chilled. Then she ran a hot bath. She plugged up her portable CD player and loaded in Marvin Gaye—the one good thing her mother had given her—put up her hair in a towel, then slowly descended into the steaming water. She closed her eyes until that special levitating calm set in; then, heaving a deep slow breath, she'd reach for the latest *Fifty Shades of Grey*.

When she'd had enough, she'd step into her cold bedroom, her body steaming, and slowly towel off. The feeling was pure exhilaration.

❦❦❦

THERE WAS SOMETHING FAMILIAR about the lighted numbers on Gary's cell, although the phone said Unknown. He held his finger on the delete button, then stopped and reached for his wallet. He studied the red numbers on the business card. He drank his morning coffee. The only sound in the duplex was a hissing from the toilet in the half-bath three feet away, the spray of wasted water that meant another call to the landlord, another big water bill.

On his way home from work, he detoured past the house he had re-modeled, the one that Deidra and Trip Trotter were sharing. "This is not me," he whispered. He reached for his phone and dialed the number.

"I'll have to get back with you," Denise Trotter said. "I'm at the beauty parlor."

❧❧❧

"WHAT'S THAT SMILE ABOUT?" Trish, the owner of Beauty World and Spa said, indicating the phone in Denise's hand. "That's one devilish look on your face." She opened the nail polish bottle with a deliberate I'm-waiting-for-an-answer twist of the wrist. "Now that you're an available single female, you're getting a little aren't you?" she said, nodding a big uh-huh.

"Since I started selling real estate and was inducted into the Kiwanis, I've not been starved for companionship, if that's what you mean, Trish."

Trish said, "I know a couple of Darlington firemen who would just love to set a fire under you. You're looking gooood."

"Thanks but no thanks. I'm working on a little arson project of my own."

"You go, girl," Trish said. "Give me your left hand, the one without the ring."

❧❧❧

WHEN GARY ENTERED THE library, Pepsi Cola Hickman stood with her back to him, checking out a stack of books.

"Accounting?" he said. She turned. He smiled. "Powerful, engaging reading," Gary said.

"Hey, Gary," she said. The librarian slid the stack to her. "Don't look." she lifted the books, clutching them to her chest. "I have a date—with a Romance novel. After a day at the bank, I just want something mindless." She gave him a little wave. "See ya," she said.

As she walked away, Gary realized he'd not had a date since the separation.

"Psssstttttt!"

Gary turned. Denise motioned to him from the Harry Potter section. She handed him an envelope. They spoke in hushed voices.

"What's this?" Gary said.

"It's the number for the tuxedo place at the Florence Mall and your script."

"Script?"

"Didn't I say I'd do the work? Dial a number and read this script. That's all I'm asking."

Gary looked down at his assignment. "I don't know, maybe it's best to leave the past in the past. Just get over it."

"I'm all about getting over it, Gary. I'd say in that category I got a big head start on you. But sometimes you have to *do* something if you want to move on. Dial the number and read your lines." She could see the hesitation in his eyes. "Your Deidra left her mark on you. Trip left his mark on me. Don't you want to remove that mark?"

Denise didn't need to hear his answer. She saw it on his face.

"This is not me," he said, watching her walk away. "This is not me."

"You look like baked Alaska, sugar lips," Trish said to Sissy Stuckey, who had just crawled out of a tanning bed at Beauty World and Spa.

"I never had baked Alaska," Sissy said. "I don't even know what baked Alaska looks like."

"Me neither," Trish said. "Sometimes when I get this stoned, words I don't even know just come flying out of my mouth."

"Good deal," Sissy said. Good deal was something she often said to truckers. She said it now because she was as stoned as Trish.

Sissy Stuckey and Trish had a good deal. Sissy used Trish's tanning beds free of charge, and Sissy gave Trish the free samples of drugs she didn't want.

Denise Trotter opened a cold bottle of Chablis and reached inside the china cabinet for a wine glass. Then while the Chablis was catching its breath, she undressed and slid into her new satin panties and matching camisole top. Her hair looked good and her nails were gleaming. She lit a candle, although the warm afternoon light still filled her bedroom, poured generously into the chilled glass then opened the drawer of her bedside table for the pad and pencil there. She dialed the first number on her list. Wanda, the owner of Wanda's Dress Shop, answered.

"Hey, Wanda? This is Deidra-soon-to-be-Trotter? I'm fine. Look, you've got to take up my dress. Oh, Wanda, I hate to tell you this. I'm trusting in your confidence." Denise gave it a good long pause. "I'm a recovering bulimic. And with all this wedding stuff? My nerves? Well, I hope I can count on you. That's right. Yes. Can you cut it down from a size ten to a snug six? Oh, Wanda. You're a miracle maker. A miracle maker, that's what you are."

Denise lifted her glass in a toast to the universe then took a good long drink. She drew a deliberate line through the word "dress" on her list. Then she dialed the next number, the one beside the word "cake."

By nine o'clock when all the shops closed, Denise had worked her way down the list, from caterer to flower shop. She opened a second bottle of Chablis and put in an old movie called *Fatal Attraction*. She hadn't eaten. And when she ordered, her voice was a little slurred.

"Too late to order?" she said.

"No ma'am," the young man said.

"What time can you get it here?"

"Well, Miss, it *is* Friday night. Might be eleven."

"Eleven? You sure?"

"Yes, ma'am," Tim Walsh said. "I'm the driver. I'll get it to you while the cheese is still hot."

GARY WAS A LITTLE troubled by how easy it had been to make the call to Francis Marion Formal Wear. Once he'd dialed the number and heard the voice at the other end, he became the man Denise had scripted.

"*What?*" the man on the line said. "From a forty-four regular to a fifty-long? That, that's *unheard* of."

"Well, let me tell you what *is* heard of, pal," Gary said. "Anabolic steroids and four hundred pounds at the weight bench. You got that, pal? I'm gettin' married, okay, and I want to look good in that tux, and one of the unfortunate side effects of getting into this kind of shape is that the enhancements make my temper just a tad short. You listenin', pal? You hearing me, mutherfucker?"

"Yes, Mr. Trotter. Fifty-long."

DENISE AND GARY SAT in his truck with a small cooler full of ice and a fifth of Jack Daniels. They drank and stared at the house their former spouses shared, the house Mr. and Mrs. Trotter would return to after their Myrtle Beach honeymoon. Denise and Gary had no concern about being "discovered." Their former mates were attending their rehearsal dinner.

"What I'd give to be a fly on the wall tomorrow," Denise said.

After dropping off Denise, Gary stopped at The Paradise Lounge. He had nowhere else to go. There he could have a little solitude, a little liquor.

"It's okay. You can run a tab, Bo," George Miles, the bartender, said when he saw Gary reach for money to pay.

"Better not do that," Gary said. He laid his wallet on the bar and slid out a ten. He saw Denise Trotter's business card, held it before him. He drank slowly. "Hey, George," he said. "You got a phone book?"

"I got my hair up in a towel. I'm standing here dripping," Pepsi Cola Hickman said.

"I'd like to buy you a drink," Gary said.

"Is this a date?" Pepsi Cola said.

Gary had moved from the bar to a booth and opened a tab when he saw her walk in. He raised his hand. Although he didn't say so, he thought she smelled like a spring bouquet. George Miles brought their drinks.

"I want to ask you a favor," Gary said.

"Is this payback for doing my homework?" She smiled.

"No, P.C. A real favor. There's a wedding at The Country Club tomorrow. I'd like for you to videotape it."

"Don't you think I might stand out just a little bit at The Darlington Country Club?"

"The couple, they both work at Social Services."

"Gary Sheppard, you are going to hell for being a racist."

"Lots of their co-workers are black. There'll be other black folks there." She watched him lift his glass, then pause, holding it suspended before him. "You know, you might be right about that first part, about me going to hell." Then he looked into her eyes. "But you're wrong about the second part."

"Your wife's wedding?" she said.

"Ex-wife," he said.

A video of your wife marrying another man? Pepsi Cola thought. That's so, so sad.

🐝🐝🐝

Custom says it's bad luck for the groom to see the bride before they exchange vows. If so, that bad luck was running up faster than the national debt, for it seemed that every ten minutes Deidra was hammering on the door of Trip's dressing room. The flowers hadn't been delivered. The cake hadn't come. The caterer said there had been a misunderstanding.

"Which one is she, Trip Trotter? I want you to go out there right this minute and point her out to me. I know you've had other women. Show me the bitch."

A little more than an hour before the service, Trip was doing shots with his best man and the minister when Deidra crashed in. This time brandishing a six-inch metal nail file. "The piano player is late," she snarled. The combination of tears and mascara made her eyes look like a raccoon's. She shouted, "There's another woman out there, right now!" She pointed to the wall. "She's out there, Trip. And when I find out who she is, I'm gonna kill the bitch. And if you don't tell me who she is, I'll kill you too!"

One of the bridesmaids was dispatched to the Bi-Lo grocery store for a cake. The groomsmen pitched in with the Country Club kitchen staff to quickly fry chicken wings, compose cheese and veggie trays, and Crockpot three gallons of finger-sized weenies. Somebody had mind enough to call a church to find a last-minute piano player.

🐜🐜🐜

TRISH AND SISSY STUCKEY were catching some rays out by the Darlington Country Club pool. One of Trish's boyfriends was a member. Both were stoned out of their minds.

Trish sat up and opened the cooler for another beer. "Look at all the cars," she said. "Where'd they come from?"

Sissy shielded her eyes from the sun. "Everybody's dressed up."

"Must be a wedding," Trish said.

The two watched as a line formed outside the door. "That means food," Sissy said. "I'm starvin'."

🐜🐜🐜

TIM WALSH WAITED OUTSIDE the entrance to the Country Club tugging at his snug collar and fingering his badly knotted tie. His shirt smelled of warm pizza. A church elder had called him saying that a piano player was needed for a wedding, that there was a quick hundred bucks in it for him if he could hustle on over. But the elder wasn't attending, and so Tim studied the faces of everyone coming in or going out, looking for somebody who looked like they were looking for a piano player.

That's when he saw Sissy Stuckey, almost naked beside another almost-naked woman, the two walking toward him.

His knees went Gumby as she and the other woman sashayed up the walkway. They stopped at the end of the guest line.

"Do you know that guy?" Trish said.

"Never seen him," Sissy said.

"Look at them eyes, girl. He's eatin' you up."

"Think he's a undercover cop?"

"Looks mighty young for that," Trish said.

"We'll see," Sissy said.

As the two stepped beside him, Tim felt woozy from hyperventilating. He looked at Sissy. His mouth fell open like a puppy's. He couldn't speak.

"Come with us," she said.

Down the hallway toward the lady's locker room, Tim whispered, "I know you, I know you." Sissy stopped and lifted her sunglasses.

"*Really?*" she said.

"Every Friday night," he said.

"*Me?*" She pointed at her breast then looked over at Trish, who did that I'm-way-too-stoned-to-follow-any-of-this head tilt. Sissy looked Tim over, shrugged, then took his hand. "In that case," she said, "Let's party."

Trish stood guard outside the janitor's closet. Inside, under the single bare light, Sissy fingered inside her bathing suit top and removed a small square plastic bag of pills of various size, shape, and color.

"Is this where we party?" Tim said. He was so erect his testicles throbbed.

"No," Sissy said, holding open the baggie. "But this is where the party starts. Git-chi some."

"Just give me the littlest one you got. I'm playing the piano here in a little bit."

Sissy handed him a pill smaller than a BB.

"What's this," Tim said, looking down into his hand. "It's tiny."

"It's called microdot," Sissy said.

"Gimme two," he said.

❦ ❦ ❦

PEPSI COLA HICKMAN SAW that the folding chairs in the main dining room had been arranged to face the stage, where the service would be held. She took an aisle seat as near the front as she could. While she waited for the chairs to fill, she tore open the package of new batteries for her camera.

❦ ❦ ❦

FORTUNATELY FOR TRIP TROTTER, his best man worked for an insulation company, and in his truck were pliers and an industrial-quality stapler. Trip gathered the tux fabric by the fistful at the waist and cuffs, pulled the staple gun trigger, then closed the staples with the pliers. Somebody found a wooden yardstick, and Trip stapled it to the shoulders and across the inside back of the jacket.

❦❦❦

Through the lens of Pepsi Cola's camera, the man in the tux looked like a scarecrow in a strong wind. When the air conditioning kicked in the air filled the suit like billowing sails, and when it shut off the sails collapsed, creating the image of a man tilting first this way and then that. Perhaps, she thought, panning back, everyone is waiting for the service to begin. But there was no bride. She focused the camera on the silent piano. A young man sat staring at his fingers on the keys, but he didn't play. Heads bobbled. People began to fidget and squirm.

Then all eyes turned to the bride. Pepsi Cola pressed the record button. Deidra had borrowed a white shawl to cover the back of her dress, where the zipper would go up no farther. The sleeves were so tight that the veins in her arms looked like a map of purple tributaries. She held her head high, but the muscles in her neck throbbed sporadically, like a reptile's. Somebody whispered to the piano player to begin, but he seemed lost in his palms. Finally the minister gave a deep nod and the bride moved up the aisle. Because of the restrictions imposed by the gown, her steps were minced into inches. Hers was a long walk to the altar. At the stage, two of the heftier bridesmaids held her elbows and lifted her step-by-step.

When the minister asked the bride and groom to face one another, Deidra whispered to Trip, "I hate your guts, you fuckdog."

Tim Walsh couldn't take his eyes from the piano keys. He'd look at a black one, then a white one, and in that instant he would hear that note, and its sound would rise from the keyboard in a burst of color, each note a different color, the keyboard a wild and wonderful spectacle of color. That music and its endless rainbow filled him with ejaculatory joy. And when a voice said, "And now I pronounce you man and wife," the kaleidoscopic image of naked Sissy Stuckey performing in an adult movie blasted open his brain and his fingers flew into a flurry of wild celebration upon the piano keys.

The raucous melody stunned the audience.

The tune was somehow familiar to Pepsi Cola but she couldn't name the song. It had the tone and swing of a barroom romp, and it was only after the young piano player began belting out the lyrics that she recognized the melody, the theme to *The Mickey Mouse Club*.

🐦🐦🐦

IN THE COUNTRY CLUB lot, Pepsi Cola sat inside her car watching the video. She thought of Gary Sheppard. He had asked a favor and she had delivered. But looking now at the playback, she didn't feel the satisfaction that she should have felt. Gary would see the debacle, would probably experience mild satisfaction, maybe a good laugh. But would anything have changed? Trip and Deidra had exchanged vows. They would go off on their honeymoon. They would return to their home, the one that Gary had built. A year from now, all of this would be a joke, even to them. Gary had asked her to give him something, and she wanted him to have that thing he needed.

When she looked up, the remaining guests blew bubbles at the departing bride and groom. Trip and Deidra Trotter waved and drove away. And without a second's thought, Pepsi Cola resolved to follow them to Myrtle Beach.

🐦🐦🐦

PEPSI COLA WOULD BE the first to tell you that the benefits of an accounting degree are often overrated. She had always been a resourceful problem solver, an agile thinker, a champion schemer. But sometimes, she thought, if you read novels of a particular nature, you learn things that you can actually use to improve your life and the lives of others.

Ninety minutes later, Trip and Deidra Trotter shared a hotel elevator with one Pepsi Cola Hickman.

In the Yellow Pages under Myrtle Beach Escort Services, the first listing was an outfit called Ace of Hearts. "That's just too good," Pepsi Cola whispered, punching in the numbers.

"Yes," she said, "that's right, D-e-i-d-r-a Trotter. We're at the Marriott." Pepsi Cola gave the Escort Services agent the room number. "I hope you'll accept cash. Trip and I tip well, very well, when we get good service, something extra for every shade of grey you can deliver." She explained to the sex worker that this was a very special occasion, a surprise for her husband. She hoped he'd receive a grand entrance when the sex worker arrived. "Yes," Pepsi Cola said. "His name really is Trip. And I promise you that when he answers the door—if you're all you say you are—you'll see that the name fits."

At a quarter till twelve, P. C. Hickman ordered a frozen strawberry liquor drink at the Marriott bar and walked to the pool area. She stretched out on the plush beach recliner and felt inside her purse for the video camera. At a patio table near the diving board, three couples sat quietly in the reflection of blue pool light. The ocean was calm, the breeze content. She sipped her cocktail and counted the balconies up to the eighth level. She looked at her watch and waited. She considered the tide, the eternal pull of one heart upon another, the romance. She lifted her camera, zoomed in on the eighth floor balcony and counted down to midnight.

Even from eight stories, the naked woman's shrill cursing was distinctive, and, Pepsi Cola thought, intricately elaborate, a looping embroidery of obscenities that first preceded then accompanied the avalanche of suitcases, televisions, end tables and coffee tables, cheap wall paintings, chairs, lamps, pillows, pots and pans, silverware, handcuffs, riding crops, latex and studded dog collars that rained down from the balcony and crashed upon the cement patio near the diving board.

❦❦❦

WHILE TRISH APPLIED A second coat of fire engine red nail polish, Denise Trotter spoke into her phone, "Done deal," she said. "But I could lose my license if you told what I did. I'm supposed to represent the seller, you know. Price is rock bottom. No fee to me, although you could buy me a fifth of Jack Daniels. It's your dream home. Work out the financing, Gary, and you got a new life."

❦❦❦

WHEN GARY ENTERED THE bank, he saw P.C.'s mock double take. She stepped back from the counter and gathered her fists under her chin, prayer-like. He smiled and spread his arms wide. "I know, I know," he said. He gestured toward his red and gray tie then pulled at the lapels of his jacket.

"You dress up good," she said. "That's the real you."

"This weather, who knows how to dress? October in South Carolina? What's it gonna be, hot or cold?" He pointed at the manager's office. "Ms. Grimes in?"

"She's with a customer. Should only be a minute."

Gary took off the jacket, hung it on the back of a chair. He looked around conspiratorially, then stepped up close to the counter. "Can you keep a secret?" he whispered.

"What's my track record so far?"

Before he could speak, Ms. Grimes called: "Mr. Sheppard. Won't you come on in?"

Pepsi Cola Hickman was a model bank employee, smart, ambitious, a quick study. She was a woman of sound ethical character. And now she stared at the man's jacket hanging from the chair across the lobby. She decided that it was her professional duty to hang that jacket in the employee's closet to ensure that someone of lesser character couldn't walk out with it. If Mr. Sheppard asked for his jacket, she'd give it to him and he would thank her for being a model employee and a dear friend.

She took the jacket.

Thirty minutes later, Gary was all smiles when he emerged from Ms. Grimes' office. The two shook hands and he headed for the door. He turned and mouthed the words, "I GOT IT!" then gave her a thumbs up. She held her breath as she watched him drive away. Then she looked up at the clock.

It had been a hot one for October but the days were growing shorter. A cool breeze escorted Pepsi Cola Hickman to her car. She carried a man's jacket over one arm. And before she drove off, she opened the slip of paper with Gary Sheppard's address written on it. She knew that there was probably a bank policy somewhere that said she shouldn't write down his address for personal reasons, or drive to his apartment to return his jacket so that he might share his good news and that she might share with him something special. Surely what she had in mind was inappropriate under company policy. But she didn't think that Gary would object. She really didn't.

There's Someone's Shadow in This One

For two hours, Tess Killingsworth and Karen Russell sat in Karen's minivan outside their father's vacant house drinking Sapphire Gin from giant Styrofoam cups. The gin was cold. They'd kept it on ice inside the cooler along with the tonic and lime slices during the five-hour drive from Atlanta. Now the sisters held their cups before them like resolute beggars and stared at the empty house. After a time, their conversation, which had rested for a stretch, lurched forward again.

"I thought you'd had the power disconnected," Karen said.

"I thought so, too," Tess said.

"Wasn't dark when we parked. It got dark in like five minutes. Has the porch light been on all this time?" Karen thought her sister was considering the question.

"Yoooo Liiiite up my liiiife." Tess lifted her cup and searched for the melody.

"That's, ah.... Who the hell sang that?"

"Mama sang that, remember?"

"Debbie Boone, that's who recorded that. Debbie Boone." Karen wagged her head from side to side like it was sad news. "Name like that? I'd have been a heroin addict."

"At the beach that summer. Why the hell did Mama resurrect that piece of shit song? It was ancient twenty years ago."

"It was like her theme song all summer."

"We both could have used some good heroin that summer." Tess looked at her older sister.

"We were too busy smoking pot." The two drank. "A looong, looong time-ago...." Karen was no singer either.

"That's not Debbie Boone. That's *American*… shit. *Pie*. Pie shit," Tess said. The dull weight of their words sank into silence again. They both lifted their cups and looked at the empty house. "Are we getting started now, or what?"

"What do you think? The place is a mess inside? Did you notice the yard when we drove up?"

"We could hire somebody to clean it up," Tess said.

"We drove up today to start this today."

"That was before you insisted I pack this gin," Tess said. "Who could we call? Do you know anybody who lives here? I sure don't."

"We should have made the effort."

"Daddy's little girl." Tess said.

"That's not even funny, Tess. We're sitting in a dead man's drive."

"Thanks to you, I should say. This was your idea, Sis."

Karen thought and then said, "What if there's stuff in there that belonged to Mama?"

"After twenty years? She'll never miss it; she didn't take it with her. God knows she took everything else. Why should we care?"

"I just can't stand the thought of something of hers going in the trash without our knowing it."

"I rest my case. We wouldn't know it."

"We have to go in there now."

"Not before we finish this gin, we don't."

"Okay, then we have to get started."

But they didn't go inside. After they finished the gin, Karen drove as best she could, following what hotel directions Tess could read. For an indeterminate time they were lost in the small city where their father had lived alone for twenty years. Then, in a synchronized moment, they looked up from a stoplight and saw their hotel beside them, like a wish come true.

"I think I believe in God," Karen said.

"I think you'd better shut up and drive," her younger sister said. "The light's green."

❦❦❦

THEIR HEAVY BREAKFAST OF grits, eggs and toast, had shored up their hangovers, but now the world was painted a mawkish gray. They didn't talk on the drive to their father's house. Karen again parked at the top of the steep drive. When Tess opened her door, a Styrofoam cup tumbled onto the gravel. She watched as the wind lifted it and sent it skittering down the scabby lawn toward the street. She remembered a childhood moment at the beach.

Karen stood on the porch. "I hope you have the house key," she called.

Tess handed Karen her purse. "You look," she said. "I'm going around back and throw up."

"Do it here," Karen said. They were not completely sober.

Tess was already walking away. "Neighbors," she said.

"Never stopped Dad, I'd bet."

When Tess walked in, she saw her sister, hands on her hips, conducting a 360-degree survey of the interior.

"I'll make a deal with you," Tess said.

"No. No way I'm cleaning up this mess by myself."

"We'll call someone with a giant vacuum to back up to the door and suck all this crap out of our lives."

"What's the deal you're offering?"

"I'll put a bullet through my brain."

"Tempting. We'll start with the books. Stack them on the porch. Take them to the library."

"Why didn't they go at the estate auction?"

"How would I know? Nobody reads anymore would be my guess. Make sure there's nothing in them before you put them outside."

"In the books? You mean money? Our old man? Not likely."

"Something of Mother's."

"In a book?" Tess said.

"Some of them were *her* books. Just look, okay?"

❧❧❧

ON THE DRIVE BACK from the library, Tess stopped for trash bags. Her sister was sitting on the floor of their father's study when Tess walked in. Karen didn't look up from the binder on her lap. "I'd forgotten these. They were taken when we were babies." Tess looked over Karen's shoulder.

"Look at how young Mom was," Tess said. "She was a baby too."

The two sat shoulder to shoulder on the floor, the photo album between them. "There's another of these albums in the closet. How did they end up here? I wonder if Mom even knew he had them," Karen said.

"It's not the sort of thing you just forget, your history in pictures, I mean."

"I'm sure she must have had her reasons." Karen pointed. "That was your fourth birthday."

"Where are we?" Tess lifted the album and tilted the picture for a closer look.

"Swan Lake," Karen said. "Look at those dresses—My Little Kitty, huh?" She pointed at a picture of the two of them petting a cat.

"Missy!" Tess said. "That was one surly, spiteful quadruped. I think she died of meanness."

Karen said, "Notice who's absent from all of these? No surprise, huh? He wasn't there even when he was there." She closed the album and looked at the clutter around them.

"We'll look through the other pictures at lunch, over a bucket of chicken. Fried chicken sounds good for a hangover. And beer. Definitely beer." Tess took a deep breath. "What's our plan of attack here?"

"Since you are the lawyer and I'm the minivan mom," Karen said, "I'll get rid of everything left in the kitchen and you go through the filing cabinets. I wouldn't know what we ought to keep, or for how long." They each took a roll of trash bags.

Tess filled the first bag with amber-colored warranties for long-discarded appliances, tools, mowers, tillers, TVs, stereo equipment and the like. Another trash bag overflowed with hundreds of newspaper and magazine articles and clippings on everything from ways to save electricity in 1980 to how to wash a dog.

Tess called to the kitchen: "Did Dad ever have a dog?"

"Hundreds of them," Karen shouted back.

"I mean the four-legged variety."

"Not that I know of."

Tess was tempted to forget the sorting, fill the bags and get the trash to the street, pronto. But when she saw the file folders marked Taxes, Credit Cards, Insurance, and Investments, she acknowledged what she already knew: the dead couldn't clean up after themselves. They could organize, but the sorting out belonged to somebody else.

When her older sister left to buy chicken and beer, Tess opened up a wobbly, molting card table and two folding chairs in the kitchen. She thumbed through the photo albums as she waited.

"These were all taken at the beach, not long before he moved out," Tess said when Karen walked in with their lunch.

"See this bag?" Karen said. Tess nodded. "It's not a very big bag, is it?"

"Big enough, I guess?" Tess said.

"But not huge, not massive though; am I right?"

"Well, no."

"But what we see—or what we think you see—can be deceiving, wouldn't you say, Madame Prosecutor?"

"My professional experience bears that out."

Karen began unpacking the bag. "I'm stronger than I thought," she said. "I never would have believed a bag this size could hold ten thousand calories. Or that I'd have enough muscle power to lift so much fat."

❧❧❧

TESS WOULD HAVE TO stop the automatic drafts for magazine subscriptions, pay off the final charges for utilities, turn in his cable equipment and cancel his phone. His car had been sold at the estate auction.

Their father neither asked nor informed Tess about assuming responsibility for administering his estate. But when the registered letter arrived addressed to his executor, she'd not given it much thought. In fact, had Karen's call been to tell Tess a long-time client had died, it could hardly have registered higher on her scale of emotions. Her father's passing was another item on a list, to be addressed when she got to it. Now she had gotten to it.

❧❧❧

FROM THE PORCH, THE brown garbage bags at the bottom of the sloping lawn looked like a line of praying monks in the dwindling yellow light. Karen and Tess sat on the steps, knees apart, condensation from their beer cans beading on their fingers. Karen lifted her beer to the moon. "Next round's on you, Mom, for cleaning up his mess."

"Look at all that," Tess said, tilting her can toward the assembled garbage.

"I would have left him too," Karen said.

"I wonder what she would think, if she'd feel anything. You know, she did marry him."

"You stand there." Karen looked down at the beer in her hand. "You say the vows. I mean you *say* them, but you don't really know what you're saying." She looked up at the line of trash bags. "How can you?"

"It's always a risk. One I'm not willing to take, thank you very much," Tess said.

"Are you happy? Single, I mean?"

"Are you happy? Married, I mean?"

"I have my children."

"So did Mom, and she was so happy."

"She tried."

"Mama's little sword and shield."

"We have a lot to thank her for."

"Speak for yourself." Tess slowly got up, one hand pressing the small of her back.

"I'm speaking for us both."

"Okay, big sister, you just go on speaking while I calculate the cost of back surgery."

"She was our mother. You should show a little respect."

"Why? You got mom's great boobs. Not me."

"You got her brains though."

"No, Sis. 'Fess up. Those came from Mr. Vacancy here."

"Where are you going?"

"I need food," Tess said. "Again." She trudged inside.

Karen imagined her husband, Tom, and their two children. She insisted on a routine, at the center of which was family. Insisting upon a carefully crafted life she had never had seemed like a design for happiness. She glanced down at her watch. Tom would be reading *Charlotte's Web* to Caroline, closing in on the final chapters. Mark had ten minutes more of his allowed PlayStation time.

"Help!" Tess called.

In the kitchen Karen saw all the empty cabinet drawers pulled open.

"You don't think we threw away the phone book do you? I'm ordering delivery." Tess picked up the phone. "How do you call information?"

"I'll get my cell," her sister said.

"Wait." Tess touched her finger to the wall beside the phone. "I'm calling this number."

"Dad's last girlfriend?" Karen said. "Think she delivers?"

"If Dad wrote her number on the wall, I'd guess so." Tess waited for someone to pick up. "Really!" she said. Her eyes flew open wide and turned to Karen. "You sure *can* help me. A large veggie pizza. Yes, that's the correct address." She hung up and turned to Karen. "Go figger," she said. "The pizza joint. We've got time for a beer."

The kid who delivered the pizza was all pimples and brown teeth. At the bottom of the steep drive, the rear of his squat orange car wagged to the beat of rap music hammering its trunk.

"What's this?" asked Tess, exchanging a ten and a five for the steaming pizza box and a small plastic cup.

"Extra sauce," said the kid. "Mr. Killingsworth, he likes the extra sauce. He's always ordering from us. He's my regular customer. Most people, they snatch the box and slam the door in your face. Not him. Sometimes he be standing here still talking when I drove away. Always a smile and a extra skin from Mr. Killingsworth. Mr. Killingsworth, he called me his friend."

❧❧❧

"I HURT IN PLACES I didn't think I had," Tess said. "Do we have another trash bag?" She folded the top to the empty pizza box. "What's left?"

"I'm leaving most of his clothes on hangers for the Salvation Army," Karen said.

"We have to be out of here tomorrow by noon, Karen. I'm administering some hardcore justice at ten on Monday. I have to be able to walk again by then."

The two sisters surveyed the remains of the kitchen. Karen said, "I guess we can leave the drapes and blinds up. Still, the bathrooms are a mess. Everything has five years of dust."

"I'm done. I'll call a cleaning service from the office. We should have called someone from the start." The sisters inhaled deeply and looked about them. The solitary overhead light cast grotesque yellow shadows. "None of Mom's pearls in this oyster, huh, Sis?"

"Peace of mind," Karen said. "Doesn't that count?"

"Peace of mind?"

"Are all lawyers born cynics, or does practicing law just make you that way?"

"I'm proud to say I come by it naturally."

"You can thank Dad for that."

"Thanks, Pop, wherever you are."

"We do have the photos," Karen said. "You forgot the pictures. I'd call that a pearl. We found something we couldn't replace."

"Yeah. Right." Tess pushed herself up slowly from the metal chair. "Time for a little walk?"

"What?"

"Down memory lane, Sis. Let's share a few obligatory saccharin moments before we fold this tent."

Even after the beers, Tess looked like a lawyer, the way she carried the albums, one tucked under each arm. She said, "Which ones haven't we seen?"

Karen opened one. "Ahhhh," she said. "These are all from the summer at the beach."

Tess sang out of tune, "We liiite up our joints."

Karen pointed. "We've got some teenage angst happening in this one, don't we, Tess?"

They studied the pictures. "Hey," Tess said. "Look at these. They are all the same picture." She pointed. "You. Mom in the middle. Me."

"She's looking right into the camera, isn't she?" Karen said. "Damn, that's a little spooky."

"She looks a little drunk in this one," Tess said.

"God, you're cynical. Just because she looks happy—"

"Look at me," Tess said. Karen turned. "Smile." Tess studied her face. "Yeah, Mom's a little loaded there. I can see it in your face. Besides, check out that hanging bathing suit strap. Mom's about to lose one. And she seems pretty happy about it."

"Tess—" Karen was laughing.

"Wait, wait." Tess said. She pulled the album in front of her and opened it to the last few pages.

"What are you doing?" Karen's face was one big bright smile.

Tess sighed. "I need another beer," she said. "I've just discovered through careful photo analysis the source of my adult cynicism, its foundation, the before and after of that summer that has made me the woman—the unmarried woman, I might add—that I've become. Here lie the roots of my discontent."

Karen was still laughing. "I'll get you that beer." When she sat down again, Tess held a page at the back of the book.

"Look at this *before* picture," she said. "What do you see?"

"You. Mom in the middle with those smiling eyes looking through me. Me on the other side. What else? We're standing on the beach, the surf behind us."

"Very good," Tess said. She was mocking the lawyer in herself now. "Now Ms. Russell, look at this other photo, and tell me what you see."

"Same thing."

"Look closely, Ms. Russell. Closely. You must take into account what hangs, so to speak, in the balance here. How is this one different from the first one?"

Karen studied the two pictures. "Our tans are darker."

"Very good. This one was taken at the beginning of the summer, this one at the end."

"Mom is holding a glass in this one."

"Gin and tonic. That's a lime there, floating on top. What else?"

Karen looked at the picture, then up at her sister. "I don't know."

"You wouldn't."

"There is someone's shadow in this one," Karen said.

"You're still not looking," Tess said.

"I don't get it."

Tess pointed at Karen in the first picture, then at Karen in the second. "Boobs. You grew a whole cup size in one summer. I hate you."

"I'd forgotten. The summer I turned eighteen. My summer of breasts."

"Summer of secret birth control pills." Tess pointed at the picture, at their mother's breasts then at Karen's. "I look like a boy beside you two. I was a woman in a boy's body. I think I was a gay man. Now I'm a cynical lawyer."

"But you were only fifteen. Now you have breasts."

"Huh!" Tess said. "Compared to what?"

"But I've had babies. You wouldn't want to see them now."

"Liar! Look at Mom's. They're beautiful."

Karen's hand covered her smile. "She's kinda letting them show, isn't she?"

"Perfect. You got the perfect breasts. Let's see yours. Take 'em out, Sis." Tess crossed her arms and tilted her head to the side. Karen turned away, laughing.

Karen said, "I half expect her to speak to us from that picture."

"And what would she say?" Tess said.

"You light up my life?" They were both laughing now.

"Voice like hers? No wonder we spent so much time on the beach, huh?" Tess said.

"And at the movies."

"And at the arcade."

"And at the pool."

"And at sleepovers."

"We did light up up our joints." The sisters tilted up their beers. "I guess Mom needed a break from us, too," Karen said. "I mean with Dad that spring. It was not a pretty time for her. Don't you think that's why she let us run free that summer, so she could have time to clear her head?"

"Or clear out his bank accounts?"

Karen looked away from her sister. "I could use some mental health days." The beer had taken a bad turn.

Tess lifted the photo book. Her smile faded. "How did he get these? How did Dad get these pictures? Doesn't that strike you as odd?"

"Maybe after Mom died—"

"Who, other than you or me, would have even known about these?"

"Well, I'm glad we found them. Some memories here, huh, Tess?"

Tess studied the shots: herself, her mom, her sister. "These pictures all say the same thing." She brought her hand to her mouth. "They all say, 'We are here, and you are there. We are a family and you are not.'"

"Earth to Tess."

"No. Look. Look at Mom's eyes. That's what they say."

"That's not what I see," Karen said, drumming the side of her beer bottle with her nails.

"She sent these to him; that's how he got them. She sent them."

"Why would she do that? You don't know what you're saying."

"She sent them, Karen."

"She wasn't like that. Besides, even if she did, even if what you say is true, we *were* a family, you, Mom, and me. We were. Always. Look." Karen reached for the other album. "See? Even when we were babies. Look at them, Tess. You, me, and Mom. We were always the family."

"Who took those, Karen?"

"What are you getting at?"

"*He* took them. Why didn't Mom take pictures of you and me and Dad?"

"I don't like what you're saying."

"I'm saying that he's not in any of these because he was taking the pictures. What I'm saying is that maybe we're looking at an act of love here."

"I can't believe you're defending him."

"All I'm saying is that there was someone behind the camera, okay, someone who was present each moment that these pictures represent, that he is the reason we see what we see here. He was a participant in every one of these."

Karen drained the last of her beer, held the bottle high. "Thanks, Dad, you shit."

"Gee, Karen, I didn't mean to—"

"It was you and me and Mom. That's where it starts, that's where it ends. She was the one who took us shopping and came to our soccer games and made us up for prom and dried our tears when our young hearts were broken. And where was he?"

"At work."

"He moved out."

"Uhmm. What were his choices?"

"He was a jerk."

"Yep. The man was a jerk. No argument there."

"You make your living winning arguments, Tess."

"I withdraw the question."

At the hotel, they showered and then watched TV in silence.

Karen nodded toward Tess's open suitcase. "You still have that?" Tess lifted her nightgown from it.

"Yes," Tess said. She pointed at her mother's raised initials in the leather. "It was my gift from her estate."

In bed, Tess closed her eyes.

When she woke, the room was dark. The dim light of Karen's cell phone cast distorted shadows on the walls. "Just because, Tom," Karen whispered. "Just *because*, I said."

🦌🦌🦌

AFTER LOCKING THE DOOR to the house that had been their father's, Tess offered to drive. Karen handed her the minivan keys and slept until Tess stopped in Augusta to fill up. Then Karen took the keys while Tess slept. When she woke, the afternoon clouds over Atlanta were a red and purple tide retreating into the darkness. Karen parked in the drive in front of Tess's garage.

"Want a cup of coffee, Sis?" Tess pulled a small wooden fruit crate from the back seat. Inside were their father's remnants, folders containing his assets, his liabilities.

Karen looked at her watch. She was now in full-fledged minivan mode. "Can't do it," she said. "Call me."

"Okay, I'll do that." Tess stepped into the bright lights of the van when she heard Karen's window come down.

"Wait," said Karen. "Take these."

"You don't want them?"

"No."

"When you're over, we can go through them again, maybe find some nice frames."

"I don't want them," Karen said.

🐞🐞🐞

TESS STARTED A HOT bath and then poured herself a glass of red wine. She was already into Monday, into the mind that she would take to court. She undressed and tested the water. She thought she might review tomorrow's cases and soak her tired bones. Walking naked from the bathroom to her study for the briefs, she reflected upon the small pleasures of nakedness. No husband or children to shield herself from.

Easing into the steaming bath, she closed her eyes and felt the release of her limbs. Then she was seeing the snapshots from that summer. Her sister, their mom, herself.

There's someone's shadow in this one.

Tess couldn't remember the man's name. Mr. Finch? Dove? It was a bird's name. The man with the mustache. The man three houses down the beach. The man with the camera hiding most of his face. Darling? Starling. Mr. Starling. "Say hello to Mr. Starling, Tess," her mother said. "He's one of my bridge friends. He's going to take our picture."

Their mother had spent most of that summer with her "bridge friends." And when she and Karen and their mother were on the beach, Mr. Starling, who had been a professional singer and actor, seemed always to appear. When just the two of them ran into Mr. Starling, he never took his eyes from Karen, even when he spoke to me, Tess thought. He had given Karen two tickets to see *Dirty Dancing*, claiming he'd won them from a local radio station he couldn't name. Mr. Starling drove them to the movie theater, Karen up front, she in the backseat. After the movie she had said to Karen, "Do you think his name is really Starling? I mean, isn't that like so fake sounding?"

"He's gorgeous," Karen had twittered. "What other name *could* he have? He's soooo hot!"

Their mother picked them up. Her hair was still wet.

Yes, someone's shadow in that one.

Tess sat up in the bath.

She was alone on the beach, sunbathing. Where was Karen? Tess remembered now that it had been their last week at the beach. She was reading a crime novel, determined to finish it before they packed to leave. She'd challenged the late summer sun. And her skin, even after almost three months of tanning, was tender. She dropped the book inside her beach bag and folded her towel. Above the horizon, a shroud of bruised clouds promised evening rain.

After spraying the sand from her feet and legs outside, she entered the house barefoot and padded down the carpeted hall. The quiet house felt empty. Then she glimpsed a reflection in the full-length mirror that hung from her mother's bedroom closet door. Tess wanted to turn away, but she felt trapped between embarrassment and fascination.

Her mother stood naked, arms loosely at her side, the white skin in sharp relief against her dark brown flesh. Tess watched as her mother's hands slowly traced her hips, her fingers floating at her stomach. Then her shoulders trembled, and when her hands went up to cover her eyes, Tess tiptoed past. She had seen her mother cry, but she'd never seen her naked mother cry. At the end of the hall, she closed her bedroom door, threw herself on the bed, plugged in her Walkman headphones, and then cranked up the volume to blast away the indelible image of her mother's sadness.

Now Tess stepped from the bath and turned to the mirror, gently drying with a soft white towel. She thought of her mother, naked and crying: two teenage daughters, eighteen and fifteen, a broken marriage, a summer lover she would never see again, maybe her last. Like Tess now, middle-aged. She studied her own nakedness.

In bed, Tess closed her eyes again, thinking of her mother and Karen. Her father behind this camera, Mr. Starling behind that one. Picturing her father, she considered motive and opportunity. Her mother's motive. Starling's motive, Karen's opportunity. Motive and opportunity. She reflected upon the years that had stretched from that summer to now, the ones that would extend from here to some unknown future. She searched for the right word. Not forgiveness. Something else.

Then she slept, comfortably, in that place of semi-darkness and no time, without dreaming even, and in the morning woke a minute before the alarm could shatter the serene place that was no place. Rising slowly, feeling the aches from her father's house, she followed the smell of coffee into the kitchen, allowing her gown to hang open for no one to see. She poured her first cup and sipped it with eyes closed, listening to the silence. She pictured the contents of the small crate beside a chair in her study, her father's papers and the two fading collections of snapshots. She allowed herself to linger over the coffee.

When she stood, Tess felt tightness in her limbs and muscles. She would be sore for a day or two. She walked barefoot down the hallway to begin sorting and filing her father's life. With the kitchen light behind her, she considered how each step took her to the edge of her own shadow without quite entering it, and at the sight of her mother's suitcase, a word formed on her lips.

"Generosity," she whispered.

These are the Eyes of Norah Jones

ADAM'S RIB WAS LOCATED near the office where we spent our days cursing the stock market and counting down the hours, where Robert, Peter, Wess, and I no longer sold high-end real estate. Wess referred to the bar simply as "The Chain" although to my knowledge it belonged to no franchise.

"Nooo," Robert said—this was ritual, "not The *Chain*." Robert's ex-wife was Jane. But after an hour or two of Scotch, she became "Chain."

Adam's Rib was mahogany and soft light, no clocks, no televisions, and never crowded. Dark and cool in the summer. Its bartender, Derik, had become our friend. At that time, about the only things we hadn't lost were our companionship and one corner of the bar.

Our unspoken covenant was that we check our failures at the door because our unspoken conviction was that the falling value of some things does not necessitate the falling value of all things.

It was Peter and Robert on one side, me on the other. When Wess entered, the bright light from outside produced his silhouette. We watched as he lifted his arms high and waved them side-to-side in a kind of hallelujah cha-cha routine. He was returning from a showing, the only one for any of us all week. His gin and tonic was waiting on the bar when he sat beside me.

"Drinks are on you, pal," I said.

Peter lifted his glass in a toast to Wess. "I know that smell, the smell of a closing."

"Sorry, gentlemen," Wess said, "but I have to save my pennies."

"You can keep the pennies," Robert said. "Take out the plastic."

"Can't do it. I'm getting married," Wess said.

"Derriiik!" Peter called. Derik smiled.

"Norah Jones," Wess said.

"Make it a triple," I said.

Robert said, "Not my Norah."

Ms. Jones had become the symbol of our salvation. When the conversation drifted too near the landmines of our broken marriages or the carcasses of our careers and our jokes passed into corrosive mockery and bitterness, one of us would seize a dark introspective pause and say, "But we still have Norah." And then we would collectively spin off on her enigmatic beauty and boundless talent and quote her lyrics word-for-word. She became that thing we all could count on, a mystery we could believe in, a fate we could bow to.

"When's the wedding?" Robert said.

"Not before her husband goes to prison," Wess said. Derik, who had been standing near the register, stepped closer.

"Norah has no husband," Peter said.

"The woman I just spent the last hour with?" Wess lifted his glass, held it before him like a chalice, slowly drank, and then nodded affirmatively to the out there. "She has the eyes of Norah Jones."

"My Norah would never hook up with a criminal," Peter said. He signaled Derik for another round.

"There's mystery and mischief in those eyes," Wess said. "That's what makes her Norah Jones."

"No, the mystery is in your ex-wife's eyes," Peter said.

"Mystery, I said, not treachery."

"Your wife would kill you if she could," Robert said. "Peter is right. You have a death wish."

Derik set down the drinks all around.

"I dreamed my wife tried to kill me last night," I said. "I'd forgotten until just now."

"How? How'd she do it?" Wess said.

"She held a gun to my head and handed me the telephone."

"She ordered you to swallow the phone," Peter said, "or to beat your brains out with the receiver?" We all laughed.

"No, she forced me to call the funeral home and make arrangements for my own funeral."

"That's no dream," Robert said. "It's called divorce court."

"Is Norah's husband going to prison for murder?" I said.

Peter said, "Norah has no husband. She's saving it for me."

"No," Wess said. "This woman's husband was convicted of making ec-stasy—the drug—in their upscale basement. When he's shipped off to the land of widespread cheeks, she'll get a huge settlement, everything. She said she was devastated. She told me that. She said it with these Norah Jones eyes, you know, sad but filled with hopeful expectation."

"He's making drugs in the basement and she knows nothing about it?" Robert said. "Not likely."

"I'm telling you, you should have seen those eyes."

"Well, sometimes you can be married to someone and never know her," I said.

Robert said, "Ecstasy, that's the new love drug. That's what I see in Norah's smoldering eyes. That's why the husband took the bullet for her. Each of us would do the same."

"She's a child," Wess said. "A woman child. A woman but innocent as a child."

We all lifted our glasses, closed our eyes, and went our separate ways with our Norah Jones.

"The less you know a person sometimes, the easier it is to love them," I said.

❦❦❦

"What kind of arrangements did you make?" Wess said. "For your funeral?"

"Oh, that wasn't the half of it," I said. "I really don't like talking about this."

"Sure you do, Billy," Peter said.

"Carry on," Robert said.

I signaled Derik for a round. "After I'd made arrangements at the fu-neral home, she ordered me to call an ambulance. 'I won't do it,' I said. 'Somebody's got to clean up the mess,' she said. 'And it's not gonna be me.' I said I wouldn't do it. She pulled back the hammer and rested her finger on the trigger."

"What was it?" Wess said. "A .357 Magnum?"

"Smith & Wesson," I said.

"Long barrel?"

"You bet."

"Oooooh," he said. He drank. We all drank.

"*My* dream," Peter said, "goes like this: Somehow I'm sitting in a wooden kitchen chair, blindfolded, my hands tied behind my back. I say,

'It was an accident.' And she says, 'Nobody screws another woman by ac-cident!' I say, 'I didn't know what I was doing. I was drunk.' And she says, 'Do I look like Mother Teresa for fucking out loud?' And then she puts this plastic bag over my head. This is scary, I tell you. And I say, 'What are you doing? What is this?' and she says, 'Plastic serum. I want the truth.'"

"'Plastic serum,'" Robert said. "I like it." Robert and I taught high school right out of college, when we still believed in something. I was History. He was English.

Peter has this way of leaning in confidentially when he gets excited. "The thing is, in my dream, if I remained very, very calm, I could breathe. But if I got excited, a.k.a. lied, I'd breathe in that thin plastic, you know, like your dry cleaning comes in? I'd suck it up my nostrils."

"You mean it was like a truth drug. You lie and you suffocate," Wess said.

"It was a nightmare," Peter said.

I said, "What does that dream mean? How would you interpret its meaning? It's full of symbols: The chair, i.e., the electric chair. The blind-fold. Is it literally about blindness? Or is it about justice?"

"Yeah," Wess said. "The plastic. Does that symbolize plastic?" We all laughed.

"What it was about," Peter said, "was life and death. I tell you, when I woke from that dream I was so tense my sphincter ached."

"Aching Sphincter." Robert looked at Wess. "Maybe that symbolizes that *Peter* will be Norah's next husband."

"Peter wouldn't stand a chance with Norah," Wess said. "She's too much woman for him."

"Those eyes—" I said.

"I would present her with a gift," Peter said.

"She'd be in ecstasy," Robert said.

"A song," I said. "One about life and death."

"Life and death? I have the perfect symbol for that combination," Peter said. "Tits."

"Those eyes," I said. "Sometimes, you just know she'd take a dare. But other times she looks like a tender, innocent debutante."

"A debutante who'll take a dare. That's my kind of woman," Wess said.

"She is from Texas, you know. Famous for its cheerleaders and debu-tantes," Robert said.

"Not cheerleader," I said. "She's too shy. Too smart."

"She could shy me till I begged for mercy," Wess said.

Peter said, "I'd beg, too, if I could, but I can't. Permanent knee injuries from the divorce."

"Hey, Billy," Robert said, "did you beg in your dream? You know, before the ambulance came with the clean-up crew?"

"No," I said. "After that, she put the barrel of the .357 in my ear and told me to call the cops. I dialed the number. Told them there'd been a murder at our address."

🦌🦌🦌

"TEXAS FIGURES INTO MY dream," Robert said.

I don't know what time it was, but it must have been late because Derik poured himself a beer and pulled up a stool.

"May I join the Coroner's Corner?" he said.

"How did she kill you?" I asked Robert.

"Do you mean in real life or in the dream?"

"The dream."

"I don't know. In the dream I'm already dead." He looked at each of us. "Do y'all ever have movie dreams?" We all nodded that we did. "This is a movie dream, and I'm in it *and* I'm watching it. I see myself in the coffin, like in a close up."

"How do you look?" Peter said. "I mean, Billy is about to make a very important call. He needs to know he's calling the right funeral home."

"Dead," Robert said. "Very dead."

We all drank.

Robert said, "The camera slowly pulls back and Chain and a group of her friends, people I don't know, are there. We're all in a tiny chapel, only it's a cocktail party. Some guy taps his martini glass with a spoon and the room goes silent. Chain hands the guy a piece of paper then mops her false tears with a cocktail napkin. The man speaks in a kind of broadcaster's voice and raises his arm indicating the paper he holds. 'Because I Could Not Stop For Death,' he says, in the voice of death itself.

Wess turned to Peter. "That's a famous poem by Gertrude Stein, I think."

Robert continued, "Everybody circles the wagons as he begins."

"Was Gertrude Stein a Texan?" Peter said. "Her name sounds Jewish, there are no Jews in Texas."

"I'm getting to that," Robert said. "You see, the guy doesn't read the poem. He *sings* it."

"Thaaat's the Norah connection," Wess said, giving Peter a big uh-huh.

"Norah would never do such a thing," Robert said. "Y'all know `The Yellow Rose of Texas'?" We all did. Robert sang its melody:

> Because I could not stop for Death,
> He kindly stopped for me;
> The carriage held but just ourselves
> And Immortality.

> We slowly drove, he knew no haste,
> And I had put away
> My labor, and my leisure too,
> For his civility.

I thought the beer he was drinking might pass through Derik's nose. We laughed until our faces glowed.

"That's not all," Robert said. He was trying to tell the rest. But we couldn't stop laughing. "There's more," he said.

Derik brought us another round.

"There's symbolism here," Robert said. "The chapel? Where I'm lying in state? It's a *wedding* chapel. In Vegas!" Our eyes were red from crying. "It's called Chapel of Love. That's some heavy symbolism, right?"

"Stop it," Wess said, motioning like a traffic cop.

"No, I can't," Robert said. "Because I'm dead and the whole thing is a set-up. They leave me there. I'm left there alone to die again. Don't you get it, the party, everyone at my funeral, all these strangers, they leave me there. The whole thing is a set-up. Chain calls a limo, the partygoers get into their cars, turn on their headlights, and the Vegas traffic parts like the Red Sea so that they can get to where the real party is happening lickety-split."

We couldn't stop laughing.

"But you still have Norah," I said.

"I'm about to pee myself," Wess said.

"Me, too." Peter said.

🎜🎜🎜

"THESE ARE ON ME," Derik said. We knew nothing about him, except that he was a fine bartender. The best bartenders? You know nothing about them. They can carry it all inside. And keep it there. That's why we need them.

We all drank. Derik locked the door and picked up the newspaper and sat in a booth near the kitchen. He had already set up the bar for tomorrow. He knew the dark path we had entered.

"Name the moment—upon reflection—when you knew it was over," Robert said. We weren't laughing now.

Peter spoke first. "When she said, 'I won't be your somebody else.' Trouble is, I don't remember when she said it. You?" he said to Robert.

"We were at an Italian restaurant. She'd come home from a professional conference, and as she told me about a man she met there, I knew she was lying. It was like that moment when you're watching a poker player, the instant you get inside that person's head. And I wasn't jealous or angry so much as I was fascinated by her acuity, her skill as she redesigned the pattern of truth. And I knew that's who she was. The woman I'd married."

Tonight it was Wess who grabbed the helm. He heaved an overly animated deep breath. "We were having a conversation, too. And I said, 'I'm gonna buy that bass boat I want.' And she said, 'If you do, I'm gonna buy that tummy tuck I want.' And I did. And she did. And that was that."

I thought it might end there. Wess's effort was a fine one. We drank. Then at some point they looked at me.

"We were in the car," I said. "Don't know where we were going or where we had been."

"That could be any one of us," Peter said.

"And out of nowhere she turned and looked at me, as if there were something I should have intuited but hadn't. 'So,' she said. 'What do you make of a line like this: The less he loved her, the more he told her so?' I didn't know how to answer. It was like a riddle or a self-fulfilling prophecy. And so I said nothing. And that was the beginning of the end."

"You should have seen her eyes today," Wess said. "I couldn't remember the specs on the property. All I could do was look at her eyes. If I get a follow-up, I'm taking you guys with me. You, you, and you. Yep, we're all going. Norah's the charm. I'll of course introduce you as somebody you're not; I mean four realtors might frighten her off. Sometimes her eyes get this frightened look, you know." He turned to me. "You, Billy, you'll be the electrician, there to check out the wiring. Peter can be my friend from the bank who just happened to see my car parked outside." Robert lifted his credit card from the bar and reached for his jacket.

"I'll pass," Robert said. "A woman's eyes? That's not enough."

"It's a start," Peter said. "You gotta start with something." He looked from Wess to me for backup. "These are not just any woman's eyes," he said.

Robert pulled on his jacket. He turned for the door. "Not enough."

"Norah Jones," Wess said.

"These are the eyes of Norah Jones," I said.

"Got to be more than eyes, even if they're Norah's."

Derik unlocked the door. Wess stood.

Robert shook Derik's hand. "Wait," Wess called.

Robert stopped and turned.

"I'll make you a drummer," Wess said.

"A full kit, cymbals all around." Peter said.

"A drummer?" he said.

"Norah's."

He opened the door. "Norah's drummer?"

"Damn straight," I said.

He paused, tilting his head slightly. He looked at each of us. There was something about his eyes. "Okay," he said. "Okay. I'll be there."

Winner Take Nothing

I'M SITTING ON OUR ragged sofa holding my triple-aught Martin and experimenting with open tunings, looking for a kind of Keith Richards' "Start Me Up" chord, when my girlfriend, Beverly, answers the doorbell. I'd written the lyrics for a song called "We Both Loved You Best," but I had no music. I'm channeling Keith when I hear Beverly squeal.

She's already dressed for work, Hooters' T-shirt and those skintight hot pants, bright orange ones. And now she's standing before the mailman doing this cheerleader thing where she goes up on her tiptoes and smacks her pompoms together just under her chin. The mailman, who's getting a good eyeful, holds out a pen.

"No thanks," I say to him.

"Sign," Beverly says in this real breathy voice. "That's what you do when you've won a contest. That's how they verify the winner."

"No thanks," I say again to the postman.

"I've been entering every contest there is," she says.

The postman looks at her chest.

"Then why isn't it addressed to you?" The mail guy begins his impatient marching in place thing. "Thanks but no thanks," I say. He starts down the sidewalk.

"What?" Beverly shouts. "This could be it for us, the ticket. You got no job." Her whole body kind of vibrates. "You're such a loser! Either—"

When they say "either" what they mean is "or."

"Hey, pal," I call to the guy. He's already in his little mail truck, but he waits for me and hands over the pen. I sign.

We sit on the sofa, and Beverly wiggles her behind against my thigh. She smiles a big one. "I have a feeling about this," she says. She repeats the pompom thing.

"So do I," I say. "Certified mail." I point at the return address. "Lawyer's office."

"That's how they do it, to make sure the winner is legit," she says. "Open it, open it." The letter inside says that I've been named in a paternity suit.

That was the end of Beverly. After she announced she was moving out, I hocked everything we'd bought together and a few items we hadn't, enough to pay for a visit to a lawyer's office and replacement locks on the house.

❦ ❦ ❦

I HELD A FINGER under the number as I dialed, expecting a secretary, but I got a guy's voice. "You've called the right man," he said. "There's a reason my name's at the top of the list of Myrtle Beach lawyers."

"Yeah, Alec Aimes, it's at the top of the yellow pages."

Aimes laughed. "You're a smart guy, I like that."

I read the contents of the letter into the phone. "What's this going to cost me?"

"I don't conduct business over the phone," he said.

His office was not, as he'd led me to believe, in the heart of Myrtle Beach. It was a good ways south, between Surfside and Garden City, in a rusting '80s strip mall. Aimes's office was easy to find. There was only one car in the lot, a faded gold Mercedes, size of an aircraft carrier, its bumper and trunk charred black from diesel exhaust. I opened the only office door that didn't have a For Rent sign posted next to it.

Inside, the dim office was all grays and tans and smelled of mildew and stale Freon from the single window unit. The curled edges of the carpet samples lapped the chair legs and filing cabinets.

After a false start, Aimes lumbered from his desk chair and waddled toward me, hand extended. He was maybe five-foot six, a dark guy with thinning black hair, barrel of a chest, and massive legs. He walked like a short fat guy on roller skates.

"Good to see you," he said. His handshake felt like a big fat soft tit. I held up the letter. "Let's take a look," he said.

He collapsed into the chair and reached into his shirt pocket for glasses. The cheap prints on the wall behind him spoke volumes: Mallards like a squadron of fighter jets getting the hell out of town.

"Ummmm," Aimes said. "Ummmm. Looks like you're screwed."

I stood. "Thanks." I made for the door.

"That'll be a hundred dollars," he said.

"Screw you," I said. "I don't need you to lose in court."

"That's when you need me the most." I stopped and turned. He lifted a magazine. "See this?" He read from its cover. "*Time Magazine*, dated May 30, 2011. That's now, son. That's the way things are right now." He thrust the magazine toward me. The cover said, **Sex. Lies. Arrogance. What Makes Powerful Men Act Like Pigs?*** In the lower corner, beside the photo of a pig, in what looked to be about a three-point font, was another asterisk with the words **No offense**.

"What does this have to do with me?" I said.

"What you're looking at is judge and jury, pal. When they look at you, they're thinking Sex. Lies. Men are pigs."

I tossed the magazine on his desk and turned again toward the door.

"Think about it," he said. "What you won't see, what you'll never see on the cover of *Time*, is this: Sex. Lies. Arrogance. What makes women who chase powerful, married men act like cows? No offense." His words stopped me. "Catch my drift, boy? This is the now: You can call a man a pig as long as in tiny letters you print, 'no offense,' but you can never call a woman—no matter who she is or what she does—a cow. Justice, it ain't blind." I took a deep breath and looked out the office window. In the parking lot, waves of heat coiled above the gold Mercedes.

"You better think about what it's worth to minimize your losses," Aimes said.

I handed him the hundred.

༰༰༰

My attorney offered to drive up to Myrtle Beach, where we'd meet with my accuser, Tina Talbott, at the offices of Slater, Cross & Rugar. I took the passenger seat. My door didn't quite shut all the way, and Aimes produced this little fake cough when he saw me staring at the duct tape covering the air conditioner controls.

"If it's okay with you," he said, "we'll ride with the windows down. I'm trying to be environmentally conscious, you know."

On the drive, he mopped the sweat from his face and questioned me about the plaintiff's affidavit. "Do you remember Ms. Talbott?"

"I don't know," I said. "More than three years ago, that's a long time."

"Letter says your band performed at The Wave, a Rock club here. That correct?"

"Yeah. Before the crash, I played every club in the Southeast."

"And you don't remember screwing a waitress at The Wave?"

"Before the crash, I played every club in the Southeast."

We stopped at a red light. The interior of the Mercedes filled with black diesel smoke. Aimes fanned his nose. "Stinks," he said.

In the elevator up to the offices of Slater, Cross & Rugar, Aimes nodded at the brass trimming. "Impressive," he said.

"Name's Steven Slater," the man in the Brooks Brothers suit said. He was tall, well-tanned, one of those professionally handsome guys who could shave every fifteen minutes. "Have a seat," he said in a theatrically professional voice. He gestured toward a chair.

"Nice place you have here," Aimes said, nodding affirmatively as he rubber necked the spacious, elegant office. "Who's your decorator?"

"Gentlemen," Slater said, "we all know why we're here. In a minute, my associate, Ms. Cross, will bring Ms. Talbott in. You can imagine how emotionally painful this is for her."

"Yes," Aimes said. He heaved a heavy sigh and nodded approvingly at the plush burgundy carpet.

"Where's the evidence?" I said. "This is not exactly a vacation for me."

"Shuuuuuh!" Aimes whispered.

"My ass is on the line here, pal," I said to Slater. "I want to know the grounds for this summons."

Slater passed a sheet of paper to me. Aimes tried to take it, but something about my look made him reconsider. Slater read from the copy in front of him.

"These are the dates your band performed at The Wave, where Ms. Talbott was working, correct?"

"If you say so," I said.

He handed me a second sheet. "This is a signed affidavit from Ms. Talbott's obstetrician, the doctor's judgment of time of conception. There is some room for error, of course, but your band had a seven-day engagement at that time, three days of error on each side of the doctor's target date."

"All this does is place me in the vicinity of a woman who got pregnant," I said.

"That's good," Aimes said. He patted my shoulder. "That's gooooood."

Slater handed over a press kit photo of my band. "She pointed you out," he said. He let me stew for a minute before he picked up his phone. "Yes," he said.

The two women, a blond and a brunette, held hands as they entered the office. Their eyes were strawberry red from crying, and the runoff from the brunette's mascara had done that Alice Cooper thing down her cheeks. Each carried a fistful of tissue in her free hand.

It was quite a damsels-in-distress performance, one likely to be repeated in a courtroom. As they entered, I didn't know which woman was the associate and which the accuser.

My question was answered as the two sat down. Tina looked away. Ms. Cross-with-the-Alice-Cooper eyes glowered. Slater allowed a long minute of sorrowful, petulant silence.

Tina was a beautiful woman, long sun-bleached hair, flawless tanned complexion, perfect features, green eyes. So beautiful I knew I'd never slept with her. She was a woman I would remember. But my feelings of exoneration were mixed ones. She really was sad, truly so.

"Ms. Talbott," Slater whispered. "We need for you to take a good look."

She drew in a deep, deep breath and slowly lifted her eyes toward me. It was a sad but strong face. She tilted her head slightly. Her melancholy eyes moved over every inch of my face. I was the man in a lineup, the bright lights nearly blinding me. But at the same time, I wanted to touch her shoulder and say, "It's okay. It's okay."

She looked from me to Slater. "I can't. I can't do it."

Instantly, Ms. Cross yelped and burst into tears. She stood, sopping her cheeks with tissue, and placed a hand under Tina's arm in an effort to deliver her from the evil, but Tina didn't move.

"Do you need a minute?" Slater said again in that Hollywood voice.

"No," Tina said. She turned her dry eyes to Cross, who then sort of wilted apologetically as if this were the Oscars and she'd stood when somebody else's name was called.

"I can't say for sure it was him." Glances ricocheted all around the room. "I was twenty-one years old. I was working in a nightclub, going to parties."

Slater looked at me. "Will you agree to a blood test? DNA, if necessary?"

"No," Aimes said.

"Yes," I said.

"I'll pay for the tests," Tina Talbott said to me. "I want to know. I want to know for sure."

Slater and Cross exchanged lawyer looks. Slater picked up his phone.

I stood and walked to the office window. Ten years ago, I would have been able to see the ocean. Not now. "What is it?" I said.

"Papers. For the tests," Slater said.

"No," I said looking at Tina.

"A boy," she said. Her eyes did not leave mine. "He doesn't look like you. He looks like me."

Slater's secretary brought in the legal forms.

"As your attorney, let me caution you," Aimes said. "You should read that very carefully before you sign."

I took the pen from the secretary and signed.

"No," Tina whispered.

When I looked up, her face was streaked with tears. She turned to Ms. Cross and then to Slater. "It's not him. It's not. The guy…he was left handed. I remember."

Downstairs, Aimes was dredging his deep pocket for car keys. I looked up at the clouds piled atop one another a few miles inland above Conway. A thin dark halo surrounded them, a threat of rain later.

"Here," he said. In his meaty palm was the money I'd given him. "I really can't take this."

"What about your time?" I said.

"Take it," he said.

"Let me pay for your gas," I said.

"I'd rather have a drink," Aimes said.

"Okay," I said.

I slammed the door to the Mercedes twice, but it still wouldn't shut all the way. Aimes fired up the engine. Exhaust shrouded the sunlight.

"The Showhouse?" he said.

"Make another selection."

"You don't like titty bars?"

"Do I have to remind you what it was that got me where I am today?"

❦❦❦

THE REPEATING CHORUS AT the end of "Third Rate Romance" faltered above the thick salty air, then wafted down the length of The Pier at Garden City. Under the giant gazebo out over the water, the band began its next selection, Don Henley's "End of the Innocence." Their song choices were clearly aimed at middle-aged, family-oriented vacationers. But since the crash, the tourists were few.

Aimes had suggested that we have drinks near his office. And it wasn't long before I knew why. After two gin-tonics, he was line dancing with drunk, sun-baked, Pepto-pink Midwestern housewives. He smiled this goofy, toothy smile and moved with the grace of a circus elephant as he sang, "Ain't Too Proud to Beg." Sweat gushed.

I sat on a wooden bench that smelled of shrimp bait, looking out at the calm, slate-colored ocean. I drank. The movement of the tide rocked the pier ever so slightly.

"I got to get going," I said when the song ended.

"Okay," he said. He smiled and bowed to the pinkies beside him.

"Byyyyye, darlin'," the really pink one with black roots said, affecting a southern drawl.

The lights that stretched down the pier created a kind of dim tunnel as we headed back, and for a moment I felt that weird sensation of being an observer of myself. It's hard to explain unless you've had that experience. But I'm walking beside Aimes down this long, narrow pier, and you've got to know that he's huffing from dancing, pacing along on legs like tree trunks in this gunfight-at-the-OK-Corral swagger. And I'm thinking, Where am I? Who am I? Look at me. It was like I was both participant and observer to this pageant.

I didn't realize Aimes was two-drinks drunk until we entered the pier's arcade and gift shop. The cheap Vegas whistles and strobe lights startled him. He stopped abruptly and pointed at a large sign above a counter where kids were trading in tickets for trinkets, to the word REDEMPTION.

"What's that?" he said, slurring his words.

"Where you cash in," I said.

"You ought to go to Sunday school," Aimes said. "Redemption," he said, "that's where you cash out."

I helped him down the two long flights of steps to the sidewalk. "Let me buy you a sandwich," I said. We crossed to a burger and breakfast place, Sam's Corner. I ordered coffee. He raised his cup, studied it for a second then turned to me.

"It was a good day today," he said. "Thanks to you, I got to dance." He looked down. "Legs like these, you don't get to dance much." He thought for a second then looked up. "I'm a shitty lawyer," he said. "When I was in college, I was a wrestler. Never guess it to look at me now, huh? I wanted to be a high school wrestling coach. Or I thought I did. By the time I got my degree, my body was a wreck. Look at me, I walk like a dwarf. I didn't want to lead kids down that path."

He was mostly sober when he dropped me off at my car outside his office. We shook hands.

"Thanks," he said. "I enjoyed it."

❦❦❦

DURING THE BOOM YEARS, Myrtle Beach's Hard Rock Theme Park symbolized promise for musicians like me, the illusion that a fan base existed to support our dreams and ambitions. Now abandoned, the park was a vast black desert of asphalt and sand spurs. And as I drove past the compound's bolted gates, I considered the concept for its Hard Rock Café—a pyramid. Must have come from a true visionary: a tomb for the dead kings of Rock.

I checked my watch for the time. I was at that crossroads between driving home and stopping for another bourbon when I passed a Hooters Restaurant. Then the question was, Where will I have that drink? I'd drive north to the House of Blues. I had no place to go, no place to be, nobody to do that nothing with. That nothing was me.

These thoughts slammed back and forth like bad reverb inside my head.

And then I saw the sign for The Wave. It was dimly lit, and the V was missing from LI_E MUSIC! Not exactly a good omen. Inside, what had been the stage belonged to squatters, four pool tables. A karaoke machine was tucked just behind the curtain. Randy, the former bouncer turned bartender, didn't remember me or my band.

I asked him to check The House of Blues website to see who was playing. He opened his phone. Behind me, I heard a flat, distant voice. "Hey," Tina Talbott said. "Feeling nostalgic, huh?" She was dressed in a thin white button down and black hot pants. She lit a cigarette.

"You're still working here?" She blew the smoke up toward the ceiling then looked back at me. "Somehow," I said, "I just thought you'd, you know, moved on."

She looked at Randy but spoke to me. "I'm constantly reminded of how lucky I am to still have this job," she said. "Maybe one day that idea will sink in." Randy slid his phone over for me to see.

"Another bourbon?" he said. He turned to pour my drink.

"You want to sit?" I said.

"How long are you going to be here?" Tina said. She looked around at the mostly empty booths and tables. "I'll probably be cut by eleven or twelve if you want to stick around. You can buy me a drink for not fucking me."

❦❦❦

I PRETENDED TO WATCH a Braves–Giants baseball game on the screen at the end of the bar, but mostly I watched Tina in the mirror. She'd pulled her hair up, and the line of her neck accentuated the perfect symmetry of her face. I thought, She'll be beautiful when she's sixty. Randy smiled when he saw me staring at her.

For two hours, I was invisible to Tina. I don't think she looked at me once, not even when she stood at the wait station at the end of the bar while Randy filled drink orders. She seemed perfectly at ease, but at the same time that look seemed rehearsed, like a model on the runway or the trained smile of a performer, real but not real. Participant, observer.

In the top of the eighth inning, I went to the toilet. Tina was sitting at the bar beside my drink when I returned.

"What will you have?" I said.

"Got one coming," she said. "Mind if I smoke?"

"Huffing smoke, that's a part of my job description." I smiled.

"Mine too," she said, indicating the scabby red carpet and cracked Naugahyde booths. "Long day, huh?"

"For both of us."

"Yeah," she said.

She glanced over to the far end of the bar at Randy, posed like a sentry, bulging arms crossed, pretending he wasn't listening.

"You know, it could have been you," she said turning back now. "You're a lucky guy."

I watched her lips work the cigarette. "At the minute," I smiled, "I'm not feeling particularly lucky in any respect."

"That could change," she said.

"That's what's bothering me."

Randy called to her and the two of them disappeared behind the walk-in cooler. She didn't seem like the type to say goodbye. I finished my bourbon and then watched the final out, a swing and a miss. I looked around to pay my tab. Tina was alone behind the bar pouring us both a drink. She took her seat beside me.

"So," I said. "What's next?"

"You mean after-Community-College-slash-fulltime-work-slash-single mom? Desperate times call for desperate measures. I'm just not sure what those measures are." We both drank.

"Mind if I ask you a personal question?" I said.

"I'd say you're entitled."

"Why did you wait so long?"

"Denial. Fear of my mother's guilt trip. I had a choice. I could have gotten an abortion."

"No. I mean why wait this long before tracking down the father?"

She lifted the pen from her pocket and slid a pad in front of me. "Make a list," she said. "All the women you've slept with." I looked at her. "You can't even name a number. How are you going to name names? You can't, I can't." She lit a cigarette. "Times are hard for a lot of people. There are some desperate people out there. I happen to be one of them." She seemed to go off someplace in her head. Then she came back. "What are you?" she said.

"What do you mean?"

"Guitar? Bass? Drums?"

"Guitar," I said.

She touched my hand. "It could have been you." For the first and only time she smiled. I'll never forget that smile.

"So," I said, "what're you going to do?"

Again she indicated the bar. "Looks like this is it." She smoked. "You know," she said, "I did think about an abortion before he was born, but I guess I intentionally waited too long to get one." She squashed the stub of her smoke. "Now, I can't remember a time when I had choices."

"What do you mean?" I said. "That you regret not doing it?"

"No, I never think about that. What I mean is—let's say you are who you are, only you've got a kid. What would you do?"

"I never thought about it."

"But it could be you, right? Beginning tomorrow, it could be you." She looked over at Randy, who had suddenly reappeared. She bumped out another cigarette. "It's all I think about."

"I don't know. I don't know what I'd do."

"Sorry, but that answer is not an option. You have a three-year-old boy, okay? What would you do? He's three years old."

"I guess I'd do whatever I had to do, you know, to see that he's taken care of."

"And what are the limits of what you would do?" She looked away, blowing the smoke from the corner of her mouth, then looked at me for an answer.

"I don't know," I said.

"I don't either," she said. "Walk me to my car."

Raindrops the size of quarters strafed the parking lot. Tina turned as she opened her car door. "Follow me," she said. "I owe you." I looked into her eyes, but I couldn't see anything there. "You've done the time," she said. "You may as well do the crime."

❦❦❦

IT WAS DARK AND the liquor kept moving the key away from the lock. We were both soaked by the time we got inside Tina's '60s-era apartment. In the kitchen, she switched on the light and reached for vodka and bourbon from the cabinet. Her blond hair was dripping. She turned. The white transparent shirt stuck like cellophane. She was arrestingly beautiful. "Make us a drink," she said. "I have to put Charlie in the crib." I'm not sure what she saw on my face, but she said, "Don't worry, I'm on the pill."

"And you weren't before?"

"I was on everything before," she said. Her words made her suddenly uneasy or maybe embarrassed. She looked away and, drawing a deep breath, raised her hand as if to explain, then dropped her arm limply at her side. Just as quickly, she lifted her head and she was herself again. "If I don't put him in the crib, he might, you know, sometimes in the middle of the night he crawls into bed with me, okay?" She turned. I could see the boy's open bedroom door, his bed, and the crib against the wall.

"Who's been with him? He's been here alone, hasn't he?"

Tina sort of lunged for me. Suddenly her mouth was on mine, her body pressed hard against me. "How's that?" she said, her frightened eyes darting up to mine. "Okay?" She attempted a smile. "You like that?" She waited for an answer I didn't have. Then just as abruptly, she walked away. "No," she said. She stopped and turned, lifting a strand of wet hair from her cheek. "I could never do that. The sitter, she was here until twelve. I told her I'd be home at twelve. The bitch won't wait five minutes. I'll be right back."

I watched as she neared his bed. She must have whispered his name because his arms floated up toward her, yet he was still asleep. He was a big boy and the lifting was not easy. She stopped at the doorway, where the light from the kitchen slanted over the two of them. He was blond like his mother, and his profile was hers. A beautiful kid. "I told you," she said. "He looks like me." She laid him in his crib.

Tina crossed from the boy's bedroom to the other one. When she came out, it was pleasantly apparent she'd tossed the bra. Her shirt was unbuttoned half way. In one hand, she held a guitar.

"I didn't know you played."

"I don't. People are always leaving things here. The place is a regular lost and found." She offered the guitar. "How's about that drink," she said. I looked at her kid's bedroom door ten feet away.

"How's about not," I said.

"Just one. Then a love song? One that tells a really, really big lie? One that has the word 'forever' in it."

"It's been a long day," I said.

❦❦❦

TINA'S RINGTONE WOKE ME the next morning. I sat up on the sofa as she stumbled into the bathroom, the phone jammed against her ear. I must have dozed because when I opened my eyes, she was standing over me, one towel around her, another drying her hair.

"I need a serious favor," she said. "See, I have this job interview and I've got to go for it."

"Where?" I said. "What kind of job?"

"A good job," she said.

"What about your sitter?"

"She's a bitch. I've got to go to this interview."

"At seven in the morning?" I said.

Tina dropped down onto the sofa, her fists knotted at her chin.

"You have to help me," she said. "Look. I'm in trouble."

"What kind of trouble?"

"I'm not in trouble now, but I'm gonna be in trouble. I've got to make plans and provisions for Charlie. I've got to do some serious groveling at the feet of my mother, see?"

"Why?"

She looked around for cigarettes, but there were none. "I got a call from this friend. They're making a string of arrests, you know, a sting, this morning. I don't have much time."

"Drugs?"

"Yes."

From the kitchen window, I watched Tina's car pull onto the street. As she drove away, I thought of how the camera imperceptibly pulls back at the end of a movie. Then she was gone.

I found the flour above the dish drain, a mixing bowl down below, and a cast iron frying pan in the oven drawer. There were eggs and milk in the refrigerator.

I sat on the sofa and stared at Charlie's bedroom door. About eight-thirty, I heard him stirring, and a few minutes later he was singing to himself, "The Wheels on the Bus." I waited until he called for his mother. And then I waited until he called for her again. He was standing in the crib when I opened the door.

"You're not Randy," he said.

"Do you like pancakes?" I said.

I turned on the TV. I watched him as I cooked.

Taking turns, we built a fort with wooden A-B-C blocks as we watched TV. We read a few books and watched TV. When he asked to go outside, I picked up the guitar. It was an old Yamaha, not expensive but well made. The action was too high and the intonation needed work, but the strings were fairly new and the instrument's resonance told me that it had aged well. We sang "This Old Man" and "Old McDonald." I affected the voice of Donald Duck as I sang "Three Blind Mice," and Charlie's eyes widened in delight. "Wait! Wait!" he said.

He slid off the sofa and sprinted into his room. He handed me a small black photo album filled with pictures of a not-so-sober Tina holding Charlie, taken, it appeared, at various parties. "That's my mommy; that's me," he said. Then he'd turn the page. "That's my mommy; that's me."

I made banana sandwiches and chicken noodle soup for lunch. We watched TV. Charlie fell asleep on the floor. I lifted him, then stretched him out in his crib. He slept for a long time. And sometime between three and four that afternoon, I suddenly realized that Tina wasn't coming back.

❦❦❦

I DIALED THE NUMBER for The Wave. I heard a man's voice.

"Hello, Randy?" I said.

"Who's calling, please?"

I told him.

"Let me see if I can find Randy. Hold on."

I held for a long time.

"I can't seem to find him. What's up?"

"Is Tina there?"

"Tina Talbott?"

"Yeah, is she there?"

"Can I have her call you back. She may have stepped out. Where you calling from?"

"Her apartment, I'm calling from her place."

"Her apartment?"

"That's what I just said. What's going on?"

"Good. Hold the line, please."

There was a knock at the door. "Wait, let me check the door," I said. "Maybe that's her at the door."

"Yes," the man said. "That would be a good idea."

Although I offered no resistance, the two police officers threw me to the ground and slammed the cuffs on me before I could speak. Then I was offered a phone call.

❧❧❧

CHARLIE WAS STANDING ON the sofa looking out the window. One of the cops held a precautionary hand at the boy's back. The other cop sat in a kitchen chair facing me, taking notes as I answered his questions. He had taken off the cuffs when he saw that Charlie and I were the only ones in the apartment.

"That car!" Charlie shouted and pointed. "It's on fire!"

A black cloud hovered above the gold Mercedes as Aimes shut his door. Inside the apartment, he spoke with the cops, then called the detective in charge—the guy who had answered when I phoned The Wave.

Aimes gave me the lowdown. Randy and Tina had been dealing pot and pills. When the cops showed up at The Wave with an arrest warrant, they saw that the bar had been robbed. Randy and Tina weren't answering the detective's calls.

"What about the boy?" I said to Aimes. Charlie was turning the pages in the photo album, pointing, whispering his name, his mother's.

"Well, given the result of the paternity suit, he'll go to DSS."

"What about Tina's mother?"

"There is no Tina's mother," he said. We both looked at the kid.

The two cops were outside. One was on the cruiser phone while the other stood nearby carefully concealing the cigarette he was smoking.

"I'll see what I can find out," Aimes said. "Soon, they'll need a more detailed statement from you, of course. But I don't think you'll have to stick around. Sometimes it takes the folks from DSS a little while to get here. They're pretty shorthanded. I'll stay with the kid if you need to get back home."

I watched as Aimes padded down the steps toward the police car. Behind me, Charlie said, "That's my mommy; that's me." Only he said it like a question.

❧❧❧

IT SOUNDS LIKE A clichéd country song, but it's true. Sometimes music is the only thing to reach for when you feel you've got nothing else to hold onto. I picked up the Yamaha. "You want to sing something, buddy?" I said.

Charlie held his finger on a photo. He shook his head no. I watched him as I played a little, just random chords. There was no song, at least none I'd learned to play, none that spoke to the moment.

"Why do you do that?" Charlie said.

"I like the way it feels," I said. "You want to hold it?"

He nodded and slid down from the sofa. He set the photo book at my feet. I pulled him up onto my lap.

Aimes opened the door. "They got DSS on the phone again," he said, looking down at his watch. "Someone should be here by now."

The Yamaha's body was too tall and thick for the boy to reach over and touch the strings, and I thought, If I had my Martin triple-aught the kid would stand a better chance.

"Is this the way it feels?" Charlie said.

"Yes," I said.

"You can go now," Aimes said to me, nodding at the boy. "I'll wait on them. You're done here."

Charlie pushed the guitar to the side and shimmied down from my lap.

"No." I said. "Let me show you how it feels." I held the guitar at arm's length and pulled him up so that he fit snugly against my chest. "Here's what you do," I said. "You hold the body of the guitar tight against your body. Like this." I wedged the boy against me. "Then you play a big ol' open G chord, play it full and clean. The sound inside that guitar, you see, it goes round and round, like a tornado, until the box can't hold it, and that feeling moves through the wood and into your body. It fills up your body," I said.

A dirty white van with a city emblem on the door pulled to a stop at the curb. "Close your eyes." I played the chord. "Do you feel it?" I said. "Do you feel those vibrations moving through you?"

"Yes," he said. Eyes shut, he raised his face to the sunlight, resting the crown of his head against my throat. "Do it again," he said.

I played the chord.

His eyes were still closed. "Again," he said. I felt his small body breathing against me. I played the chord, full and clean. His face was soft, serene. "I feel it." he said. He turned, pressed his palm to his chest. "Here," he whispered. "Do *you* feel it?"

"Yes," I said. "Yes, I do."

Safe Storage

H E WOULD MAKE THE twenty-minute drive from the hospital to his daughter's school. He would observe traffic laws and keep his eyes on the road. Because now he knew that anything could happen.

The doctor had assured him that his wife would sleep, but he didn't trust the doctor. The doctor said there was no reason for him to take chances on the road. You've not slept all night, the doctor had said to him. He was taking no chances, but it had nothing to do with the doctor. He hardly knew the man. He didn't trust him.

Still he was taking no chances. He'd called his daughter's second grade teacher. He hadn't given the teacher a time, but the teacher would be expecting him to show.

He'd have to make sure that his seven-year-old daughter didn't start asking questions before he could get her inside the car. He didn't know how to do that. She would ask the moment she saw him. It was one thing he could still count on, that she would ask. She was a very bright little girl, with blond hair and a missing front tooth and a funny way of covering her mouth—now that she'd lost the tooth—when she laughed. He'd have to find a way to keep her from asking.

But first he had a chore to do. He couldn't let her come home to the way things had been. The teacher would have to wait. It was something he had to do for his daughter. After all, she was only seven, a second-grader. He couldn't let her down, and his wife would be sleeping. He was sure of that. He told himself to concentrate on the traffic.

He didn't know what time it was because he hadn't slept all night in the hospital and the sky was overcast and you couldn't count on anything. But his daughter was in school, so it had to be before two o'clock because she was always waiting for him at two o'clock, and he was always there. He had talked to the chairman of his department at the university where he taught literature and logical thinking and where he had told his students that one day they would learn that in the world not all things are negotiable. He had arranged through his chairman to teach in the mornings so that he would always be at his daughter's school at two o'clock, so that maybe she would grow up remembering that her father was someone she could rely on.

As he sat at a red light now, he assured himself that he would not be late, that he had time to take care of the thing he had to do before he picked her up from school and that when he did get to her school, he would know what to do to keep her from asking what he knew she would ask.

A horn sounded behind him. He pressed the accelerator. He would speak before she did, and he'd keep it going somehow at least until he got her outside the school, until he could get her into the car, where they could sit close and he could say it to her the way he wanted her to hear it. He would begin by saying that her mother was sleeping, that she had been up all night, that it had been a very hard night for her but that she was sleeping now and that maybe at that very moment she was having dreams. And then as they walked he would ask how his daughter had slept and if she had had any dreams and what they had been. That would maybe get him outside. Then he would say that her mother had been talking about her at the hospital during the night, and he would make up some of the things she might have said and say some of the things she had said.

But he wouldn't of course say what his wife had said to him and about him. That this wouldn't have happened if he had not insisted upon their moving back to South Carolina from the mountains; that in the mountains, where they lived an hour away from any hospital, the doctor would never have waited the extra two weeks, that it would have been too risky. That two weeks ago everything was fine. Two weeks ago this never would have happened.

Try to imagine the worst, he would someday say to his students. You can't, he'd say. You can't. And neither can I, he would say.

He pulled into the drive and sat looking at their house, feeling so tired he didn't know if he could stand. It was a small, simple house, not what either of them had hoped for, but the best they could do. He had taught summer school to make money to pay for their move, and that hadn't left much time to find a place.

He shut off the engine and walked around back to the small wooden shed, which had a narrow enclosed space not much wider than the door itself, a space for keeping gardening supplies, rakes, and shovels. He needed to make sure that everything would fit in there, that his daughter wouldn't see anything. It would be hard enough for her without that.

The house had just two bedrooms. They had bought a portable kerosene heater. His wife didn't like the idea, but they'd agreed it was better to be warm. They had converted the room that had once been the front porch. The room had been enclosed long ago, and though it was small, it would do. Everything, they'd said, was temporary. In a year or two their lives would be better. They had made plans for things to get better. Besides, the room was big enough to hold what they needed. It would do for now.

He began. The stuffed animals on top of the blanket were his daughter's and she had arranged them just so. They couldn't go in the shed. He wouldn't put up with that. He tucked them under his arms and carried them to his daughter's room and set them on her bed. Then he emptied her toy box, laid the stuffed things gently inside, and piled her toys on top. She'd find them sooner or later, sure. But maybe not too soon. You never could tell. There were things you couldn't know. Things that happened without explanations, even from doctors who were supposed to know such things.

He heard the echo of his own footsteps as he left his daughter's room.

Next, he neatly folded the blanket and sheet and set the small pillow on top. Outside, under the shed, he found a cardboard moving box for the artwork his daughter had created. He collected the things his wife had laid out on the table under the window: lotion, towels, a small silver hairbrush, a tiny mirror, and a plastic lamp. He set the box on the floor beside the table and used the sheets and blankets as packing material, to keep things from colliding. He brought a chair in from the kitchen so that he could reach the mobile that he had hung from the ceiling.

He couldn't close the top to the box filled with things from the small room. He didn't like the thought of the dust and the dirt that would soon cover everything. So he put the box inside a large black plastic bag that he'd bought to hold the leaves he had expected to rake when his wife came home from the hospital, and he set the box in the small storage space where gardening tools belonged. He pushed it all the way along the narrow dark storage space to the back, where she wouldn't see it, even if by chance she opened the wooden door. He wiped cobwebs from his face and went back inside the house.

He would tell his daughter that he had discovered Charlotte's web, and he would launch into that, her favorite book, before she put together two and two, before he told her the real story.

Next, he turned the mattress on its side and carried it out. It wouldn't stand on its side, but if he leaned the metal springs against the wall, he could secure the mattress inside the shed. They'd bought everything second hand, but it was fine. Everything had been fine enough.

The crib folded diagonally and became longer than you'd think. But he managed to lift it and angle it through the tight places, and although two of the casters fell off as he made his way down the cement steps at the back of the house, he got the crib out to the shed's storage space without having to stop or think too much. He should have put it in first, though, he realized. He had to take out the mattress and the metal springs and start again. If she opened the door, there was no hiding the crib. No hiding it. The box of diapers sat up on top.

Now he stood in the room that was as empty as the day they moved in, and he didn't want to think about his daughter seeing it like that. He didn't want to think of the look on her face, but he really had no choice. Certainly not the choice of her seeing it as it had been.

So he'd done the thing he had to do, and now he had the other thing to do. Now he had to drive to his daughter's school and present himself at her classroom, and not let her know, not let it show on his face, until he could get her some place where she would be safe, some place where it wouldn't have to be any worse than it had to be, so that he could one day say that he had, as best he could, told her what he had to say.

Available Light

THERE IS NO PRETTY exit from this scene," Rachel said.

"What are you talking about?" the man said.

"Telling a woman she looks bored? That's the worst pick-up line I've ever heard."

"That dress makes me think you've heard them all. Am I right?"

"Maybe detached, disenchanted. Bored, that's your word, not mine."

The young man smiled. "Okay. What amuses you?"

"Is that a question or a come-on?"

"You decide." He had announced that he was buying her a drink. In the looks department, he was interchangeable with the other MBAs in the bar. "Feminine prerogative," he said. "You can have it any way you like, right?"

"Is that an answer or a come-on?"

"I'm amusing you, aren't I?" His smile was all he had going for him.

"In that trip-to-the-zoo sort of way, I'd say yes."

"You're a voyeur?"

Scanning the room, she spoke more to herself than to him. "I can't resist a man who knows a big word." Her husband's lover wasn't there. "Want to try again, or is that the only big one you know?"

"You like the big ones?" He was working that smile. "Words, I mean?"

"Go away."

The bartender set drinks before Rachel and the man.

The man lifted his glass. "If you're not here for conversation and company," he said, "then what's the deal?"

"If I wanted to meet someone, I'd be sitting down there in your department, the meat section, at the other end of the bar."

"What department is this?"

"The fuck-off department."

"I like you."

"You're sick."

"You're amusing."

Although she had never seen her husband's current lover, Rachel was certain she'd recognize the woman. Again her eyes swept the room. "I'm just here for the show, you know, to see a bad movie performed by bad actors."

"I've seen this movie before. You're the star of it," he said. "You've been the star since you walked in."

"No. In case you haven't figured it out, I'm looking, not performing."

"You don't have to sell me on that. One glance at that dress and how you fit into it? You're a looker, all right."

"If you could resist watching yourself perform in the mirror," Rachel said, "you'd hear what I'm saying."

"I'm watching the movie. Ours."

Rachel reached down for her purse. "How about a little reality, an ounce of truth." Their eyes met for the first time. "Are you always attracted to older, bored women?"

"When they look like you?"

She set down the purse. "I think we've already covered the subject of my looks."

Leaning forward, he whispered. "Truth is, if you thought you could do better, you wouldn't be here."

She whispered back. "You're wrong. When you're the best I can do, I'll order a double—and a bullet."

The man looked toward the end of the bar, at the other accountants who were watching. He smiled. His lips hardly moved when he spoke. "Do you find this amusing?" he said.

"There is no this."

"Maybe you're looking in the wrong place." His trousers brushed her thigh. "This is this," he said.

"That's it." She pushed away the drink. "You have to go. You and the midget are invited to leave."

"No problem," he said. He looked down the bar at his friends. One smiled and gave him a thumbs-up.

Rachel dredged the purse for cigarettes, for the pack she'd not opened. She tore the wrapper and bumped out a Marlboro, then paused with the pack in her hand. Rachel didn't smoke. Not looking up at the man, she said, "Are you still here?"

The muscles in his false smile drained flat. He turned and walked to an empty space near the wait station, leaned back pressing his elbows into the bar, and assumed the stoic pose of the other men there. The accountant beside the man said something Rachel didn't hear. In the mirror, she saw their heads turn. The two sized her up. "She looks *way* better from a distance," the man said. The two laughed.

The bartender swooped a flame beneath her cigarette. "Can I get you something else?" he said.

"Magic dust," Rachel said. She meant to make the men disappear. Her eyes skimmed the crowd, pausing at the face of a woman with thick black hair and dressed in a green silk blouse. The woman turned. Their eyes met.

The bartender thought she meant drugs. She was a stranger in his bar, maybe a cop. Appearances were not to be trusted.

"Can't help you," he said.

"Then call me a cab," she said.

🐾🐾🐾

THE DRIVER HELD THE door. "Where to?"

"You tell me," she said, looking out the taxi window and feeling inside her purse.

The cabbie ticked his index finger against the steering wheel and glanced up into his mirror. Rachel freshened her lipstick. She sensed his eyes. "Look at me," she said. The driver had a face carved by thirty years of cheap bourbon and black coffee. His eyes didn't waver. His voice had that May I help you? inflection.

"I need an address?"

"Look at me," she said. "Where would you find a woman like me?"

The driver pulled away from the curb. "You want some music?" he said. "Some music might be nice."

"No," she said.

At the first light he assessed the traffic. "Someplace nice," he said. "You look like you could use someplace nice."

"Mind if I smoke?" she said.

His eyes flashed up into the mirror, a look of disbelief there. "Not in the cab, Miss."

"Just some place where I can smoke then," she said.

🐾🐾🐾

THE BARTENDER WORE AN elegant black bustier and dark purple satin pants. She smiled and slid Rachel's martini and credit card across the brightly lit bar. This place, mahogany and marble, was, like the other bar, inside an opulent international hotel, the kind of hotel familiar to her corporate husband. And gliding effortlessly on the currents of youth and money were fashion ornaments with pouty lips and sullen eyes, the kind of women her husband slept with in these hotels. The kind he might be sleeping with now in San Francisco.

After ten years of marriage, Rachel knew her husband's taste in all things, his habits, his wanting and her power over that wanting, his in-securities and predilections. She knew exactly what to do with his erotic impulses, what and when to submit, what and when to withhold. Rachel had created a profile of her husband's current lover from his menu of privations, from those things she couldn't or wouldn't give him, from his pathetic neediness. She would certainly know the woman when she saw her, no question.

She lit a cigarette she didn't smoke, ordered another martini, dirty, and fingered the stem of its glass.

Neither jealousy, nor insecurity, nor love incited her. Their marriage had been one of low returns and diminishing expectations. She had loved him and not loved him, felt passion and disdain for him, missed him while he was away and distanced herself from him when he was not. She had mar-ried him for the reasons some women have children. She didn't particularly want him, but she didn't want to be deprived of him either. She couldn't claim sexual fidelity, fidelity of any kind. But the constricting tentacles intrinsic to every affair ran contrary to her deeper impulses and essential needs. Intrigue's aphrodisiacal promise had failed her like bad cocaine. Each had become a placeholder in the other's life, a presence felt only by its absence. Hence, Rachel held no animosity toward her husband's lover. She certainly did not fear her, for the constant throughout their marriage had been the shared understanding that while Rachel could leave him, he could never leave her. So convinced was she of this that Rachel often fantasized other women making love to her husband while she watched and directed.

Curiosity was the fire that burned brightest. But simply imagining the other woman no longer moved her. She had lost interest in that. She wanted a real face, a name. Imagining had become the antithesis of living. She would wait, assert her will, and the other woman would appear, no question.

Rachel brought the glass to her lips and lifted her eyes. In the mirror behind the bar, she surreptitiously followed the unfolding narratives of couples on the dance floor, of others entwined in softly lit leather booths. As she drank, she studied the eyes of one woman, another's hands, committed to memory the lips of a third. A titillating tremor of readiness passed through her, a feeling of expectation, of promise. It occurred to her that she stood at the thrilling precipice of something new. Lowering the martini, she raised her head and breathed deeply, absorbing the ambience of the bar. A warm tide of passion filled her.

❦ ❦ ❦

BESIDE RACHEL, A VOICE: "I've had that dream before." The woman's red hair and perfect complexion were enough to draw the attention of every man at the bar, but it was her eyes, wide and green, that Rachel saw first.

"Pardon me?" Rachel said. Mechanically, she reached for her glass.

"Hi, Rachel," the woman said. "May I sit down?" She took the leather barstool.

"Who—?"

"I'm Julia." She motioned to catch the bartender's eye. "You were out there. I go there all the time." And now she looked at Rachel and smiled. "Dirty martini"—she nodded toward Rachel's glass—"good choice."

Rachel tilted her head and smiled. She was certain she had never seen this woman. "How do you know who I am?"

The bartender stood before them. "What can I bring you?" she said.

Julia turned to Rachel, studied her face for a second before she spoke. "Is it possible to define a thing by what it is not?" Rachel and the bartender exchanged smiles. "My future former lover and I were just having that conversation. Now that love is gone. I considered it an intellectual exchange. You know, a kind of existential discussion. So, Rachel, is it possible?"

"*What?*" Rachel said.

Julia said, "By the looks of you, I'll take that as a yes. It *is* possible to define a thing by what it is not. Thanks, I'm happy we have that behind us." To the bartender she said, "I'll have what she's having."

"Dirty?"

"As dirty as this one," she said lightly touching Rachel's hand. As the bartender walked away, Julia sang the words to a corny old song, "The Impossible Dream."

Rachel covered her laugh with a hand. "What *are* you talking about?"

Julia raised Rachel's glass, looked down into the remains of her drink. "Make that two," she called to the bartender, "another for Rachel."

"Do I know your lover, have we met?" Rachel said. "Is that how you know me?"

Julia looked up and pulled back her red hair, cradling the curve of her face in her palm. "My mother read tea leaves. I took it to the next level. I read olives."

"Sooo," Rachel said, joining in. "Your mother was a Gypsy?"

"No. She was Chinese." She bowed slightly, her green eyes slowly easing down Rachel's neck. "Ahhhh-soooooo," Julia crooned. The smiling bartender set down the two martinis.

"You're funny," Rachel said.

"You're Rachel," Julia said.

Rachel's smile disappeared. "Have we met?"

Julia reached for her glass. "In a former life, I'd say. You're not the type who believes in *the universe*." She smiled. "It's taken fate—the Mother of All Things—this long to bring us together. Like every other woman here"—she sang again—"you've been wait-ing, anticipat-ing." Julia was no singer. "You've been dreaming, I've been dreaming. That's what the olives say." Julia lifted her glass, then handed Rachel hers. "For what, nobody knows." She lifted both glasses. "To us," she said. "To destiny, fate, fortune, chance, karma, the stars; to exquisite doom and lavish waste; to sweet dissipation; and most and foremost—to these olives."

"Not your first martini, this one?" Rachel said with a crooked smile. They both drank.

"Nor is it my first life," Julia said. "I am a woman of many martinis, a woman of many lives. And so are you, Rachel."

"How do you know who I am?"

Julia again bowed slightly, her red hair framing her eyes, her lips. "Like soooooo," she said. She pointed at Rachel's name on the credit card nearly hidden beneath her purse. "It's a subversive habit I picked up in a former life, when I used to go on a manhunt." The two women laughed. "A carryover from a former self," she said. "Do you know the secret self? You know what I mean, don't you? The secret self. Everybody has one."

"I have no idea what you're talking about," Rachel said. She was smiling.

"It's okay," Julie said. "I'll teach you. But first I need your help." She lifted Rachel's wrist. "We should formalize the departure of lost loves." She looked up as if she'd suddenly heard a voice. "Byyye," she sang brightly. The two women waved to the room. Julie lifted her glass to Rachel.

Rachel looked away and reached into her bag. "Mind if I smoke?" she said.

"No. I accept it as part of the swearing off process. Yours," she said, waiting for Rachel to look at her. Julia smiled. "Not mine."

Rachel dropped the Marlboros back into her bag. "Well, Madame Mystic, oracle of the olives," she said, "if you know so much, trace this call and tell me where I am."

Julia smiled and raised her glass. "You and I—all of us," she said gesturing to the room, "we're aboard this cruise ship, the one we signed on for." They laughed and drank. "Tonight is my present to myself," she said. "And to you. It's my birthday. I'm thirty."

Rachel extended her drink. "I remember thirty," she said. They touched glasses.

❦❦❦

RACHEL HAD ORDERED DRINKS, and now the two women watched the bartender bring them.

"Soooo," Julia said, lowering her voice two octaves, "love that dress, what brings you here, what floats your boat, come here often, didn't I see you in a porn film?"

Rachel laughed. "You're right. We have met." Both women were a little drunk.

"I knew it," she said. "In a secret life."

"No," Rachel said, "in a former bar, earlier tonight. Is that why you've sworn them off—men, I mean?"

Julia held her glass suspended before her. "Men?" she said. "Ahhh, yes, men." She closed her eyes in search of the netherworld and spoke in a mock trance. "You mean because they are all so *rudimentary*?" She turned and looked into Rachel's eyes. "As a species, I'll admit that most men live in a perpetual world of false starts, which makes the single life of some women unbearably predictable. I'm at that point where I meet a man, and within fifteen minutes I've run all the tests—I've become one of those computerized diagnostic instruments at the car dealership. I know before the end of the first drink."

"Maybe you don't know what you want," Rachel said.

"Speak for yourself." Julia lifted Rachel's cigarette pack and hummed the melody of "The Impossible Dream." She smiled, held it for an extra beat, then set down the pack. "Long ago I reduced what I wanted from a man to its essence. Two things. Only two things. One: that when the shooting starts, he'll take the bullet for me. And—"

"And that he'll beg you for sex."

"The combination doesn't exist."

"Let me guess" Rachel said. "Your lover is the 'I'll take the bullet'?"

"And yours," Julia touched Rachel's wedding ring, "is the 'I'll beg you for sex.'"

"To seem so different, how can they all be the same?"

The bartender set down two more martinis. "On me," she said. "My therapist charges two-hundred dollars an hour for this." She smiled and walked away.

Rachel said, "How about your. . . older lovers? Are they the same?"

"They're more attentive and sometimes less self-centered, you know. But most of them carry around this kind of sadness that can be unbearable. You know what I mean. I know you do." Julia turned. "What sort did you come here looking for? Younger? Older? Richer?"

"I came here looking for a woman; I mean—that—didn't come out right," Rachel said.

As she drank, Julia's eyes held steady over the rim of her glass. "Sounded right to me," she said.

Rachel fingered the stem of her glass and looked away. At once it seemed the room had become crowded with businesswomen and professionally manicured men. "Who is that singing?" She looked around the bar. "I've never been here before." The lights had dimmed to a pale yellow. "The music, I mean. Where is it coming from?"

"I came here looking for another woman, too," Julia whispered. "The woman I'm to be in my next life."

"The after-thirty life?" Rachel said.

As she spoke, Julia gestured like a maestro. "Here's the problem: I've learned that a woman can never truly love a man. You see, the whole idea is oxymoronic. What I mean is, what we have to give up—I don't mean in bed, I mean that part of ourselves necessary to *love* someone—makes us incapable of loving him. To love a man is to be vulnerable to the power of men. Vulnerability and love are mutually exclusive. You and I have been here for, what, two hours? And we have everything to gain and nothing to lose, right? This is just you and me. If either of us were with a man now, we'd have an invisible force field surrounding us, one necessary to protect us from the essence of men. What kind of love is it that requires you to wear that kind of armor?"

"Yes," Rachel said.

"So for our own happiness, yours and mine you see, it's become necessary to select men incapable of exerting that power over us, men we can… predict."

"You mean control," Rachel said.

"I don't mean in a vile way; I mean men less strong than we."

"That's safety, not love" Rachel said.

"Yes, absolutely."

"But," Rachel said, "over time we come to resent their weakness."

"The thing we require of them," Julia said.

Rachel turned and looked into Julia's eyes. She whispered, "And we come to despise them a little, don't we, their weakness?"

"Voilà!" Julia said, raising her arms. "That's my girl!"

"And the sad thing is, the truth is, that this is a conversation we can never have with a man," Rachel said.

"Maybe it's not so sad," Julia whispered. "The truth, it shouldn't make you sad."

"No," Rachel said. "It shouldn't."

"But it does?"

"Yes and no. This thing we're talking about? It's the opposite of what it is."

"You got it." Julia said, tossing her arm over Rachel's shoulder. "Look," she said. "Look."

"What?" Rachel said. Julia nodded toward the enormous mirror behind the bar. Rachel saw the two of them.

"That's the future you," Julia said. "That's the future me. The future us."

Rachel said, "You are a charming woman."

Julia lifted her glass like a chalice and pressed it into Rachel's palm. "To the not-so-secret-self," she said, nodding into the mirror.

OUTSIDE THE HOTEL, THEY stopped at the curb. Julia said, "Seems we've arrived at that awkward intersection, the corner of What's Next and Where?" Rachel looked left and right. She didn't know the time or where she was, but the quiet street meant it was very late.

"I know a place," Julia whispered.

"I should get home," Rachel said.

"You can't get there from here," Julia said. The two women stood unsteadily, waiting. "I'll drive," she said. Neither moved.

Rachel looked down the dark, empty street. From inside a shadow behind her, the hotel doorman said, "Get you ladies a cab?"

"No," Julia said.

"Miss?" the voice inquired of Rachel. "Miss?" Ahead, a yellow taxi at a stoplight pulled toward them. "Miss?"

"No," Rachel said.

✾✾✾

SMILING, JULIA SAID, "As captain of this cruise ship, I'd like to welcome you aboard."

"You okay to drive?" Rachel said.

"I'm the captain, you're my first mate. Or, we can do it the other way around. I'll be your first mate. However you'd like." Julia started the engine, turned and gave Rachel a little salute. "Whatever floats your boat."

A light rain had glazed everything. The late night was dark and quiet. They listened to Diana Krall. After a time Julia said, "How do you feel?"

"Like I could just sail on," Rachel said, "you know, on and on."

"I do know," Julia said.

✾✾✾

WHEN RACHEL OPENED HER eyes, she realized she'd fallen asleep. "Oh," she said.

Without looking away from driving, Julia extended her hand to Rachel's. "Dreaming?" she said.

"No," Rachel said.

"Good," Julia said. "That's good."

Rachel sat up, eyes wide, and drew a deep breath. She looked all about. "Where are we going?" In answer, Julia turned and smiled. "Where *are* we?" Rachel said.

"Almost there."

"Where?"

"The future."

They stopped, their faces bathed in the red traffic light.

"No," Rachel whispered. "I don't recognize any of this. This isn't where I live."

"And where would that be?"

"Home," Rachel said, but the answer sounded like a question.

"I want to take you someplace," Julia said.

"Where?" Rachel said.

"You'll like it."

"Yes?" Rachel said.

"You'll see."

"Where?" Rachel said.

"You'll see."

The rain had stopped, and Rachel lowered her window. The air was warm and damp. "Okay then," she said.

The green traffic light lit their faces. Julia looked both ways before she eased through the intersection. They entered a thick cloud of fog.

"There must have been a thunderstorm," Julia said.

"I love that ozone smell," Rachel said, "new air. A thunderstorm creates that smell."

Before them, morning light the color of rosewater swelled from the horizon. Rachel turned, resting her head against the window and watched as the breeze gently lifted Julia's red hair.

Rachel said, "Your idea, the secret self. I think I know what you mean."

Julia smiled. "Of course you do. Some secrets are not meant to be kept."

Rachel said, "Maybe we can define a thing by what it is not."

Julia said, "You're awake. You've sobered up. So, what do you think? What do you say?"

Rachel said, "I have no idea what I'm going to say ten minutes from now."

"But when we get there, you'll know." Julia smiled into the windshield.

"Yes, when we get there," Rachel said, "I'll know."

That Place Love Built

HAPPILY MARRIED EXPRESSES ITSELF in code, in that music-like combination of word and gesture that you feel but never talk about. I was happily married. I knew what that meant. If you've ever been that way with a man for a long time, you know too. That we-can-read-each-other's-mind, that puppy love, is not what I'm talking about, and not that stretch of hot-and-bothered infatuation either. I'm talking about long-haul love here. Carl and me.

So Carl and I spent the weekend in Myrtle Beach Christmas shopping then came home and watched a special about Johnny Cash on TV. We stretched out on top of the sheets in our underwear and sipped a beer. We held hands and sang along. We'd been married seven years.

When it's time to shut off the lights, Carl, who looks like a teddy bear in boxers, skates on his thick hunting socks into the bathroom, and while he's in there I lower my regular voice about four octaves and sing, "Folsom Prison Blues." Carl returned as I sang, sporting a full-face grin. He held our vitamins and Tums in one fist and the front of his boxer shorts bunche dup in the other. "I think I can, I think I can," he chugged, doing his hips in that humping in-out motion. We both busted out, Carl laughing so hard he dropped one of the pills on the floor. I feigned martyrdom by scrambling for the pill and tossed it into my mouth. And then I, dressed in bra and bloomers, went all spastic by acting out that I'm choking on the Tums like it was poison from being on the floor, which made Carl laugh even harder and caused him to choke for real on the Tums. But actually it was his heart stopping that killed him, a deadly virus that had invaded the muscle, not the Tums.

It was the last thing on earth I expected to happen. I loved him.

When you lose somebody you love, that loss leaves a hole equal to the size of that love. So I think I know what it's like when a soldier says he can feel his lost arm or leg. Which means its absence. I know in my heart. And just as the veteran would do anything to get that arm or leg back, the time comes when a woman will do most anything to fill that emptiness of the heart. I'm not trying to cover up for anything. It's just that sometimes hindsight informs us of how deeply we can be hurt, how great that loss is, how vulnerable we are. And how stupid. We tell our women friends that we can never love again. But at night when we're lying there on those same sheets, we feel the weight of loss on our chest and our heart hurts, and I mean hurts as in hurts. And you want it to go away. To just go away.

I'm not making excuses for my stupidity. I just want you to know. You can love somebody, really love that person, and come to discover from the one you've lost that you can't live without love. After enough time has passed, you come to know that you can live without that person, but you can't live without that thing. Some of us have to have somebody to love. You might find that hard to believe, but some of us have to have somebody to love. And to love us back. We can't shake off that need, that blessing, that curse.

That's how I got Ted, my second husband. I don't want to talk much about Ted because whereas Carl had been my life's fortune, Ted was my life's failure. I won't try to explain too much because it comes out sounding like a mouthful of excuses. No, that's only partly true. The real truth is that when I think about Ted now, I hear my mother's voice in my head: "When you talk dirt about your ex-boyfriends," she used to say, "it only makes you look stupid for having them in the first place." And she's right. So I'll only tell you two things about Ted. The first is that he made me laugh. And at the time, that laughter was like nourishment to a starving person. But funny does not make a person good. The second thing I'll tell you is that Ted wanted a bass boat and he wanted to buy it with the little bit of money Carl left me. Sure, Ted and I were married, but I still felt that money was really Carl's money. I never dreamed of touching it. It was all I had left of Carl.

So Ted and I are eating breakfast and he's quizzing me about Carl's money for his bass boat and I'm paying him as little mind as I can until I've heard enough. You never plan that moment of "heard enough," it just comes over you. I've taken a spoonful of Raisin Bran into my mouth when that moment arrives. "I really don't want to talk about this anymore," I say to Ted with a mouthful of fiber-rich cereal. As a way of expressing his disapproval, Ted slaps his knee with a big HA! HA! and says: "Shut your mouth. You look like a fat mullet with a half-chewed worm in his mouth!"

And that was the end of Ted. I'm not sure if it was the image of a half-chewed fishing worm or that he used the word "fat." Either way that was the beginning of the swift end for Ted.

Other than a list of unoriginal one-liners, the only thing of value Ted brought to our miscarriage of a marriage was a three-year-old red Cadillac. But when we went out of marriage, he demanded half of everything. I didn't have a leg to stand on.

There are things about me that I'm ashamed of sometimes. For a time while the lawyers were having it out, that tender place Carl had made of love became an ash pit of venomous spite. I would have that car. Come Hell or high water. Call it childish because that's exactly what it was, and now I'm embarrassed by the whole thing. I didn't want it, but it was as much justice as I could get. And so get it, by God, I did.

I parked the Cadillac in the front yard, and I hate to say it—it doesn't make me feel good about myself—but I parked it there with pure malicious intent. So that every time Ted drove by in his purple exhaust pickup truck, he'd see the shiny red Cadillac. Just sitting there. At first, the lame revenge I felt masked my emptiness, but not for losing Ted. Ted had nothing to do with it. That emptiness had a life apart from Ted. That emptiness was that place love had built, a space that Ted couldn't fill.

I'm not the kind of person who can hold a grudge. That doesn't make me better than someone else. If I could have held one, Ted would have been the perfect object of animosity. But I couldn't, like I suppose some people can't curl their tongue.

For a time I thought I'd sell the Cadillac. The grass had grown up around its tires and just seeing it out my kitchen window reminded me of Ted. It became just a hangover. But I did nothing, and time passed. Every few weeks someone, some man, would stop and ask about buying the Cadillac or leave a note with a number on the windshield, under the wiper blade. But their conversations were always the same. They talked to me like I was stupid. They all turned into Ted.

I began having dreams about Carl, and once I woke crying. I shouldn't have told that. I should have kept that bit to myself; it makes me look pathetic. But I don't mean it like that. Carl was teaching me again that I couldn't live without love.

Time passed.

And one day the following April, after fertilizing and watering squash and cucumbers and tomato plants, I sat absentmindedly at the sunny patio table near the garden with a For Sale sign from the Dollar Store in one hand and a permanent black marker in the other. I turned the sign over, and on the back I wrote: FREE TO THE RIGHT MAN. As I placed the sign inside the Cadillac, between the steering wheel and the windshield, a horn blew from the highway: Ted's pickup, black exhaust enough to kill mosquitoes, a new bass boat attached to the bumper.

When I think back today, I realize that what those words, "right man," meant to me then are not what they mean to me now. Those words didn't mean anything then.

My childish spite, justified as it might have been, was doing more harm to me than to Ted. Besides, it was springtime, when I always feel the urge to bury seed in the garden and to turn the mattress over. I was only thinking of disposing of the car to someone worthy of having one, that's all. I thought I'd taken the trouble out of washing that Ted right out of my world.

What I got was the zoo coming to me, one beast at a time: I got the king-of-the jungle types and rabbits, a couple of hyenas, and every variety of snakes. I got cockatoos and Labradors, and monkeys—lots and lots of monkeys. Some came with flowers, some with chocolate, some with a swagger and a look in their eye. One arrived wearing a T-shirt with big letters that said MR. RIGHT. "*Guess who?*" he shouted, throwing his arms open wide.

"Guess not," I said, closing the door.

"I'm gonna make you sooooo happy," said another.

"When you're gone," I said, closing the door.

"Can we pray together?" said another.

"God favors solos over duets," I said, closing and locking the door.

I never dreamed it could be so hard. I considered crossing out MAN and making it Free To The Right WOMAN, but I just knew I'd get the country music version of the Oprah show. I put the sign in the trash. But word was out and they kept coming. Even after I stopped answering the door.

Time passed.

Cooking for one is not really as hard as some make it out to be. It's harder in the winter than in the summer. In the winter it's macaroni and tomatoes with smoked sausage, mustard greens with side meat, sweet potatoes with boiled cabbage. They're good eating but not so good left over. But in the summer when you have fried chicken, sweet corn, squash, string beans, fresh tomatoes, cantaloupe, and watermelon, you can mix and match, and some of it tastes even better if you let it set, let the juices mingle. So I'd picked enough butterbeans to nearly fill my short apron when I heard the sound of brakes up front. As I stepped to the side yard, I heard the wrecker's engine shut off. The driver sat behind the wheel with his head bowed, listening to a country music song as the fade began. When the song was over, he opened the door and made for the Cadillac. He didn't see me looking.

His walk was slow and graceful, the way you'll see an athlete leave the field of play, his chest thick and wide. A smudge of red was scrawled above the pocket of his pressed blue shirt. Nearing the car, he pulled off his cap, uncovering neatly trimmed hair, black and abundant. Even from a distance I could see the dark pattern of his freshly shaven face. I walked toward him carrying my butterbeans like an offering.

The man tucked his cap into his back pocket and leaned down to the driver's side window. He brought his hands up to either side of his face like blinders and pressed them against the window. His arms were thick and deeply tanned. I blush to say it, but I advanced as stealthily as a cat. As I got closer, he shifted to inspect the inside of the Cadillac and his hips swayed this way and that. I couldn't help looking. When he stepped back, he saw my reflection in the glass. He turned and smiled, but it was not a happy smile. He seemed a little shy, and his eyes turned down and to the side when he spoke.

"I can carry this to my shop if it needs work," he said nodding toward his wrecker. "Do you know what's wrong with it?" His khakis and blue work shirt were severely pressed. The name Marion in red letters hovered over his heart. His eyes were abalone blue.

"Just needs driving," I said. He nodded in agreement and looked down at the soft tires. I cradled the butterbeans in my apron with one arm and pulled a loose ribbon of hair behind my ear. "I've driven by here—on the job." He nodded again toward the wrecker. Then his blue eyes moved up all of me, to meet mine. I mean really.

He offered his hand. "Marion Walker," he said. And in that shy way he motioned toward the truck again with the words Walker's Wrecker Service on the door.

"Becky Carter."

"Do you want to sell it?" he said.

"Maybe," I said. I'd forgotten the effect of a hint of aftershave.

"Mind if I take a look?"

"It's unlocked."

I stood behind him as he lifted the hood, stepped up, and leaned way in. The back of his thighs were tight with muscle. When I caught myself looking again, my fingers flew up to the strand of hair already fastened behind my ear.

"I don't see anything," he said into the engine.

"Me either," I said with a rush of breath. I stepped up beside him, mechanically patting my cheek and bobbing my head in a big uh-huh, before glancing over again. "Not a thing. Nothing," I said. His thick dark fingers went from one rubber tube to another gently pinching and tugging. A white band of flesh stood out where a ring had been.

"All of these need replacing," he said.

"Want to see if it'll start?" I said. "I can get the key."

Now he reached for the battery cables, giving each a yank. "Your battery," he lifted his blue, blue eyes, "needs water. Cells are probably dry. Think you have enough of a charge to fire up anything?" He smiled at the engine. I was speechless. "If you want it fixed or if you want to sell it, I'll take that key."

From the kitchen window I watched. He circled the car as I felt blindly for the pile of butterbeans on the counter and shoved handfuls into a plastic grocery bag. Facing me from the driver's side door, he reached for his cap, then crossed his muscled, brown arms over his chest and rested back against the Cadillac. The afternoon sun cast a light on him just so, making a picture I can still see.

I had already opened the screen door when I remembered the car key.

"Won't you take these?" I said. "Butterbeans." You should know that all else aside, this is the country way. Nothing forward about offering fresh vegetables. Nothing. "They come off all at once," I said. "I'm cooking for one."

Now that the car business was over, he smiled at me. "You're one up on me," he said. When he saw me looking at his ringless finger, the smile disappeared.

"I knew a man when I was a kid," he said quickly, looking away from me. "Swung down from a hayloft? Caught his wedding band on a nail—"

He looked at me again, his eyes the color of blue pearl. I looked back. "So far," he said, "I haven't learned much about cooking besides opening a can. I'm kinda new to it. But if you don't mind, thank you very much. I'll give these to my mom if you need to do something with them. Her house is right on my way."

"Your wife don't cook?" I had to be sure.

He looked away again. "No." He weighed the bag in his large brown hands.

"They'll make good seconds, left over I mean." It just came out.

"Yes ma'am," he said. He covered the empty ring finger with his right hand.

"Second time's the charm, they say," I said.

"I believe it," he said.

I reached up for imaginary stray hairs.

"Thank you," he said. He looked at me again, waiting—I thought—like the next move was mine. Time stopped. "Can I have that key?" he whispered. It took me a second.

At the window, I watched as he backed the wrecker and hooked the chains underneath the front bumper of the Cadillac. Marion had a very delicate way with the lever that worked the hydraulic action, which tenderly lifted the car's rear end. He climbed inside the truck and parked in the drive. My eyes shut involuntarily. Even when he knocked at the screen door, I seemed unable to move. Then I was standing at the door looking up at him. He spoke through the gray screen mesh.

"I'll take it in and see what needs done to it. Think about if you want to keep it or sell it."

"Oh, I don't want to keep it, I want to give it away." Flew out of my mouth, just like that.

"Then if it's okay, when it's running good you can tell me your pleasure, if that's all right."

"That's fine. I'll do that," I said. "That would be fine." My eyes followed the back of him as he walked away. "Fine," I whispered. He stopped, turned.

"If you've got a scrap of paper—"

"Yes," I said.

I drew a deep breath to steady my hand, then wrote down my number.

From the door, I studied the wrecker, Cadillac in tow, until Marion Walker disappeared behind the ridge.

I watched my fingers shell the butterbeans. And though I wasn't thinking about anything in particular, off and on I'd get the feeling that a part of me was somewhere else in the room *watching* me shell those beans. Either you know what I'm talking about or you don't.

I washed them gently in cool water, put them on with a little bacon grease—not as much as my mother would have used—brought them to a boil, and turned them down to simmer. I rested on the sofa with a book, what Carl called a trashy Romance novel. I don't know its title. I must have fallen asleep before I read a word. Out like a rock. And I know I dreamed, but all of that was gone when I woke. It was the smell of butterbeans that woke me.

As I ate my supper, I wished I hadn't taken a nap. My sense of time was messed up. I decided I'd run myself a hot bath—which I almost never do. I made it good and hot so that I would feel extra cool afterwards. Then I retrieved my book. The idea was to relax so that I could get my normal sleep. Just lying there at night was a loneliness that I don't like to talk about. So I put my hair up, inched into the steaming water, and reached for the book. I read until the water was tepid, but even that wasn't such a good idea. The story left me feeling more wound up than relaxed and sleepy.

The steam had gotten to my hair, so I decided I'd go ahead and wash it. To rinse, I slid way down, feeling my shampooed hair float up, and held my breath for as long as I could. Then I did it again. And again. And once, when the water rushed into my ears and I lay there without breathing, I thought I heard a voice. But it was nothing. After that I shaved my legs. I felt light and cool after toweling off, but not sleepy. I combed my hair but left it wet. I felt clean all over.

In the kitchen, I took down my vitamins. Some habits just stick with you. I stood at the sink and filled my glass. From way off I heard thunder, a sound like the slowly unfolding tide at the beach, the sound that promises summer rain. I thought about how happy my garden would be in the morning. A distant flash of lightning brought my eyes up to the window, and a second flash illuminated the space where the Cadillac had sat for so long, that empty space. "Yes," I whispered aloud.

I still wasn't sleepy. I wanted sleep but my body felt alive all over. I got a beer from the refrigerator and turned on the TV to catch the score of the Braves game. I hit the mute button and looked at the screen, but I wasn't seeing anything. The empty beer can left me no choice but to go to bed and wait for sleep.

The sheets were crisp and cool, my hair still damp. Outside, rain off the roof sounded like lapping waves. I closed my eyes and thought of the gutters overflowing, the ditches along the road in front of my house softly spilling over, emptying into the river and finally into the sea, that place made for and awaiting rain. And though I didn't know how long it might take, I knew that sleep would come and that in the morning I would wake, and that everything would be fine. I can't tell you how I knew it. But I did. There was no doubt. I just knew that everything would be fine.

Things That Smell Like Food

I'M LACTATING," DOTTIE GOLDFISH said.

"So?"

"Look," she said. "If you knew how long it's been since I had my teeth cleaned, you wouldn't want to put that thing in my mouth."

"It'll clean up," Jim said.

"Stop it. Why do we have to go through this again?"

"We came here, Dottie, because we agreed anything can happen here. City of hope."

"Hope and disappointment and desperation, despair. Don't look at me like that. Put that thing away."

"Admit it, this could be it."

"Illusion. Fantasy. All you want is reproductive access."

"Timing is everything, Dottie. You said so yourself. Open up."

"No."

He lifted his hand to her forehead. Dottie pushed it away.

"The smell of all this rabbit shit makes me gag," she said.

"Lift your arm," he said.

"I'm not lifting my arm."

"Dottie—"

"Try to make me, I am *not* lifting my arm."

"Luck and chance, Dottie, they don't seem to be working for us. The odds are no good. Come on, open up."

"I'll gag!"

"Okay. Okay, okay, okay, okay, O-*kay*," Jim Goldfish said, reaching for the small black rectangular box beside him. He didn't smell the rabbit droppings anymore. The stacks of cages had become home to him.

Jim looked from Dottie to the thermometer in his hand, laid it inside its black case, and closed the lid. He collapsed onto the love seat. Dottie reached for his hand and gave it a soft pat.

"Nature's way requires patience, commitment, and diligence," she said, "without the use of technology, the way it was intended to be. Nature's way or no way, Jim."

Shifting into professional mode, Dottie dropped his hand and stood at attention. Looking into the small mirror on the wall, she unbuttoned her blouse and tested the snap of her nursing bra. Jim studied the thermometer case in his hand. When he looked up, his wife was rummaging behind a tower of rabbit cages. She spotted her bag. "I do love you, Jim," she said, lifting her heavy backpack. "But the timing is all wrong. I can tell. I just know. Maybe soon."

"What time is it in Moscow, Dottie?" he said, looking over at the humpers in the cage on top of the TV. She didn't answer.

༓ ༓ ༓

ON BLUE DIAMOND ROAD into Vegas, Dottie Goldfish read aloud the address she'd scribbled on a scrap of paper, then folded it.

"You know what to do with this, don't you?" She tucked the paper into Jim's shirt pocket. He gave her a look. "Say it," she said.

"I know the routine," he said.

"Say it."

"I'll feed it to the rabbits."

As a La Leche League Leader, Dottie selected the meeting sites and communicated in code with the women who attended. The locations changed whenever Dottie suspected infiltration or sensed federal electronic listening devices.

Jim headed toward Las Vegas Boulevard, the old Strip. After a time, he couldn't tolerate the silence. "What is it today?" he said with a sort of Mr. Rogers' inflection. Small talk was better than no talk. There is a grain of possibility in small talk. "Support group counseling?"

"Adoptive mothers," Dottie said. She wouldn't look at him.

"It's a miracle," he said. He hoped she'd get his point about miracles, that she would include him in her life's possibilities. If Dottie got the hint, she didn't let on. "Mendela Supplemental Nursing?" he continued, "or Lact-Aid Nurser Training?"

"The former." Dottie's folded hands rested on the revised edition of *Breastfeeding the Adopted Baby*, which lay like a holy text on her lap.

"They don't appreciate you, Dottie. Your methods, they've become too extreme. You're less tolerant." Just off Industrial Road, Jim stopped at a light in front of an abandoned liquor store, one that awaited demolition. "They've never forgiven you for the hedge clippers and the bare breast. You're paranoid, obsessed."

"I've not filled the trailer with crippled rabbits," Dottie snapped, not taking her eyes from the windshield. "Don't bother parking," she said, "I'll get out here." She reached for her backpack of adjustable neck straps, bag hangers, strainers, funnels, cleaning syringes, and instructions. Jim held her wrist as she opened the door.

"You're leaving me, aren't you?" he said.

"We're sitting in traffic."

"You're going back to Russia, aren't you?"

"This is a city *built* upon obsessions, Jim." She shut the door and was gone.

❦❦❦

HORNS BLEW BEHIND HIM.

At that very second, men all over Las Vegas, men as desperate as Jim Goldfish, their hearts and pockets empty, flailed about the city in timeless, perpetual darkness—arms outstretched, zombie-like, feeling for a drink or a roulette wheel—while others followed the scent of cheap women or bad cocaine. Still others pursued acts so perverse that an obsession hardly described them. Jim pressed the accelerator of his Subaru Brat and headed for North Mojave Road, for his obsession.

"Collard greens smell like rotten eggs when they're cooking," he said aloud, "but there's no better eating. Garlic smells like toxic waste, but it makes for some good spaghetti sauce. The whiff of Dottie's lactating breasts first thing in the morning smells like love, like there's a baby in the house." He paused to let that one sink in. "Rabbit shit smells like rabbit shit," he chimed, "but it means there's life there. The smell of a dead rabbit smells like death."

The image of thousands of charred bodies, *miles* of human bodies turned to black ash, flashed before him. He wanted to stop thinking. But he couldn't. It was the smell.

He closed his eyes, pressed the accelerator, and shot through the red light at Wyoming and Main. But the odds fell in his favor.

On Oakley, Jim topped seventy miles an hour. True love, he thought, may be the least likely of life's possibilities, more rare than a monkey's rendition of a Shakespeare play. In the absence of an infant or a small child, all of nature works against a sustaining and abiding love. Even more remote under the sovereign laws of physics and probability is love at first sight. But that is what it had been. No matter her feelings now, Jim was sure that Dottie would agree, even if her love for him had turned to Nevada dust, that theirs had been love at first sight. Throw in the location of that shining moment—Washington, DC, steps of The Senate Office Building, 1999, and Vegas' most prophetic bookie would bow his head to the odds of that love.

❦ ❦ ❦

AT THE SIGHT OF The Animal Foundation up ahead, a weight like a cement block lifted from his chest. When Jim pushed open the door to the office of the Special Rescue Unit of the Las Vegas Animal Shelter, Rhonda Reardon, the squad leader, didn't look up from her screen.

"You ought to monitor your messages, Jim. It's bad." She handed him a memo. "Bunnies on the run don't last long. They are prey to everything."

Rhonda was too young to remember the sixty-mile stretch from Mutlaa, Kuwait to Basra, Iraq, too young to know about humans on the run, about human prey.

Jim committed to memory the locations list. He numbered his stops, starting in Henderson and working his way around the western and northern beltways, circling back to North Mojave. He checked the gas gauge and fired up the Brat's engine.

Had they been bald eagles, he'd said to Dottie, or Alaskan caribou, or those freaky walrus-looking manatee in Florida, the slaughter would stop. The dirty little secret of America's fastest growing city would be a 60 Minutes wet dream. But the cries of thousands of maimed and murdered rabbits terrorized by the city's new construction—its progress—were as silent as the sound of a breaking heart.

He thought of Dottie as he exited Boulder Highway. In a matter of minutes, if he was lucky, he would be counting the broken limbs of the black-tails, white-tails, cottontails, and pygmies he'd rescued. Later, with Rhonda Reardon's help, he'd decide which would die, while at the same time Dottie would be instructing and consoling adoptive mothers who wept at the possibilities for the maternal life Dottie symbolized. Jim's eyes watered.

If this woman so dedicated to La Leche League that she had held a pair of hedge clippers to her bare breast on the steps of The Senate Office

Building, this woman so dedicated to life and love and giving that she had been handcuffed for those beliefs, if his Dottie had lost all feeling for him because he could never give her the one thing she most needed—in strict accordance with the laws of nature—then all happiness was lost. He glanced at the gas gauge again as he entered the freeway and felt in his pocket for the twenty he hoped would still be there.

He and Dottie had gotten by on his military disability and VA benefits. But as the city Rafael Riviera named "the meadow" had grown, the brutality compounded. George II's war had driven up the price of gasoline. Then there were the costs of rabbit food and cages, stacked now to the ceiling, cramming one bedroom and transforming the other rooms into an elaborate maze—pillars of reproductive psychopomps.

"I told you it was bad," Rhonda said. Rhonda Reardon, who had come to Vegas as a stand-up comedian before her conversion to animal rights, looked up at Jim with exhausted, haunted eyes. Coffee and cigarettes and the endless cries of the defenseless had transformed her laugh lines into troubled wrinkles as deep and hopeless as the cracked desert floor.

During the past three hours, Jim had circled the city from new housing development to road construction to strip-mall replication, stopping to save the living and collect the dead. The rescue total was forty-two. The wounded lay on a crib mattress in the back of the Brat, the dead deposited into black trash bags. There is no food that smells like rabbit blood.

"*Lepus californicus,* fourteen. *Sylvilagus audubonii,* thirteen. *Lepus townsendii,* ten." Rhonda pointed down at the five remaining casualties. "*Brachylagus idahoensis,*" she said. "Maybe I'll find a zoo that will take these. They're endangered." She dropped her cigarette stub on the asphalt and squashed it under her boot. "Eighteen bucks, twenty-four doe. Half of these are goners," Rhonda said, looking down at the bloody crib mattress.

"And the other half?" Jim said. He thought of the euthanized rabbits. He remembered the fit of the gas mask he'd worn in Iraq. The glazed brown eyes of the wounded stared up at him in shock and awe.

Rhonda looked away, reached for a cigarette.

"How many are out of the woods?" he asked, motioning toward the fully recovered rabbits out back, knowing what Rhonda's answer would be. He didn't give her time to speak. "I'll take them to make room for these."

She reached for a new pack, then looked up at Jim Goldfish through gray cigarette smoke, her brow as furrowed as an old woman's. Six years ago she had been a college girl whose combination of caustic feminist theory and anal sex jokes had made sell-out audiences at The Riviera, Comedy Stop, and Improv wet their pants in laughter. Now she was all business.

"You building onto your trailer? The idea to double-up on their caged accommodations is *faux* brilliant, Jim. A real problem solver. I'll bet Dottie is lovin' it."

"I said I'll take care of it," he said.

🦌🦌🦌

A BLAZING EVENING SUN hunkered down on the city when blue lights flashed in Jim's mirror. If rabbits understood English he would have had a word with them before the skinny cop reached his window, but instead, the cab of the Brat looked like a popper of ricocheting brown, furry popcorn. Jim lowered his window just enough to pass his license and registration to the officer.

Pygmies rebounded off the dash and windshield. An orgy of Vegas dimensions dented and bubbled the back of his seat. "Have I broken the law, sir?" Jim asked. Before the cop could answer, a black-tailed jackrabbit delivered a World Federation Wrestling–inspired head butt to Jim's chin.

"This is dangerous," the officer said. Another black-tailed jack streaked past the tip of Jim's nose at thirty miles an hour and slammed against the window, just inches from the startled cop's thin young face.

"When the sun goes down," Jim said, "it's only natural that they—"

"What are you doing with all these rabbits?"

Jim went eyeball to eyeball with the young, skinny cop. "What happens in Vegas…" he said.

The cop was still doing that bobble head thing when he closed the door to the police cruiser, shut off the blue lights, and merged into the traffic.

Jim checked his phone, hoping against hope that Dottie had left him a message. There was no calling her. Her line was open for La Leche emergencies only. He dropped the cell into his pocket and hit the blinker.

On Blue Diamond Road, Jim Goldfish repeated to himself that his wife would not be at home when he got there, that he'd save himself some grief by wiping the thought from his mind. But he couldn't hold back the prayer that her earthly possessions would still be in the trailer, that she was merely off someplace answering the needs of a sobbing new mother with aching nipples or soothing the postpartum depression of another's recent delivery.

Jim parked, shut off the engine and escaped the Subaru without free-ing a single rabbit. He looked up at the canopy of stars. The smell from inside hovered like waves of heat over their trailer. Inside, the kits had already eaten through the carpet, one leg of the love seat, and through the cheap composite door to their bedroom.

When he inserted his house key, he felt the walls quaking from the humping of hundreds of rabbits. He reached for the light switch inside. The room rocked softly like a speeding boxcar and the towers swayed and rattled.

At a glance he spotted the worn copy of *The Womanly Art of Breastfeeding* on the kitchen table. Dottie hadn't left him. Not yet. He felt inside his shirt pocket for the address of the abandoned liquor-store-turned-safe-house where he'd dropped off his wife.

He looked around at what had once been their living room. No one need remind him of the cunning, greed, and power of corporate forces to direct people's lives away from what was good for them, of the awesome firepower of multinationals to destroy life, to incinerate it. On the steps of The Senate Office Building, Dottie had cited the enormous sums of money generated by brainwashed consumers who denied their babies breast milk. She'd enumerated the tragic consequences. He, in turn, had shouted the grotesque Halliburton profits generated by the Gulf War and the con-sequences of what came to be known as Gulf War Syndrome and Post Traumatic Stress Disorder.

But he never told Dottie about mopping up on the Highway of Death, the sixty-mile stretch from Mutlaa, Kuwait, to Basra, Iraq. Never told anyone about the eyes of the dead children. Or the smell. He couldn't.

"Everything you need to know about American culture," she'd said, opening and closing the shiny new hedge clippers like a giant pair of scis-sors, "can be understood in terms of the relationship between money and ignorance."

Jim looked down at the address in his hand, and fed the scrap of paper to a cottontail as he'd promised. He didn't know where Dottie was, when or if she might return.

He collapsed into his recliner, sighed again, and closed his eyes. "I want to give you a love that smells like… Krispy Kreme Doughnuts," he'd said to Dottie Goldfish that first day at the foot of the Washington Monument.

She looked up at Jim, her eyes beaded with tears. "There should be a monument like this to women," Dottie said shading her eyes. "Ours is a penis nation."

"What about Stonehenge?" Jim said.

"There should be a monument to mother's milk," she had answered, looking up. "But that's impossible here. In Russia it would be possible."

Jim dropped to one knee and took her hand. "I'll find someplace for us where all things are possible," he'd said.

"Where?" she said.

"Where there's always a chance."

"For what?"

"Where the once barren land now teems with life."

"Where defenseless rabbits are dying and new mothers despair?"

"Yes," he said.

And she took him into her arms.

JIM WAS NO MORE a Mormon than Dottie was a Russian. He was a Baptist from Darlington, South Carolina who at nineteen had come home from George I's Gulf War only to find disappointment in the two things that had mattered most to him: a Dale Earnhardt racing tire that had done laps at The Southern 500 and a penis, his, incapable of rising to the occasion of a lap dance. Dottie had given rise to Jim's lost libido, and like Joseph Smith the two lovers had answered a calling, their beacon of fate from a singular plot of western desert. Where rabbits were being slaughtered by progress and new babies needed suck. But while Dottie had helped provide suck to hundreds of Vegas infants, Jim, hydraulics restored, failed to supply the seed for their own child.

Outside the trailer, the Brat's horn wailed. Jim's eyes opened. "An accident of nature," he said aloud. "A bunny bounces chaotically about, strikes randomly a mechanical device that sends a sonic message speeding across an empty desert. As unlikely as a sperm with a suitcase. But possible. Praise be to Chaos."

On the trailer steps, Jim sat facing the Spring Mountains, waiting for Dottie. The night's breeze was cool and sweet. A dying flame of red sunlight trembled behind the ridgeline. The Subaru horn's blast had startled the rabbits into temporary hiding and the cab of the Brat was quiet and empty-looking. Still, he'd have to find occupancy for them. Above the desert, the dome of Nevada night sky glittered. He struggled to identify in those random points of light the image of a bear or a horse. He closed his eyes in quiet reverie and wished for the image of a human face, one he'd never seen: his father's. He heard his mother's voice.

"If he hadn't died in that holdup," she said to young Jim, "I would have eventually left him."

"Tell me what he looked like, Mom."

"I should'a kept a picture. You saw him. His face was the first thing you ever saw," she said. "But you were getting born. You wouldn't remember. He was a jerk."

"I don't care. Tell me again, tell me again."

"What the hell's there to tell? I'm huffing and puffing, and the doctor's yelling, 'Push! I can see the head now, push, push!' and I'm feeling like I'm about to pass a ten pound bag of Dixie Crystals Sugar, and your daddy's behind the doctor vaulting about like a monkey on a string shouting, 'Peak-a-boo! Peeeeak-a-booooo!!' I would' a left him, I'm telling you."

"Maybe not. Maybe something wonderful would have happened."

Jim's eyes slowly descended from the stars, to the trailer behind him. Inside the Subaru, the rabbits were at it again.

The word "maybe," Jim thought, was the most precious word in Vegas. Maybe he'd find Dottie back at the abandoned liquor store. He felt for his keys. Maybe.

But she wasn't there.

🐇🐇🐇

TWO HOURS LATER AS the tow truck hauled off the Brat, the rabbits piled against the windshield looked out at Jim-in-the-handcuffs. Jim stood on the sidewalk, a set of TV rabbit ears duct-taped to the top of his head. Behind him stood Officer Hawks, the skinny young cop who had stopped him earlier. He didn't bother reading Jim his rights. Instead, Hawks lifted the cuffs and whispered, "What are the odds?"

"It's not against the law to drive around with rabbits," Jim said.

"You're right," the cop said, pulling him back toward the cruiser. "It's not even against the law in Vegas to parade around with a television antenna duct-taped to your noggin."

"Then what are the charges? I'm not drunk," Jim said. The cop held the cruiser door open.

"Suspicion," he said.

"Of what?"

"Of suspicion, that's what."

"What about my rabbits?" Jim said. Seeing them that way, all wet-eyed and huddled like refugees against the Brat's windshield as the tow truck pulled away, made him sad.

"You take the cake, pal," the cop said, "the fucking fruit cake."

Like most locals, Jim usually avoided the Vegas Strip, steering away from "the herd," they called it. But tonight, getting lost in a crowd had been just what Jim wanted. He couldn't face the other members of The Special Rescue Unit who met at the Sagebrush Bar to share their occupational miseries and to wash away their collective pain. Tonight he had no quick evasive answers to Rhonda Reardon's inevitable questions about him and Dottie. About their future. Not tonight. He'd parked the Brat at a construction site, the future home of the Trump Tower just off Las Vegas Boulevard, left the windows cracked for the rabbits, then walked over to the New Frontier Hotel & Casino, where some of the herd stampeded toward women's mud wrestling at Gilley's.

Inside, he sat at a Wheel of Fortune slot machine and dug into his pocket for his only twenty. The Monkees sang the chorus of "I'm a Believer" over the casino's bells and whistles.

Jim fed in the bill but waited for the waitress to show before he lost any of it. When she did, he ordered a bourbon. She brought him two.

"How much do you know about rabbits?" he asked.

"They shit BBs and taste like rattlesnake?" She had the complexion of a vampire, but her smile was human.

"The cab of my truck is full of rabbits. Think they could find their way home," he said, "like cats or dogs lost at a rest area someplace?"

"Absolutely. Unless they wind up in a casino. Then they stay lost forever." She smiled and turned. "Lost, I'm telling you. For-*ever*."

"But things that smell like food aren't always food," he called to her as she walked away. She hadn't heard him. What he meant was that there were counterbalancing forces in the universe, that not all things could be explained by numbers, that the dazzling lights, flowing liquor, and cheering from the craps tables might produce in some gamblers a quiet place, an interior cool shade, a peaceful landscape for introspection, a soft illumination of hope. That in spite of the food chain, there was something like an anti-food chain, that rabbits, for instance, were more about creating than destroying, that a woman who felt herself to be Russian might not become a Russian, that when all reason pointed toward despair, hope might spring forward in a blaze of spontaneous combustion, a big bang. That indeed women who had never conceived had the capacity to nurse a child, that maybe, just maybe, a man without seed might produce one.

Although there were no clocks in the casino, time passed nonetheless. Jim sat before the slot machine with his finger resting on the lighted "bet one credit" square.

"Cocktail?" the smiling waitress said. "Bourbon, right?" She handed him his third drink.

"How do they do it?" Jim asked.

"What?" she said, looking away from him. The casino quivered with white noise, and a stratosphere of cigarette smoke hung just above the rows of flashing slot machines.

"How do rabbits find their way back home?"

"Whaaat?" She tilted her head and heaved a labored sigh. "They carry pagers," she said, reaching for his two empty glasses. Her smile had disappeared. "You want another cocktail?" she said.

"I'll have fate, with a twist," he said.

She looked at the Wheel of Fortune machine in front of Jim. "Cash out," she said. "Go home."

He couldn't remember where he'd parked the Brat. Exiting The New Frontier side door, Jim had been swept up by the herd and transported like a corpuscle down The Strip. He couldn't see his truck. "You float some, you jet some," he said aloud, but nobody took notice. He passed two wheelchairs with oxygen tanks attached. The force of life, Jim thought, strength to pull a handle, faith to believe in a jackpot before the end. He hummed the Monkees' theme song to the cadence of marching obese Midwesterners.

As the human conveyer moved on, he remembered an episode from the original *Twilight Zone* in which Confederate soldiers trudge endlessly past the home of a weary young belle who offers them water and asks the whereabouts of her husband. But none of the soldiers can stick around to answer her questions, for they are moving like spent sperm toward some destined, uncertain end. Finally the husband shows up, and she is so happy to see him that she forgets the war is lost. She is thinking only of their love. Then he tells her he, too, must move on, that he can't stay. And in that *Twilight Zone* sort of way, Jim realized that not only is the husband dead but the wife also, and that the couple will spend eternity apart.

Jim couldn't breathe. It was the smell.

The tourists' bodies, some tanned as leather, others pasty gray, formed a solemn creeping mass. That day he'd arrived soon after the massacre at Mutlaa Ridge. Tonight he trudged zombie-like with the herd. The dead, bloated, charred heaps: two thousand withdrawing Iraqi troops, busloads of civilians—Iraqi, Kuwaiti, Palestinian. Jim imagined the satellite photo, the gunners' view through the crosshairs. He suddenly looked up into the night sky expecting to see the in-coming, the napalm, the phosphorus. Instead he saw giant letters. The looming neon above said THE MIRAGE. When Jim looked back, the fleeing Iraqi troops morphed into rabbits racing blindly from the highway, pouring into the desert night.

There were words for it. Mopping up, the lieutenant said. For the smell there were no words.

The Japanese man Jim had accidentally knocked to the sidewalk was looking up from the concrete and swearing in his native tongue. Jim hadn't even seen the little guy, not that it would have mattered. He had to get out of there. If he reversed course, against the wave of soldiers, civilians, and tourists, surely he would end up back at the Brat. But the human tide crashed in on Jim from every direction.

He broke away from the swarm and scurried into the shadow of a doorway, dodging the pale, meaty-faced clusters, the bands of dispossessed spirits. Somewhere between Twain Avenue and Paradise Road, Jim stopped to breathe. The sign above his head said, Grant's Pawn Shop. He walked inside.

The owner sat behind the counter watching baseball on a miniature TV. His was not a face but a facsimile of one formed by fleshy lava, a freak of nature. His chin retreated from his thick upper lip and his bunched cheeks, so thick and round they crowded his nose, buried his soft brown eyes behind narrow slits. He mumbled to himself in an Irish accent.

Jim wandered the cluttered aisles looking for something, anything familiar. "Got any rabbit cages?" he called.

"Does this look like a pet store?" The guy reached for his stubby cigar.

"I've got to get back to my rabbits."

"Call a cab." He was watching the game, smoking.

A metal cylinder like an umbrella stand overflowed with ancient TV antennas, rabbit ears. Jim reached inside. "I've got to get back home."

Something happened on the screen. The old guy softly clapped his pudgy, mitten-like hands. "Try clicking your heels together."

"My wife," Jim said, "she's leaving me."

The old guy slowly turned, looked over at Jim, and shut off the tiny television. He paused, tilted his head, and lumbered off his stool. One of his legs was a little shorter than the other. "I'll call you a cab," he said, making his way toward Jim. He forced his paw of a hand into his trouser pocket and held out a small loaf of cash.

"No," Jim said. "I have a phone. I have a truck." The old man's wet brown eyes looked like a child's. "I have a question," Jim said. "What ever happened to the *Old* Frontier?"

The guy wouldn't take any money for the TV antenna or for the length of duct tape that wound under Jim's chin and formed an X over the rabbit ears to hold them securely atop his head. At the doorway to Grant's Pawn, the proprietor laid a hand on Jim's shoulder, pulled the cigar stump from his mouth and pointed to show Jim the way to the New Frontier.

❦ ❦ ❦

JIM STOOD LOOKING INTO the Brat's passenger-side window at the reflection of the TV antenna. The skinny man in the police uniform had pushed the rabbit ears down horizontally, and now they looked like an arrow through Jim Goldfish's head. The best Jim could figure, Officer Hawks must have spotted him on the sidewalk, because even before he could reach for his car keys, the cop had him in the cuffs.

The tow truck driver pressed a lever and the rear wheels of the Brat left the ground. The defenseless rabbits tumbled onto the windshield. Jim thought of Dottie, of losing her.

Through the wire cage that separated them, Jim spoke to the cop from the backseat of the cruiser. "The sweet juice from an apple will produce vinegar," he said, "but an onion that produces chick-flick tears will taste sweet if it's cooked good and slow. How do you explain that?"

"Is that the message you're picking up there, pal?" The cop glanced back into his mirror.

"If you believe in the food chain, then isn't it logical that we are food for the angels?" Jim said. The cop just looked at him. Jim's cell rang.

"That's my wife," Jim said. "I know it is."

"Lucky girl," the cop said.

"I think she's calling about the baby."

"That's some lame shit," the cop said, glancing back. "Some *really* lame shit."

At the police station, Hawks snapped a picture of Jim with the rabbit ears duct taped to the top of his head for the station's Area 51 scrapbook, then, minus the rabbit ears, snapped Jim's mug shot for the police files. In the police photo, a wide red streak like sunburn ran down one side of his face, under his chin, and up the other side. Above his ears, divot-like craters occupied space where the hair used to be.

It was nearly two in the morning when Jim was released.

"Where's my truck?" he asked the skinny cop.

"In the compound." Officer Hawks handed over Jim's phone. "It'll cost you seventy-five bucks."

"But I didn't break the law."

"Parked illegally—on Mr. Trump's property."

"But I've got to get home. My wife is going to Russia, where someday she'll build a mammary monument. She's leaving me."

At the door, the cop handed Jim the metal rabbit ears. "Maybe Scotty will beam you up," he said.

On the sidewalk, Jim checked his messages. The one call had come from Rhonda Reardon. He pressed the numbers, but there was no answer. The ten bucks he'd cashed out at the casino wouldn't pay cab fare back to the trailer.

He set out on foot for the abandoned liquor store, the safe house where he'd dropped off his wife. If Dottie hadn't left him, she would show up there in the morning. If she had left him, where he was or wasn't wouldn't matter.

At three-thirty, Jim reached the La Leche rendezvous. He sat on the low stoop, untied his shoes, stripped off his socks and slowly shook out the sand. He wiggled his toes and looked up at the sky. To ordinary people, Jim thought, Nevada sand looks like Iraqi sand, Russian sand.

Too much city light to see the stars, he thought, not enough stars to see his father's face. He hummed The Monkees' "Take the Last Train to Clarksville," rested back against the door of the abandoned liquor store and shut his eyes.

Jim tried to imagine the woman Dottie had been before her trip to Russia as a La Leche representative. The woman holding the shiny new hedge clippers to her naked breast in support of female federal workers' right to breastfeed their babies on the job was a product of her Russian experience. She had returned more devoted to the cause, less accepting of alternative perspectives. Dottie's deepest belief was that the world could be changed one baby at a time, and that a better world began at a mother's breast. Her devotion to that belief was all-consuming, for it was all-encompassing: the answer to war and poverty and human misery. Whereas her parents had believed that all you need is love, Dottie believed all you need is suck. Jim couldn't envision a pre-Russia Dottie any more than he could imagine a pre-Dottie Jim. He couldn't remember the man he had been before the Gulf War, the young man in the NASCAR cap driving the new Corvette he'd joined the National Guard to pay for, the kid resting on his cue stick and singing about having friends in low places at The Paradise Lounge in Darlington, South Carolina. He could see the memories in old photographs, but he didn't recognize the man in them.

Sitting ducks, fish in a barrel, sheep in a pen. We nailed'em, slaughtered'em, massacred'em.

The smell of pizza surfed in on the cool desert breeze. "Nothing else smells like pizza," Jim whispered.

The Subaru Brat would smell like rabbit shit by the time he got it back. He only hoped the rabbits would still be there, alive. But giving those rabbits shelter at their trailer was out. Dottie was leaving him. He couldn't risk it. Tomorrow, he would stack the cages in the back of the Brat and drive up to the mountains, maybe to Lake Mead. He would free them all. In the end, there was no protection from fate, not for them. Not for him.

The dim pink ribbon beyond the horizon said that morning was coming. Time. In the time it took rabbits to reproduce, Dottie could have her Vegas divorce. An entire country could be destroyed. What could you say about time, except that it ran out.

His cell rang.

"Hey, Rhonda," he said.

"It's me."

Jim sprang to his feet. "Dottie, what's wrong?"

"You have to come home immediately."

"What's wrong?"

"My urine smells like cheap coffee grounds." Jim was walking in circles. "I'm ovulating, Jim. This is it, I just know it. Hurry."

🐰🐰🐰

HE HADN'T PICKED UP a gun since he'd returned from the Gulf, but now Jim wished for one. He'd hold up the nearest liquor store for cab fare.

"Ovulation smells like coffee grounds," he said aloud. He reeled up the sidewalk, feet bare, legs churning. "Mint smells like chewing gum," he huffed. "Fresh doughnuts smell like Dottie's love." His lungs ached, then burned. The smell of pizza was everywhere around him. He wouldn't get home on time. Surely pizza smells like something else, he thought. He wouldn't make it to his wife, who waited now, her body's clock ticking, her one free egg disco-dancing to the heavy beat of time, her breasts swollen a little extra, her heart lying open to him.

"Pizza—" he said, charging on. "Coffee grounds." Jim glanced over at the all-night pizza shop, where a familiar looking teenager marched toward his small truck in the otherwise empty lot. Jim tried to call out to the kid. "Pizza smells like—" Jim had no breath. He looked to the delivery kid in the Dale Earnhardt, Jr. cap for the answer. The young guy lifted the lighted pizza sign from the top of his truck. He set the pyramid-shaped sign in the truck's bed and felt in his pocket for his keys.

When the kid turned, a breathless man with brown soulful eyes and craters where his hair used to be stood with his arms extended. Upon his open palms were a ten-dollar bill and a TV antenna.

❦❦❦

IN THE HEADLIGHTS, DOTTIE waited at the open door to the trailer, a large rainbow blanket folded over her arms.

"I don't want to talk," she said as he neared her. They watched from the steps as the pizza kid's taillights disappeared. She took Jim's hand.

The air was cool, the pre-dawn light behind the lifeless mountains the color of smooth, soft, warm flesh. They took the trail up toward the light beyond the ridge. She held his hand. He carried the blanket. "The stars are closing their eyes," Jim said.

"Here," she said, and he laid down the blanket. He spread it smoothly over the cool sand. When he stood, she came to him and unbuttoned his shirt. "Uhm," she said, "you smell like pizza."

"Nothing else smells like pizza," he said, smiling at his wife. "You smell like Krispy Kreme doughnuts."

She lifted her arms, pressed her soft, full body against him and cradled the side of her face into his neck and shoulder. Naked before earth and sky, they held one another. After a time, she said, "Now."

Jim and Dottie lay on the soft blanket, upon the silent, barren desert floor, without the sound or sight of another living creature anywhere, without signs of life, surrounded by clean, sweet air, folded in each other's warm arms, waiting. And neither spoke until Jim felt the sun on his back and saw the light on her face.

Glory Day

BEHIND THE COUNTER AT the Handy Pantry, the blond clerk ringing up the twelve-pack reminds Stu of his seventh-grade teacher, the one who was sexing a boy named Mel. Stu imagines himself Mel. And for a second his consciousness vacates the premises.

"This be it?" the clerk asks.

The woman's voice startles him. From the video monitor overhead, an inquisitor's eyes bear down on him. Stu watches as Stu straightens the reversed red-and-black baseball cap that conceals his thinning hair. He is here. He is there.

Stu pays. While the woman makes change, he considers making his move. She wears a faded University of South Carolina Gamecocks T-shirt. Stu likes that. Stu likes everything Gamecocks. His pride, a 1968 muscle car, is painted Gamecocks' colors, garnet with a black convertible top. In the monitor screen, Stu watches her from above. Then he remembers the last time he stood before a video camera, blue lights flashing all around him.

"Like your car," she says with a nod. "What is it?"

"GTO," Stu says.

"Looks like new," she says.

"Was new for a long time," Stu says. He snaps open his GTO-engraved Zippo lighter. "My mom's first husband bought it with enlistment money just before he went to Vietnam. Came back in a box." He sucks fire to the tip of his cigarette. "The car sat in my grandmother's garage 'til she died."

"Well, I like it." She counts back his change.

"Take you for a ride, sugar lips?"

"What does GTO stand for?"

"Gas, tires, and oil," Stu says.

She bags the beer and slides it across the counter. "Have a blessed day," she says.

"I don't think so," Stu says.

Outside he digs for his keys and considers the risks. Since losing his job at Dixie Cup—the job he got straight out of high school fifteen years ago—Stu's become a man with time on his hands. His emotions are in constant oscillation, and the sneaking suspicion that he's stuck in time collides with the giddy expectation of a revelation just over the horizon. The butterflies in his stomach remind him of high school graduation. Still like a clock ticking down, the law of averages, he knows, is working against him.

He opens a beer and starts his car. Its visceral power enters his body, lights up his circuits. But its transformational power, its magic, has abandoned him. Instead, the voice of the judge echoes inside his head. "You could have killed somebody," the judge said.

☙☙☙

STANDING OUTSIDE HIS SISTER'S apartment, the morning sun charring the back of his neck, Stu turns a slow, deliberate three-sixty and scans the neighbors' windows. He's got the heebie-jeebies, as if the eyes of a sniper are working him over. He's been knocking for five minutes and although it's only nine in the morning, the plastic bag he holds is already starting to bead up in the heat. He hears footsteps. Stu draws up his shoulders and waits at full attention.

On the other side of the screen door, his nephew Tode stands in the blinding morning light. Tode is fifteen. Through the silver mesh, the boy glows. He wears only boxer shorts. His erection looks like a kickstand. When he was a baby, he'd squat butt-to-heels and raise his enormous head as if awaiting a celestial voice. "Looks kinda like a bullfrog, don't he," Stu's twin sister, Sting, said.

"'Sup, Tooooode!" Stu says. Everything about the kid is skinny except his Martian head, and he does that screwdriver thing with his fists against his eyes, wringing the sleep and fiery sunlight from them. Stu lifts the plastic bag. "Let me in," he says. Tode staggers back from the door and claws at a tuft of hair, a tsunami on a globe.

Tode's eyes track the contents of the bag. "Almost killed anybody lately?" he says.

Stu stands at the open refrigerator door. "Want one?" he calls.

"Why are you here?"

"Where's Sting?" Stu says.

"You know where she is, what do you want?"

"I have a business proposition. There's a hundred bucks in it for you."

"Keep going," Tode says.

Stu glides into a chair at the kitchen table, cracks open a beer and waves to his nephew. "Sit, sit. Come-on, Toooode." The kid cautiously slides sideways into the opposite chair. "I want you to go to driving school for me, pal. Take my place."

"You don't have a hundred bucks."

"I will by the time you finish the course, I've already done the class-room part. To tell you the truth, Tode, I'm feeling a little spooked."

"But I already got my permit."

"Awesome," Stu says. "Get dressed."

Tode trudges toward his room. "This will never work," he says. "I want half the money up front."

"No problem," Stu says over his shoulder as he empties the ice bin into the plastic Handy Pantry beer bag.

When Stu stabs at the car's ignition, his key slides a little to the side.

"This is never gonna work," Tode says.

"You lack faith," Stu says. "You need some Jesus in your life."

"Oh, *Jesus*," Tode says.

"Oh, hell yeah," smiling Stu says, squashing down his baseball cap, pumping the accelerator. "Fasten your seatbelt, buddy."

❦❦❦

A MUSTARD YELLOW FORD Focus sits in The Darlington School of Driving lot, a dusty patch near the steps of the single-wide that serves as its office. The female driving instructor and two fifteen-year-olds, a boy and a girl, wait in the car. Stu parks the Goat a comfortable distance away.

"Here," he says, reaching in the glove box for an envelope. "Take this."

"Cash?" Tode says.

"No. Papers from the court. Show these to the instructor."

"What do I say?" Tode asks.

"Say you've quit drinking."

Tode takes the envelope and opens his other palm. "Fifty bucks."

"I'll have it when you get back." The instructor beeps a triplicate. "Go!" Stu says.

As Tode shuffles toward the waiting car, Stu feels for a cold one in the back floorboard. It's already puddled back there, he thinks. When he looks up, he sees the lady instructor escorting Tode, hangdog head rolling from side to side, back toward Stu, who briefly ponders how Tode can keep his balance with that head.

"Ha, ha," the woman says, handing the envelope over to Stu. She's too tall for a Ford Focus, Stu thinks. And way too good looking. Her red hair sparkles in the morning light. A breeze blows a red crescent against her fair complexion. But not enough to hide the green eyes.

"Awesome hair," Stu says.

"What do you think you're trying to pull?" she says.

"Whatever," Stu says.

"Whatever what?" she says.

Stu gives gorgeous the old fisheye-once-over as he unwraps a stick of gum. He offers her the pack. "'Suuup?" he croons.

"Can I quote you on that for the judge?" She turns and makes for the Focus in long smooth strides.

Stu hustles to catch up. "Wait."

"Whoa," Tode calls. "Give me the keys to your car."

"Can't do it."

"Give me the keys to the Goat, Stu."

"No way. Call your mom to pick you up," Stu shouts over his shoulder.

"Cells aren't allowed during driver's ed. You can't just leave me here."

Stu reaches for the back door to the Focus. "Sorry, kid. Don't worry. I'm still good for the fifty."

"I got my permit. I'll be careful."

"Can't risk it," Stu calls.

"I hate you," Tode shouts. "I'm drinking your beer. I hate you."

When Stu opens the rear door, the very large girl in the backseat whirls away and flattens her nose against the window. From behind she looks like a capital M, shoulders drawn up tight, head retracted like a turtle's. In the rearview he sees the smirking pimpled face of the kid behind the wheel, fists at ten and two, and the cum laude smugness in his petulant eyes as he glares at the unshaven middle-aged man behind him.

"Back the car," the gorgeous redhead says.

"Yes, ma'am," the kid says. Then he begins the lecture. "The driver must back the car for a distance of 100 feet at a slow rate of speed and as straight and smooth as possible." He turns, throws his right elbow over the seat and lightly touches the gas. He jerks his mongoose head to the left, indicating that Stu is impeding his vision. As the kid steers, the tip of his pink tongue oozes from between his thin, translucent lips.

The Focus slowly glides past Tode, who leans against the GTO, arms bound to his chest. Stu waves. Tode raises his middle finger.

"Take a right out of the lot, toward Hartsville," the instructor says.

"Yes, ma'am," the kid says, gently and deliberately pressing the turning signal device. He glances into the mirror at Stu and nods affirmatively, then continues the lesson. "You use hand-over-hand steering," he says, "when turning the wheel at low speeds."

Sometime during the next ten miles, Stu falls into a visionary trance, his vacant, impassive eyes fixed upon the unshaven man in the rearview. "If you don't mind," the kid says. "The driver must be able to see without distraction in all directions at all times. This is necessary for appropriate defensive driving. The majority of traffic accidents and deaths occur when the weather is clear and the roads are dry."

"You mean like today?" Stu says.

"Yes, like today," the kid says. He looks back to ask if Stu is paying attention. "Any questions?"

Beside him the fingers of the heavyset girl-without-a-face fidget in her lap like the fingers of a meth freak reading braille. She murmurs into the window, "The-Lord-is-my-shepherd-I-shall-not-want-The Lord is my shepherd...."

"Yeah, I got a question for you," Stu says. "Who farted?" The girl's shoulders begin to tremble. She hyperventilates.

When the instructor turns, Stu sees the nametag above her breast. "Roxanne?" Stu says. "That's a song by The Police. My twin sister and I were named after two guys in that band. Her name's Sting."

"You don't say," Roxanne says. "Please be quiet."

"Thank you, ma'am," pus-face chimes.

Stu's mouth is dry and his bladder feels tight as a morphine drip. "I have to pee," he says.

"My driving time is not up," crater face whines to Roxanne.

"Okay," Stu says. "But I can't be held responsible for the mess when my genitals explode." The girl's broad forehead thuds against the window in four-four time.

❦ ❦ ❦

IN THE RESTROOM, STU checks his phone. Voicemail from Sting but he doesn't open it. Outside, the large girl sits behind the wheel gnawing her nails. The skinny kid with the face like a relief map sits in back. When Stu opens the door, the kid crosses his arms, lifts his nose and looks away.

"I'm thinking it's my turn," Stu says. "She scares me."

"The notes from the judge would suggest that thinking is not exactly your strong suit," Roxanne says.

"I can't do this," the girl whispers. "I feel sick on my stomach."

"Foot on the brake," Roxanne says. "Gently shift into drive."

As they travel north on Highway 52 toward Dovesville, the speedometer needle never rises above thirty.

In answer to the death-ray curse emanating from Mr. Stridex, Stu looks up into the rearview, raises and tilts his chin, and begins pinching imaginary zits on his cheek. A scarlet wave rises up the kid's neck, engorging his face, and the little white pimple dots light up like a Christmas tree. The girl glances at Stu in the mirror. She begins belching uncontrollably.

"Slow down," Stu says. The startled girl burps a big one. "There's a road up here on the left named after a famous dog that could climb trees or walk on water or something." Roxanne turns slowly and narrows her eyes. "There," Stu points. "Flat Nose Road. That was the dog. Dead now." Stu speaks to the girl. "Probably got run over." Then to Roxanne. "He performed on The Johnny Carson Show in 1987. I know because that's the year The Police broke up."

His phone vibrates. Stu reaches for it.

"No calls in the car," Roxanne says.

"It's my sister," Stu says. "I have to take it."

"Safety first," Roxanne says.

"Thank you, ma'am," zit-kid says.

His cell chimes. Stu reads the text. He is blinded by tears. "No, no, no. Sweet Jesus," he pleads. "We have to go back. Now. My nephew, he's been hit by a car."

🦌🦌🦌

BEHIND THE WHEEL OF the GTO Stu slumps forward huffing for breath. He looks at the gauges, the radio, the black leather interior but he doesn't know what he's seeing, as if he's been teleported into the commander's seat of a spacecraft. He stares down at the key, its size and irrational shape, its excessive weight in his hand, and considers the consequences of inserting it, putting into motion a series of seemingly chaotic but intricately related events, events that, like fate, seem inevitable only when examined retrospectively, from effect to cause: An electrical charge, a spark, ignites an oxygen-gasoline mixture, setting off blindingly rapid and perfectly timed explosions, and the eight pistons hidden inside a steel casing propel the car to speeds in excess of a hundred and twenty miles an hour.

Stu is paralyzed in fear. But he has no choice. Sting's message said: Tode hit by car. Emergency room. He starts the GTO's engine. Its deep pulse rumbles through his body. Stu looks down at his foot resting on the accelerator and waits to see what the foot will do. When he computes the math, Tode-plus-emergency room, he feels the sudden impulse to press the gas petal through the floorboard, to bury the needle, to erase the time between the now and the then. Instead, he moves his foot to the brake and gently shifts into drive. He signals before turning out of the driving school lot.

Hands at ten and two, he says to himself, "Use hand-over-hand steering when turning the wheel at low speeds." He thinks again of Tode. The majority of traffic accidents and deaths occur when the weather is clear and the roads are dry.

"You mean like today." Stu says. Then Stu answers himself. "Yes."

Stu stands an invisible man, seeing but not being seen. Although it is eleven-thirty on a Friday morning, the emergency room of McLeod Regional Hospital looks like war-zone triage: Toothaches, tourniquets, bleeding bandages, about-to-explode pregnant moaners, drunks and strung out dopers, a landscape of obesity and chaos.

Sting does not answer her cell. At the desk he waits. In the waiting room he sits. Nothing. No Sting. No Tode. He returns to the desk. He waits. A squinty nurse studies a computer screen as she inks her scalp with a pen.

"My sister won't answer her phone," he says.

"Phones are not allowed," the nurse says, absorbed by the glowing screen. "We have no Tode," she says.

"Sorry," Stu says. "His real name is Andy, the third member of The Police."

The nurse looks up, lifts her glasses, lowers the glasses and turns back to the monitor. "Age fifteen? Yeah. He was struck by a car."

"I know that," Stu says. "How is he? Where is he?"

"You'll have to ask his doctor."

"What's the name?" Stu says.

"The one on call," the nurse says.

❧❧❧

STU CAN'T BREATHE, CAN'T move. He stands catatonically outside the main entrance to the waiting room, his hollow eyes transfixed upon the garnet and black GTO, which shimmers like a mirage in the afternoon summer heat.

"Oh, hey, Stu," Sting says. She lights a cigarette. Her face tells him nothing. Stu can't speak. "He could have been killed," she says, blowing a long string of toxic smoke. She looks down at her hands, slowly draws them apart. "This close. It's a miracle he wasn't killed. I got the goddamn shakes," she says. "Can you imagine?" she says. She turns to her twin brother. "Thanks for coming, Stu. Damned kid, what's he thinking? What's he doing on the other side of town? You don't think he was over there buying drugs, do you, Stu?"

Stu can't look at her. "How is he?" he says.

Sting points to the ground. "Ran over his foot. Broke his foot. How the hell does that happen? How can a car come so close, to run over his foot and not kill him?" She separates her hands again. "I tell you, it's a miracle my boy ain't dead. Driver never stopped."

A black orderly wheels out Tode, whose massive head wobbles to music only Tode can hear. His left foot is in a white cast. When he recognizes Stu, he smiles like a jack-o-lantern, "Far out, Stuuu!" he says.

Sting takes out her cell and speaks as she scrolls for a number. "Doug's not gonna like this. I'm down for three eight-tops tonight." Stu takes the phone from her.

"You okay?" he says to her.

"I'm broke but my kid is alive. How much happier could I be?"

"I'll take care of him," Stu says. "He's on so much medication, he won't know if you're here or not. Go on to work. If I need you, I'll call."

"Promise?"

"Promise."

The orderly speaks to Tode. "That's one bad ride, dude." He reaches for the passenger door of the Goat. "More leg room than Motel 6." He tosses the crutches onto the backseat and lifts Tode from the wheelchair. "Watch your head," he says.

"Very funny," Tode says.

Stu checks his mirrors. He checks them again and signals to exit the parking lot. Makes the turn slowly, hand-over-hand. He wants to look at his young nephew to make sure the kid's in one piece, that there are no signs of internal bleeding or post-traumatic stress disorder. But he's afraid to take his eyes from the road. After he crosses the MLK Bridge, he glances to his side. "Oh, hey, Stu," Tode says.

"How are you, buddy?" Stu says.

"Somebody almost killed me," Tode says. "I sort of felt something—you ever had that spooky feeling, Stu—and I turned; have you seen those billboards about texting?"

"How's the foot?" Stu says.

Tode looks down, then up in wide-eyed wonder. "Oh, Stu. Look. Somebody ran over my goddamn foot."

"It's okay," Stu says. "You're okay. That's what matters."

"Are you making fun, Stu? Like that time when you shut the car door on my thumb? 'Hell, Tode, you got nine more.' That's what you said."

"I ain't making fun now, pal."

"Let's go," Tode says.

"Where?" Stu says.

"Riding. In this mean-ass car. Let's go bird doggin'. I'm fifteen. I got my permit, did I tell you that?"

"Riding where?" Stu says.

"Around," Tode says. "Got any beer?"

"It's hot," Stu says.

"Too bad," Tode says. "A couple of hot babes and cold beers. You and me bird doggin'."

They ride in silence, Tode nodding off then coming back. He turns to Stu and smiles. "Let's go dove hunting," he says.

"Season's a month off," Stu says.

"So?" Tode says.

They ride in silence. Tode stares vacantly into the out yonder. Ahead, coiling waves of heat like phantom serpents ascend from the blacktop. The kid slowly turns, tilts his head and rests back against the door. His distant eyes narrow like a prophet's and he speaks in a voice not his own. He's not smiling. "You're a real fuck-up, you know that, Stu? You ain't nothing but a fuck-up. You've always been a fuck-up redneck. You'll always be a fuck-up redneck. You'll die a fuck-up redneck. The only thing that makes you different from every other redneck in Darlington is this car. If not for this car… This is one fucking hot car, Stu. I love this car. I love you, man."

Stu lowers the visor and lifts his hand to fend off the fierce afternoon sun. "What can I do for you?" he says.

"Take me dove hunting," Tode says. "All we need is a couple of shotguns and ammo. Lots of ammo.

"Okay," Stu says, "Okay."

♀♀♀

TODE LIFTS HIS HUGE head and periscopes all around. "Where are we?"

"Your great-grandmother's house," Stu says.

"She lived in a *barn?*" Tode says.

"No. Her house stood over yonder where the new church is. This barn is where the GTO sat for all those years. I'll be right back."

"Awesome," Tode says. "Why are we here? Ammo?"

"Payback," Stu says.

"I'll wait in the car," Tode says. "Somebody ran over my foot."

Stu returns with a large red plastic container. He opens and shuts the trunk. Then he's behind the wheel. He thinks: The driver must be able to see without distraction in all directions at all times.

"I'll help you clean up," Tode says.

"What?" Stu says. The blinding sunlight slants through the windshield like a laser and he's concentrating on the narrow two-lane road that connects Darlington and Society Hill. Out here is nothing but farmland.

"Somebody ran over my foot, but my hands are okay." The kid studies his hands as if he's just now discovered them. "I'll help you clean up what we kill."

Stu turns off the highway onto a dusty tractor path that divides fields of tall corn. The leaves and stalks have gone brown, and they shimmy as they applaud the soft breeze. The GTO passes through two acres of dark pines then enters another amber corn field that stretches farther than they can see. In a large bed of green grass on the high ridge overlooking an irrigation pond, Stu parks. The sun is low and the sanguine sky is tinted by broad strokes of deep grays and pale yellows.

When Tode looks up, Stu is at his window. "What's that?" Tode says.

"A blanket," Stu says.

"Where'd it come from?

"Trunk."

"What's it for?"

"Special occasions," Stu says. He descends the steep bank to the shore of the pond.

"I get it," Tode says with a big goofy grin. "Special like the redhead, huh? Bird doggin'. One day I'll have a car like this one. That'll be me. Where's the shotguns?"

Stu kneels, dips his hands in the water, and runs his fingers through his thin hair. He spreads the blanket, returns and lifts the boy into his arms. The two sit in the long shadows of the high bank looking across the water, up at the muscle car, which appears to hang in the sky, bathed in scarlet light, the last light of day.

"This pond's where we got our limit that time?" Tode says.

"Yes," Stu says.

"It was about this dark. They were coming in to roost, weren't they? Right over the water, low and fast. Low and fast. Low and fast. The sky like this. Doves all around us. We opened up on 'em, didn't we, Stu? Slayed 'em."

"Blood of the lamb," Stu whispers.

The sun is only a dim yellow shadow above the silhouette of black trees. Upon the dark water's surface, the image of Stu and Tode fades. Stu lays a hand on the boy's shoulder and pulls him close. He runs his fingers through the boy's hair. There's something in Stu's face the kid has never seen, something that frightens the boy.

Stu stands. "Where you going?" Tode says.

"For ammo," Stu says. "You wait here."

Tode looks down at the thick white cast. "Where would I go? And where were you, Stu?" he calls. He watches as Stu opens the trunk and brings out the red plastic container. "Doctor says I can't get this thing wet, Stu." Tode thinks that Stu must have lost something in the car because he's climbing around in the backseat, in the front seat.

Stu stands with his back to Tode and at a distance from the shiny garnet GTO with the black top. He steps forward ceremoniously, tosses his baseball cap into the car, and steps back. Stu lights a cigarette. He raises one hand to his hip and looks at the car. Then he tosses the cigarette lighter into the backseat, and the car becomes a fireball.

❦❦❦

THE TWO SIT ON the blanket facing the water. Stu studies the reflection of the burning car in Tode's eyes. The flames light up his pupils with wonder, like a newborn's. "What do you think?" Stu says.

"The fire is water. The water, fire," Tode says.

"Yes," Stu says. They sit. He brushes back hair from the kid's face. The wind is still and the weight of summer darkness folders over them. They do not speak. Stu waits until there's no danger of fire for the woods and fields. "Time," he says to Tode.

"My crutches," Tode says. "They burned up."

"I know," Stu says. "You don't need them."

"Those crutches, I'll have to pay," Tode says. "How will I get home?"

"I'll carry you," Stu says.

"How?" Tode says. "You can't leave me here."

"On my back, Tode," Stu says, reaching for the boy. "On my back."

It's About Time

THE THREE OF US were sitting in the baby pool at the YMCA.

I gently dabbed number 30 sunscreen on Ellen's nose, which was the color of boiled shrimp. My face was more a lobster pink. In the shadow of a low beach chair, our plastic 32-ounce cups, the kind with built-in insulation, sat on the cement within easy reach. She was vodka. I was bourbon.

We'd made a big deal of lathering up Meg, our granddaughter, who was motoring about inside a My Little Kitty float, her little chubby legs pedaling, a white sailor's cap shading her determined face. We were all feeling pretty good about things.

I watched my slick fingers trace Ellen's warm face. I wanted to touch lips, neck. When she lifted her chin, I felt warm breath inch up my wet chest. Behind the dark sunglasses, her eyes slowly closed. Her lips parted only inches from mine.

"Remember that night we slipped into the university pool?" I whispered.

She opened her eyes and lifted my oily fingers from her cheek. "Don't. Go. There," she said.

"Okay. How about that night in Jamaica?" I said. "Private pool outside our villa door?"

My wife lifted her sunglasses. Her eyes were slits. "George."

"It's something about the smell of chlorine."

Ellen smiled, turned and reached for Meg, who pressed her cheek against her grandmother's.

Age and beauty? I thought. No correlation there.

"Let's you and me go to the little girl's room," she said in that universal feminine voice, the one that disappears men. "We'll give the old man time to finish his walk—down memory lane." Ellen kissed me on the nose, I kissed Ellen on the nose, Meg kissed us both on the nose.

"Hurry back," I said, crooning my best Frank Sinatra.

Rising from the shallow pool, she gave me that fetching look of vinous mystery and carnal provocation. "Down, boy," she whispered.

She hoisted Meg and stepped from the water. "Come on, baby," she said. Meg threw her tiny arms around Ellen's neck, buried her face there, and squeezed until her small blue eyes shut tight.

"I wove you, Eeee Leee," she said.

"You and I must have a talk about The Big Bad Wolf," my wife said as her wet feet padded away from me.

For thirty-two years I've watched that walk with gratitude and wonder. I've never tired of the sight. Reaching for my cup, I called, "Remember that old Robert Goulet melody?" I was speaking in code. "*What now, my love?*"

When Ellen glanced back, I nodded toward her lovely behind.

"Stop it, George," she said, lifting a towel without breaking stride.

Little Meg turned, tilted her head, and studied her grandmother's face. Then she looked up at me with hard, pinched eyes.

As the two entered the deep shadows of the brick wall, I called again. "Okay. How about a Tom Petty song?" Ellen didn't break stride. "Don't do me like that."

From the darkness, a small, timeless voice, perfectly pitched an octave above Ellen's and exact in its inflections, echoed back to me. "Stop it, George," Meg said.

Baby's Breath

M Y WIFE MELISSA AND I were wrapping Christmas presents and watching porno movies when I got the call saying my father was dead. I hit the pause button on the VCR, sending the actors into fluttering ecstasy. Melissa picked up the phone in the other room.

Later we sat upstairs with a glass of red wine and talked down our list of gifts to buy.

❦❦❦

I'M NOT SURE WHEN the box containing my father's things arrived on our doorstep. I'm thinking mid-January. The box came the same day as the credit card bills. I didn't know the contents of the box—Melissa often shops by mail—but I had a bad, bad feeling about the credit card bills. I opened them first. I reached for my checkbook. And by the time I'd done the subtraction I wasn't thinking about the box.

That night, we were eating chicken wings and pork fried rice on TV tables in the den. Melissa sorted the mail. I was watching basketball. My wife laughed.

"When I saw 'Garden of Eden' on the package, I never expected this," she said, holding up a small catalog of sexually oriented material. "You didn't put our name on some list, did you?"

"No," I said. "Maybe they just read your mind or something."

She smiled, thumbing through the pages. Few things shock her. She teaches fifth grade.

"If you see something you really like, though, I'll buy it for Valentine's," I said.

"If it was something I *really* liked, how could you afford to keep me in batteries?"

She looked up from the catalog and smiled at me. We've been married for fifteen years.

At halftime of the game, we pushed back the trays and carried our plates to the kitchen.

"What's in the box?" Melissa asked, reaching into the cabinet for our vitamins. "It's addressed to you." I wiped my dinner knife on a napkin and slid its blade under the brown tape at the corner. "I'm gonna start a hot bath," she said. "Pour us a glass of wine?"

My mother had bought the box and the packing at the post office. Their new smell and texture made the contents seem inconsequential, as if what was inside existed for the package, not the other way around.

My business was paper. I was Quality Control and Safety.

Under the first thin layer I saw a cheap wrist watch, its band dangling from one side, my gift to him the first Christmas after he and my mother split. A scaly black wallet lay beside it. Attached to its fake sharkskin was a yellow Post-it note in my mother's hand: "This is it."

I set the watch and wallet on the kitchen table and peeled back the next layer of paper. Then the next. The box was large enough to hold shoes. I felt down its length. It was empty. There was nothing more of him there. Nothing to prove that what was inside was really his—not the watch I'd forgotten, or the wallet I'd never seen, not a fishing lure or a golf tee, not a guitar pick or a typewriter ribbon, not a ratchet wrench or a jigsaw blade. He'd not left a shrub in the ground, a fence he'd hammered, a story or a joke of his own making. I stood over the wallet and the watch on the table. I didn't know what I was looking at. Like random items from a crime scene.

Like somebody had disappeared without a clue.

When I unfolded it, the wallet made a crackling, splintering sound. Inside were a half dozen yellowed business cards and a single dim photograph. In the photo, my father stands like a Munchkin in front of a massive new 1970 Eldorado Cadillac parked outside the dealership where he sold cars. He had taken me for ice cream the day he won the car.

I suddenly breathed the smell of the Cadillac's new leather.

Stepping over to the light above the sink, I felt for my glasses. By today's standards, the car was enormous, its black hood longer than my dad's body, its headlights nearly the size of his head. A blue ribbon as big as a wagon wheel lay on its hood. I tilted the photograph to catch the light and brought it up closer.

My father's demeanor reminded me of safety posters I'd hung in the plant to caution workers about the dangers of cutting machines. His disjointed torso bent forward in protest, and his contorted face—gaping mouth and bulbous eyes—brought to mind a frozen moment of warning, or rapture. His finger pointed up toward or beyond a banner, King of the Hill, suggesting an evangelical moment of insight, as if he had, at the snap of the shutter, found words to express a revelation. His '70s fashion choices, extra-wide lapels and slightly flared slacks, only accentuated the surreal cartoonish portrait.

Why would he have kept this picture? I thought again of the warning posters at work.

I couldn't believe he'd considered this the look of the number one Cadillac man in the Southeast, a man at the top of his sales game, a guy who had won a new Eldorado. What was he thinking?

I brought the snapshot up closer. The center of the image was sharp enough for me to read the license plate and to see into my father's eyes—which stared dead-on into the camera with that haunting vacant expression you find in photographs of Confederate soldiers.

His was not the picture of happy success, of money or the swagger born of the triumph of capitalism. Instead he was a puzzle of mostly missing pieces, a joke without a punch line. My father, who had always lived in the gray mist of my imagination, floated now in an ethereal haze, suspended between memory and conjecture. It was too late to find even a shirt that would hold the scent of him.

At that moment, all I wanted was something of his hand to lay my hand on.

Opening the bathroom door, I realized I'd forgotten to pour Melissa and me a glass of wine. It was, I guess, in the back of my mind. I knew that I was supposed to bring something to her. I looked down to see the watch in my hand. But that was okay. She had fallen asleep in the bathtub. I gently lowered the toilet lid, sat beside my naked sleeping wife, and quietly contemplated the watch. I looked up at her. Melissa lay in the warm water, eyes closed, gently breathing, her knees up and open, arms floating at her side, palms up, expectantly, as if to embrace some new, welcomed arrival.

Suddenly the room was freezing, the light blinding. From I don't know where and for the first time in years, the cold delivery room and its bright lights rushed back to me: the warmth of Melissa's swollen breast through the green cotton gown against my cheek, her quiet voice saying, *"Dear God. Dear God."*

My thoughts accelerated and slowed, turned without signaling, then took an unexpected, dreaded exit ramp to someplace off the map. When I felt the imminent collision of memories, I held my breath and crept upstairs to our bedroom. After a time I blew my nose and washed my face again, hoping that Melissa wouldn't wake just now. Standing at the mirror, I heaved a deep breath then opened our closet door, found Melissa's robe, laid it on the radiator, and waited until it was warm all the way through before I woke her.

🍃🍃🍃

AT WORK, WE MANUFACTURED file folders. There, I administered tests on workplace violence and sexual harassment, taught quality control classes, and explained the meaning of safety posters. But the machine operators' assistants and the outside contract labor no longer listened when I talked safety codes or emergency procedures. They turned their eyes away from the reality videos, testimonials from mangled converts. Layoffs, not lost limbs, occupied their mind. While I taught, they stared slack-faced at the lunch they fetched from plastic grocery bags.

🍃🍃🍃

MY BOSS, MARK MCDONALD, pointed to his lips. "We definitely are *not* shutting down. No matter how electronic the world gets," he said lifting his carriage to full attention, "paper copies will always have to be filed."

Each of us, he said, was an important part of the company machine. Each was valued. To make his point, he began explaining the concept of integrated circuits; seeing that almost none of the hourly help was getting his message, he abruptly stopped in the middle of his motivational talk. After a long pause, one of the line operators asked if the plant had been bought, to be outsourced to Mexico. McDonald's face reddened and a vein in his neck fattened. What followed was a rambling no-but-don't-hold-me-to-this answer that somehow included the meaning of America, his worst childhood memory, and a long list of sacrifices the company had made for us. Somewhere in there I began thinking about how most of the ads on TV are for dot-coms, that even TV is being sucked up by something else, something nobody can see or put their hand on.

I felt inside my shirt pocket for the cigarettes I'd stopped smoking ten years ago and discovered my father's watch with its broken band. I'd been carrying it for a few days, thinking that I'd take it by a jeweler's on my lunch break.

McDonald's voice faded, his face disappeared—and I was thinking about the photo of my father and the Cadillac.

The plant was located in Florence, but Melissa and I live ten miles away in Darlington, where it's cheaper. I'd worked overtime again. The evening was warm for late January, and I drove with the window down. Before me, the full moon floated above the horizon as the sounds of the machines still swooshed and clanked inside my head.

A wave of crimson light covered my face. Ahead, a bank of red traffic lights in front of the technical college allowed night students access to the campus. Beside me, Grunge Gospel thundered from a battered, rusting cargo van. Its driver was a kid wearing a tie-dyed T-shirt and glasses so thick his bulging white eyes appeared glazed with lacquer. I turned. Across the campus, yellow moonlight reflected off the fountain near the campus entrance.

I thought of Melissa at nineteen rising from the small lake in the middle of our college campus, her flesh softly tanned, clear water sliding down the length of her, and the sight of her walking toward me in the bright, bright moonlight, wearing only those thin white panties and a soaking tie-dyed T-shirt.

Without warning a flash from a new electronic sign across from the administration buildings shattered my memory. Its blazing red-white-and-blue digital message flowed across the sky like a celestial victory banner, wrapped around an invisible corner and repeated itself: "We're Building the Economy One Student at a Time… We're Building the Economy One Student at a Time… We're Building the Economy—" The gnarly gospel music from the van beside me fled. I looked up. The moon had become a green traffic light.

When I pulled into our drive, Daniel, our next-door-neighbor, stood in the floodlights of his backyard tossing a football to his two young sons. Daniel and I have almost nothing in common. He's at least ten years younger than I and very religious. He's a cop. Daniel and his wife, Linda, are cordial, but the boys seem afraid of us. We can count on Daniel and Linda in an emergency and they on us. But neither Daniel nor I find it easy to make conversation.

What we do have in common is a dead child, ours four years before theirs. Theirs to a freak automobile accident, ours to unknown explanations.

I embraced him the night of the visitation following his child's death, and that bond remains the only thing between us.

As I switched off the engine, he gave a little neighborly wave without looking. I walked over and stood beside him like an intruder as he tossed the ball. After watching for a minute I praised the boys' passing and catching. After another pause, I asked him if it would be possible to track down a 1970 Eldorado Cadillac from its license number. I just wanted to know if it were possible. My question gave him a chance to speak professionally, which put us both at ease.

"Try the DMV in Columbia," he said. "You'd need the Vehicle Identification Number." He was throwing alternately to his boys, talking to the side of me. "If by chance the car is still running, they can tell you who has it. If it's been junked, there ought to be a junk title for it somewhere, a VIN somewhere."

"What would you say my chances are of finding it?"

"In some kind of restorable condition?"

"I just wanted to see it, you know. You have a memory, a mental picture of a thing—" I looked over into the floodlights. "It's only a picture, a memory," I said, looking down into the grass. "If that's all you have... ." Massaging the football, he turned away. "I was just curious, I guess."

"These days, rule of thumb is that a car more than thirteen years old is most likely in a junkyard. You're talking more than thirty years. But some things, like you said—" Daniel studied the ball's laces. His voice dropped to little more than a whisper. "Sometimes the law of averages—you know, you just never know. You never can tell. Anything can happen."

In our sun room I saw Melissa watering peace lilies. "Thanks," I said.

Gripping the football, Daniel turned to me. "Let me know what you find. If you run into any flack," he said softly, his eyes looking past me, not looking at me at all, "let me know. I'll try to run it down at the station."

I phoned an 800 number and got a recorded message saying I could choose information from a menu of recorded messages. The recording informed me that if I wanted to talk with a person, I'd have to call another long-distance number and pay for it myself. When I finally got through, another recorded message told me that if I held the line for fifteen minutes and nobody answered I could leave a recorded message and someone would return my call.

AT THE KITCHEN DOOR, Melissa said, "Don't look at me, whatever you do!" I glanced up from the breakfast table, where I was concentrating like a surgeon, dissecting my father's watch beneath a high-intensity lamp. She gave a little fake squeal and ran to the wall switch. Melissa's fifth grade students love her.

"That light! The x-ray vision! I'm melllllting!" she said in her famous Wicked Witch voice. The kitchen went dark except for my lamp.

I couldn't help laughing. "Lights, please," I said. She hit the switch and gave me a drive-by kiss. "What was that all about?" I said.

She removed my glasses, turned her back, then turned again, facing me. Her eyes were the size of egg yolks. I'd forgotten I'd been wearing two pairs of glasses, hers and mine, so that I could work on the tiny innards of the watch.

"You'll ruin your eyes," she said. Melissa set the glasses on the table and began unloading groceries. I held the two pairs together and pushed them up against my nose, then reached for a tiny screwdriver. It was a cheap watch. I couldn't imagine my dad's having worn it. When I knew him, he considered an expensive watch as necessary as shined shoes, a perfectly knotted tie, and a waxed and spotless ride. But its plastic face was opaque and gouged. A small web of rust darkened the stem like a dry blood spoor. I thought I'd clean it up.

"Everything can be cooked in the Crockpot," Melissa announced, stacking the cans and meat on the counter. "Beef tips, chicken, chili. How does that sound?"

I forced the back off the watch to see how the parts fit, to see how it looked in there. To maybe see how things had once worked.

"I have a cookbook around here somewhere. We'll plan a week's menu if you want."

"Okay," I said.

McDonald, repeating that we'd all have to be a little more productive, had informed me that my hours had been extended, that I'd have to work on until six o'clock every day. It was Melissa's idea that we preplan our suppers, our way of not losing that hour together.

I dismembered the watch, carefully emptying the delicate cogs and clips with tweezers and the small screwdriver. The two pairs of glasses helped.

Melissa lifted the cooker from underneath the cupboard beside me.

"What will you do when your eyes go completely?" she asked.

"I guess I'll just have to feel my way around," I said, not looking up.

"Ooh, good answer," she said. I laid the tiny works on a white napkin. There must have been fifty parts. I couldn't believe it.

"Come on," she said, setting a glass of wine before me and taking the tweezers from my hand. She lifted my double panes of reading glasses. "Let's sit in the other room and listen to music. Maybe an attractive woman will teach you to dance," she said, giving me a come hither look as she walked way.

A dozen years ago, we'd taken a few lessons. In the Carolinas the dance is called the Shag, and its music is called Beach Music. If you know the movie *Bull Durham*, our favorite, you've heard "Sixty Minute Man" by The Dominoes. I never mastered the dance moves. I'd hold Melissa's hand while she performed little crossover steps. When I raised her arm, it was our signal for her to do a quick turn and cradle back against me, then spin out and begin the steps again. On special occasions, she'd sometimes dance in her sexy nightgown and white athletic socks. From the living room, I heard the voices of Billy Scott and The Prophets on the stereo.

Pushing back from the table, I lifted my wineglass and contemplated the tiny cogs on the brightly lit white napkin. I marveled at the notion of a watch, that anything so fragile could go so long without missing a beat, amazed that so much could fit into such a tiny space, that a thing so small could slice and dice so much joy, so much sorrow.

Later, after Melissa had gone up to bed, I checked the doors, shut off the lights, and carried our glasses into the dark kitchen. In the light of the full moon, the watch's remains appeared to float like a constellation upon the soft, luminous white napkin. I stood over the tiny metal dots conjuring their connections. The picture of my father formed before me. I touched my finger to one of the tiny wheels, no larger than a speck, brought it up to my mouth, placed it on my tongue. Then I reached for the last of the wine.

I LEFT A MESSAGE for my mom, asking about the car. The next evening I listened to her three-word reply on our machine: "Not a clue," followed by a click.

AT EMERSON'S JUNKYARD, I asked if he had a 1970 Cadillac.

"Not a piece," he said, scrunching up his face as if I smelled bad. I asked about tracing the title.

"That was before computers," he barked. "Nobody knows anything without computers. Before computers? Nothing."

At home there was an electronic voice on the answering machine, this one from the DMV in Columbia. The information I'd left on their machine was incorrect, incomplete, or insufficient. The robotic voice urged me to call back during normal business hours and assured me that the DMV was eager to assist me with information or services.

❦❦❦

CHAOS LEAVES OPEN THE door for the good, even the miraculous, sometimes. I have to remind myself of that, even now.

The last weekend in February was one of those good times. After a month of darkness and cold rain, the temperatures rose to the seventies on Friday, and on Saturday we set candles on the patio table, grilled chicken, and had our drinks until after ten. Daniel and Linda's boys peeked out at us from their bedroom window. On Sunday morning, we were back outside in our robes, drinking coffee in the warm sunshine. I was reading the paper.

"I think we do harm to their children," Melissa said, looking past me at Daniel and Linda as they packed their wide-eyed kids in the car for Sunday school. "I don't know what I'd tell our children if we had us for neighbors."

❦❦❦

AT BLARNEY'S GARAGE, A thin young black guy and his very large girl-friend sat reclining like two astronauts awaiting launch in the front seat of a dirty silver Seville. The passenger door was open, and the guy had one foot on the ground. I stepped closer. They were sharing lunch on the console and holding hands. When I asked if he worked there, he nodded yes. After I told him what I was looking for, he started out of the car.

"Go ahead and eat," I said, waving that he not get up. I turned and backed away.

He wiped his mouth and walked me into the office. His boss sat at his cluttered, greasy desk eating fried chicken from a square Styrofoam container.

"Got a '77," he said, looking down into the box.

"If somebody junks a car is there a title that shows that it's been junked?"

"What exactly is it you want to know?" he said, looking up at me for the first time, chewing slowly.

"If I had a VIN and I traced it, would it maybe show that the car was in your yard?"

"All I've got is a '77."

"I meant as a rule. Is there a title somewhere that shows where a junked car is?"

"Or was. Most likely a car that old has been sold for scrap."

"But wouldn't there be *something* that would show where it had last been?"

"S'pose to be," he said, dropping a wishbone into the trashcan. "If I get a title with a car, I'm s'pose to put the information on some form and send it to Columbia. Or do some computer shit. Do you see a computer?" He was examining his second piece of chicken, deciding where his teeth would fit best. "That's the rule, anyway."

❧ ❧ ❧

I TOLD McDONALD I needed a half day off to see the doctor.

"Does that mean noon or one o'clock?" he said.

"One."

"Okay. Make sure you fill out the forms in HR," he said.

At the DMV in Columbia, I watched the clock on the wall for an hour, afraid that I wouldn't get in. When my number was called I stood behind a high counter until one of the clerks who bowed before her screen raised a hand. I didn't want to waste time.

"How could I go about finding a 1970 Eldorado Cadillac?"

The young woman wore a starched green blazer. She turned from her screen, fingered down her glasses, and smiled at the attractive college-aged guy at the next desk. "Nineteen *seventy?*" She was talking to me but looking at him: "Best place to look is Mexico. They don't junk 'em there." The two laughed.

Driving home on I-20, I couldn't stop thinking about what would happen to Melissa if I was diagnosed with a protracted, fatal disease. I don't have long-term disability insurance.

That night, I awoke suddenly.

Among the business cards inside my father's wallet was one from his former insurance agent. The next day, I called the number.

"He's no longer with the company," said the sing-song voice on the other end.

"Can you tell me how I might reach him?" I asked. "It's important."

"No sir, I can't," responded the jingle.

❦❦❦

MELISSA AND LOUISE OXENDINE are yard sale pals. Louise's husband, Harmon, has his own insurance place here. He's a hard worker and a nice guy. He knows how to get around in the insurance game.

"Got a pen handy?" he said when I answered the phone. He gave me the combination of seventeen numbers and letters that made up the Vehicle Identification Number of my father's car. I repeated them to make sure I'd gotten it right.

"Must have been a good car. And a good agent," he said. "Your dad kept them both until 1990; that's when his agent died."

"Where is the car now?"

"No telling. All I know is that your dad dropped the insurance on it, that the file is marked 'sold.' Your dad's being in the car business and all, it's no telling, unless of course the car's still running. Fat chance of that."

The woman in the glasses at the Columbia DMV didn't remember me. She was wearing the same starched green blazer as before. I gave her the VIN.

"All I can tell you is that the last title, dated 1992, is in the name of Harold Robinson, a wholesaler in Raleigh, North Carolina."

I called.

"A car that old? I'm sure it must have been sold for junk." The cell phone voice sounded as if it were in the middle of a hurricane. "We'll have these sales, we call them Cash-For-Clunkers, you know. We'll give you five hundred dollars toward a trade for anything you can drive onto the lot. Got something you wanna sell? Give you a hell of a deal today, over the phone."

"Where do you sell the junked ones?"

"Depends. Sometimes locally. But if we have a big promotion and get lots of cars, wholesale scrap metal guys from all over come and buy the clunkers by the train car load."

"Do you have the title for it?"

"No. When we sell them for junk, the title goes to the junk man."

❦❦❦

MAYBE THE DMV PAYS really poorly. She was wearing that same green blazer.

"Well," I said, "if the car's not being driven, and the guy in North Carolina doesn't have the title, and there's no junk title, where's the car?"

"I'd say either Mexico or cyberspace," she said to the smiling young guy beside her.

❧❧❧

MY COWORKERS AND I sat as if inside a cave. The dim reflection of McDonald's PowerPoint gave his face an ashy metallic-gray appearance, and when he slowly turned to stress another fascinating idea, his eyes dissolved into black cratered shadows. His presentation to the group we called Leadership explained the new Performance Evaluation Instrument. His demonstration revealed that the results of the instrument would be converted into multi-colored graphs so that we could monitor our individual productivity, evaluate our strengths and weaknesses, and plot our perpetual improvement. He stepped away from the computer cart. Our assignment, he said, was to take the instrument home, administer the tool, and submit the results to his office. He read each person's name, handed us an envelope of information, and shook our hand. We applauded and walked outside to our cars.

Lonnie, my friend who sometimes covers for me on night shift, called out as I opened my car door. He was holding up the new Performance Evaluation tool. "It's like trying to prove you love your wife," he said shaking his head in disgust, "isn't it?"

The technical college's electronic sign had been upgraded. In a never-ending parade of tiny luminous dots, bright images of Man and Woman burst from the underworld. They mechanically joined hands, turned, stopped, blinked, and smiled before they ascended, in perfect union, into the heavens of the economy—from which a new, identical generation was born. It was a dazzling, frightening display. I couldn't take my eyes from it. I wanted to tell somebody what they'd done. The battered white van at the light beside me pulsed with loud music.

"Hey!" I shouted to the driver, a guy in a tie-dyed shirt. "Do you *believe* that?"

The van's stereo blasted in thumps and waves. His ear was bent toward the music and the singing: "*Think of what it could have meant, think of what it could have meant...*" I looked back at the brilliant visionary spectacle.

"Hey," I shouted again. If he heard me, he paid me no mind. Besides, his glasses were spooky thick.

When I pulled into the drive, I saw Daniel in uniform, sitting in his police cruiser, door open, writing on a pad in the soft light of the dash. When he heard my door shut, he glanced up. I looked away before our eyes met. Somehow, though, I could feel him watching me as I walked up the steps.

❦❦❦

MELISSA AND I HAVE two anniversaries. One we celebrate at home. Each year, Melissa takes out our wedding china, silver, crystal, and linen napkins. We light candles and play soft music. We dance.

As you would expect, for the first few years the other anniversary was painfully sad. We sent each other cards and flowers and had our tears together. But you come to a point where there's nothing left to say. When you do damage to the other person by reliving certain memories, it's better to relive what you must alone. So now on that day we have dinner out. Neither of us says anything about our dead child. I'll come home from work and Melissa will be putting on makeup and one of us will say, Where do you want to eat, without mentioning the occasion, and we'll have a nice meal. We remember, of course, but there is no display of tears. This year Melissa wanted Italian. At dinner, I brought up the subject of disability insurance.

"Statistics say that I'll die first." I pushed aside what was left of my eggplant and poured the last ounce of red wine into Melissa's glass.

"Oh, great. The longevity of our marriage has been reduced to a numbers game," she said, looking into her plate. She set down her fork.

"Everything is a numbers game," I said. "That's how we explain things we can't explain."

"Not so," she said. "What did we do before we had numbers?"

"What do you mean?"

"We haven't *always* had numbers. What did people do before we had numbers? How did we explain the unexplainable? You know that thing from the Bible, 666, the Devil is 666?" She held her fork suspended, leaning in toward me. She was being pedagogically instructive. "Do you think there was no Devil before our concept of numbers?" She looked up, then back at me. "Well, people miss the point," she said. "It's not the particular number 666 that is the devil. Think about it. Why did John the Apostle identify Satin with numbers? Why not letters? Why not WWW? The point is when you live by nothing but numbers, you're living under the *rule* of the Devil. Take my word for it." She tossed her napkin on the table. "Do you think that the only possibilities are the ones that numbers give us? That's exactly what the Devil wants. Believe me, if you teach public school, you know about numbers and the rule of the Devil." She looked down at her plate, pushing it aside.

I had spoiled the mood, and I wanted to fix things. There was an empty silence that could have been filled by anything.

"Wanna go dancing?" I said, lifting my wineglass, hoping she'd look up at me. I smiled.

"Sure," she said, smiling back, touching her glass to mine.

In the car, she found an oldies station and we both sang. It was one of her favorite songs, an ancient one from The Prophets. "Give Me Just A Little More Time" by the original Chairmen of the Board came on next. "I'll lead. You can just follow," she said over the music. She lifted her left hand as if to accept a chivalrous kiss and rocked from side to side singing the chorus out of tune over and over until the song faded.

It had been Melissa's idea that we take dance lessons after the baby died. "Dancing will help take the weight off," she had said.

Following the PowerPoint announcement that we had been sold, McDonald said we should feel great. The company would expand and buy modern equipment that would boost productivity and eliminate waste in our production operation. A new site had been purchased. He was not at liberty to say where. We would be vacating in less than a year.

There would be necessary personnel changes, of course. But every attempt would be made to save jobs. We'd be able to roll over our 401(k) if jobs were lost. He asked me to hand out T-shirts sporting the new company's initials, VAC.

"That's it," I said when I'd handed out the last shirt. Everybody looked at McDonald. Somebody initiated the applause.

Then everybody went back to their machines.

A little before six that evening, I was on the catwalk, on my way to my office to pull samples, when the power went out. I froze in the black silence and removed the earplugs OSHA required us to wear. Hail pounded the metal roof and vague concussions of thunder vibrated through the darkness. After a few seconds, the emergency generators kicked in, illuminating the feeble safety lights at fifty-foot intervals along the tall metal walls. The place looked like a graveyard, the machines like mausoleums. As their eyes adjusted to the eerie yellow safety lights, the machine operators and the fastener crew began filing into the wide corridors between the machines, many holding cigarette lighters before them like candles, trudging in a silent processional toward the rear doors, their final destination, the shipping area. As they approached the open dock, random flashes of brilliant light froze the silhouette of their bleak parade.

Outside, the asphalt was covered in pellets of ice. Hard rain swept across the parking lot in gray sheets, like spray off a crashing wave. I didn't look up as I ran to my car. Somehow the unlit street made everything seem quieter, and as the rain let up, I lowered my window a little to clear the condensation from the windshield.

I listened to the hum of my tires on the black, wet streets.

As I neared the technical college, blue lights reflected against the black sky. I thought of the randomness of tornados. When I spotted the cop directing traffic, I looked to see if it was Daniel. But the figure was wearing tall boots and an over-sized hooded raincoat.

As traffic crept from the campus, I coasted to an easy stop and waited. The rain had stopped.

My first thought was that the driver beside me wearing the thick glasses and playing the loud music must be my clock-punching double. We sat side by side at the intersection in front of the college that, with or without electricity, was building the economy at a frightening rate. The kid bent forward and reached for the volume. The singer was a woman.

"What are the chances?" I murmured.

The weight of astronomical odds took my breath: The room was freezing cold, the lights unbearable. He was warm when the nurse laid him on Melissa's chest. The only thing missing was his breathing. Why? I thought. The song's lyrics entered my head like bullets of light.

> "If Ted Bundy had been Jesus
> think of what it could have meant
> to all those young women
> who came to his rescue
> or who saw his face
> as if in a dream
> how bright their lives might have been
> if Ted Bundy had been Jesus."

I saw him, his tiny hands, his face like an old man's, without breath, transfixed in blinding, timeless space.

The song was gone.

Someone blew a whistle.

❦❦❦

STANDING IN THE DARK foyer, I called out to Melissa. She didn't answer. I unlaced my wet shoes and walked barefoot down the hall to the small cabinet where we keep the candles. She was not at home. Dark rain hummed a single deep, sustained note. I shaded the candle as I hurried into the den to check the answering machine, thinking the car had given her trouble again. Without power, the machine was useless. There was a loud knock on the door. I pictured Melissa there in the black rain, clutching her plastic grocery bags.

I jerked open the door.

In his uniform and oversized cloak, faceless Daniel stood like a giant specter. The rain was coming down hard again. He held out a piece of paper. As I reached for it, he spoke from inside the hood. "I think it's there," he said. I looked down at the paper I couldn't read. "Zebulon," he said. I didn't know what to say. I opened the door wide and stepped back for him to come in. Heavy raindrops exploded into blooming shards on the steps and across the lawn.

"I can't," he said, motioning toward his house next door. "It's dark."

❦❦❦

MELISSA AND I SAT outside at the patio table staring down at the phone. Behind us, Daniel's two boys ascended from their new trampoline. One held his hands tight against his hips and thrust up his shoulders. The other folded his knees to his chest and tucked his head.

"What will you do," Melissa said, speaking toward the phone, "if it really is your father's car?"

"Go take a look, I guess."

I'd called the number. A guy in North Carolina named Kevin Asher said he might have the Eldorado. I watched as the boys lifted off, then looked down at the faded insurance agent's card in my hand, at the dead man's name on the card, a name my father could have put a face to. I turned the card over and studied the seventeen numbers and letters I'd slowly repeated to Kevin. And now I sat hoping that he'd keep his promise to call me back.

There was an odd silence. When I looked around, the boys had vanished.

❦❦❦

ZEBULON, NORTH CAROLINA, IS 175 miles north of here between Raleigh and Rocky Mount. Marion Walker, who runs his father's wrecker business, said he'd drive me up, load the car, and deliver it back to Darlington for fifty dollars, plus gas. At dawn on Saturday, Melissa and I kissed as she headed out in search of yard sale treasure. I waited at the window and watched her drive away.

I met Marion at the curb. Below the front bumper of his wrecker was a black license plate sporting a large #3, and on the back glass of the cab, in large cursive, the name of his hero, Dale Earnhardt. We aren't big talkers, either of us. After the Hi-how-are-you, all I could think of was the Eldorado, and each time Marion tried to make polite conversation, I was unable to sustain it. When we merged onto I-95, I asked him why Earnhardt was the greatest NASCAR driver of all time, then settled back into my own thoughts as he led me through forty years of NASCAR history and around the tracks at Bristol, Rockingham, Charlotte, Daytona, Talladega, and of course Darlington. The inflections of his voice became distant music to me, rising and falling, and at times he lifted his hand from the wheel and painted imaginary figures in the air.

I looked for old cars headed up the interstate to New York or down to Miami. I took in the scenery.

If you've experienced the death of a loved one, you'll remember the disembodied feeling during the drive from the church to the cemetery. You watch from the limo's window as people go through the motions of their ordinary lives, mowing the grass, strolling their kids, or washing their car. You want to scream out at them, *Hey! Don't you know what's going on here? Can't you see what has happened here? Don't you know what this means?* What you are feeling is the intensity of living. And what got you to that awareness came at the cost of a human life. A person you loved.

As we neared Zebulon, I noted the signs for New Hope, Pilot, and Spring Hope. I counted the mile markers.

A ten-foot steel wall shut off Southern Salvage from Highway 31 and from the rest of the planet. As soon as we passed through its gates, the pastoral skyline was replaced by a bitter landscape of tangled ruin. Thousands of headlights turned their empty sockets to the vacant blue sky. The view was both horrible and thrilling. The giant structures of randomly assembled carcasses, angular heaps of fiberglass and steel, were at once haunting and breathtaking, like those massive stone structures built by ancient, mysterious orders.

Marion rolled to a smooth stop in front of a mobile home that was the Southern Salvage office. Without knowing it, I'd not uncrossed my ankles for over three hours; when I tried to climb down from the cab, both feet felt tingly, asleep. My first few steps were tentative and awkward. I held the handrail and wobbled like a toddler up the three steps to the office door.

The small, dark room smelled vaguely of incense or pipe tobacco. From somewhere, the murmur of gospel music crackled from a cheap radio. I waited for my eyes to adjust to the dim light. Two very old men, one in a fedora like my grandfather wore, sat on a scarred, threadbare sofa, their faces hidden from me. The second man had shoestring-thin strands of hair that draped his baldness like lines drawn with a black Magic Marker. The two were engaged in a conversation about hunting dogs. Kevin Asher, the man behind the counter, was about my age. One of his eyes seemed to float, but the other one was bright and clear and blue. I stood without motion or word until Magic Hair was done with his dog. Then all three looked over at me.

"Great day to be alive, ain't it?" said the old man in my grandfather's hat, smiling and bobbing his head. Kevin stood and offered his hand.

Outside, at the bottom of the steps, Kevin said, "We'll take this one," pointing to a faded blue Grand Am with its trunk open. He dropped the shifter into drive and pressed the gas.

"Hell, bro, I got two of 'em Eldorados. One of 'em belonged to my uncle. It's a convertible—or was, I should say. If it hadn't burned up, there might be enough of the two of 'em to make one of 'em roll."

The dirt path was like a ghastly tunnel. Only as wide as the car and walled by ghoulish metal body parts, the road that led into the belly of the salvage yard appeared to have been recently shelled by artillery. The Grand Am had no seatbelts, and Kevin Asher drove at speeds that forced me to hold the console with one hand and the armrest with the other.

"My cousin and me are the same age," Kevin shouted. "In 1980, his daddy let him and me borrow that convertible after high school graduation to take our girlfriends to Myrtle Beach for the weekend." As he spoke, Kevin's good eye never left my face, while his bad eye rolled about like a marble in a shot glass. "His daddy, my uncle, started the first string of titty bars in Charlotte in the early '70s. He had three or four Cadillacs back then. Ain't no thrill like being in a motel traveling to the beach at a hundred miles an hour, Doobie Brothers full blast." As we probed deeper and deeper into the desolate land, its tormented landscape piled high with metal coffins, literal deathtraps, our course grew more and more unpredictable—Kevin Asher taking what I'd swear were five right turns, then as many lefts, all the while flying up and crashing down until my brains felt scrambled, my sphincter violated. Black smoke hovered overhead and even the faded sunlight was rust red. Sweat burned my eyes.

I don't know how Marion decoded the maze we were racing through. But each time I glanced back, I spotted the searchlights mounted on the top of his wrecker. They disappeared when we reached the top of a hill. A thirty-acre battlefield of smoldering mid-day metal stretched below us.

Topping the crest of a deep pit, we appeared an instant away from a head-on collision with an already beheaded Skylark. Feeling squeezed from every side, I shut my eyes. A left-angle turn slammed me against the door. I heard the piercing squeal of brake metal on metal and was thrown forward as the car came to a jolting halt.

All four tires flat, the Eldorado sat at the ready, crouched on its belly, as if it might leap at any moment. The car was streaked with dirt and rust. Its windshield and rear glass were intact, but the passenger windows were cracked. One of the headlights was broken, giving me a curious, impish wink. I half expected the car to morph into a winged dragon and spring to life.

Marion parked the wrecker behind the Grand Am. "That's what Boss Hog drove," he said, looking to me and then to Kevin for confirmation, "on *The Dukes of Hazzard* TV show. Only his was white, wasn't it?"

For a full minute, we assessed the Eldorado like three cavemen contemplating a massive bagged bison.

I stood at the driver's side and ran my fingers over the dirty VIN on the dash. These were the remains of my father. I laid my hands on the car.

"You sure you want this?" Marion Walker asked.

"It's a hoss, ain't it?" Kevin said, trying to pry open the passenger door. "500 cubic inches of whoop-ass and 400 horses of bye-bye." He turned and spoke to the car's mate, the rusted frame of his uncle's Eldorado parked beside my father's. "And a backseat built for a three-some," he added.

I stepped off seven paces from bumper to bumper, reached through the broken glass on the driver's side, and pulled the door open. The tepid grey bleached leather had ripped at the seams and peeled down in wide strips. I slid onto the seat and instantly sank to its springs.

"Dry rot," Kevin said.

I felt small and naked in the cavernous car, unable to see over the massive steering wheel. My foot failed to reach the pedals. I gripped the wheel.

"Engine's no good," said Marion. "Look at where the belts have melted. This baby got hot. Maybe a carburetor fire. All the seals are gone in it, too. A car sits like this," he said, "the worst thing that can happen to it."

From a few feet away, Kevin slowly shook his head from side to side as he ran his hand over the other car's rusted hood. A red cloud formed above his fingers. "Ricky, my cousin, took this one down to Mexico and back a few times—at very high speeds—carrying what the courts later said were heavy loads of contraband. From his jail cell he handed my daddy a hundred-dollar bill and the title and made him promise he'd park it in the back of the lot and lock the title in the trunk. The next night, it mysteriously caught fire."

"What do you want for this one?" I asked.

Back at the office, Kevin wrote me a receipt for two hundred dollars. He opened a filing cabinet drawer.

"I'll keep my eye out for the title," he said, his bad eye floating around as if it had been given the command to search. "I have had it. I know I have. I'll look for it, I promise. Only God knows where that piece of paper is," his eye twitched and fluttered in surges. "And so far He ain't tellin'." Kevin let out a sigh. "This your address on the check?"

I nodded that it was.

"Well, I'll copy down your address," he said as he stuffed my check into a small tackle box, "and if the Lord comes through, I'll mail that title to you. Not that you're gonna have any use for it."

Outside, I spotted Marion's wrecker moving slowly up the path, the Eldorado securely aboard. Across the lot, the old man in my grandfather's fedora was examining the burnt body of an '80s MG. At the sound of the wrecker, he turned and saw the Eldorado. He smiled at me and walked over.

"You found it!" he said. "What are the odds of that?"

I smiled.

He stepped closer. "I like to cut the fool," he said. "You know, just for fun. At my age, it's a good thing. And to show that no matter how old you are there's always something to learn, let me try out something on you."

Marion's wrecker passed through the back gate. He saw where I was standing.

"How many fives in twenty-five?" the old guy asked.

"Well, there used to be five, but the way the economy is—" I said.

"Take out your pen there," he said. He pulled a pad from his shirt pocket and offered it to me. "Write twenty-five." I wrote the two numbers. "Only takes one," he said, pointing at the number five. He smiled and walked back inside.

❦❦❦

OUR BACKYARD IS SMALL. We have room for pansies in the winter and petunias in the summer. Large terracotta pots of miniature roses border the porch. The only place the car would fit was between the patio and the downstairs bedroom window.

I had managed to get the hood up and the trunk open and was walking out of our garage with as many tools as I could carry when I spotted Melissa rounding the fig tree with two glasses of wine. I could tell by the sway of her hips it wasn't her first glass.

"Very attractive," she said, gliding up the walkway. She was wearing nothing under her thin white blouse, this a picture I will carry to my grave. "If you can remove the hood and trunk lid," she said, handing me a glass, "we can convert this into a double sauna."

"Don't you mean double hot tub?" I set down my tools.

"That's exactly what I meant," she said, giving me her sexy Merlot smile. She kissed me. Her mouth was warm. "Or, we could build benches in the trunk and on the hood and have a massive picnic table. Or better yet, we could drag it over into Daniel and Linda's yard and make two sandboxes and build a fort on top for the kids." Her words were soft around the edges. "Too bad it won't be here for Easter. The children could have one hell of an egg hunt in that thing."

I sipped my wine and gave her my You've-had-your-second-glass-of-wine smile.

"Louise and I have been celebrating our yard sale finds," she said. "That woman has an eye for product." Melissa nodded a big uh-huh. "She told me this hilarious story. You've got to hear it." Her eyes were wet and bright. "You see, she came home and found Harold stumbling in their attic wearing a snorkel mask and diving fins and scanning the room with his metal detector. Hil-arious, I tell you."

We stood, arms folded, looking at the car the way people study abstract art.

"So?" she said.

"So, what?"

"Well, now that the search is over, how do you feel about it?"

"I don't know exactly. I feel like I've found it and not found it."

"In that case, your feelings will be unchanged when you've lost it again, right?"

"What?"

"This thing is way gone. You can't bring it back to life."

"Not as it is. But in some other form, maybe I can."

"You know this can't stay here, don't you." Statement not question.

"I'll figure out what to do with it. I want to give it some thought."

"Okay," she said taking hold of my arm and leading me down the walk. "But come inside with me now. And let's have a nice meal, and maybe one more glass of wine. We'll listen to music." Then she stopped, leaned in close, and whispered, "It's *Saturday night*."

They say it's not rare at my age. That it happens to every man. That it's nothing to worry about, really. Melissa was sweet about it. She ran her hand across my chest and whispered, "How's about a date in the morning? It'll be Sunday." She kissed my shoulder and rolled over. I lay motionless until I heard her slow breathing. But I couldn't sleep. My brain was revving out of control.

I slipped from our bed and crept over to the moonlit window directly above the car. Looking down, I imagined a cinematic event: The show-room-new Eldorado cruising the interstate at a hundred miles an hour, windows down, my smiling father at the wheel, I hovering above—looking out for trouble up ahead.

❧❧❧

THE FIRST THING I made was a birdbath. That was easy. I removed the air cleaner cover, set it on the steering wheel, ran a threaded rod through the hole in the cleaner top, down through the steering wheel center, secured it with two wing nuts, then mounted the steering wheel onto a length of galvanized pipe, which I cemented into the ground. A glue gun was needed to fashion a ring of cheap red beads around the rim to attract the birds.

Next, a heat gun did the work of lifting the wood-grain trim from the dash. With the aid of a jigsaw, I converted the trim into circular wine coasters. With a small hammer, I cracked the glass from the side mirrors and placed the shattered pieces inside an old white pillowcase. Looking up, I saw Melissa walking toward me.

"You're gonna like this," I said. "Very original concept."

The larger pieces of the mirror reflected the first stars of the night. I folded the pillowcase and began softly crushing the mirrors into glitter-sized shards. Melissa stood with her arms folded then turned and started back inside, speaking over her shoulder.

"Recess is over in fifteen minutes. Supper will be ready."

When the glass was finely ground, I took the radiator fan blade out into the light of the full moon and sprayed it with adhesive. I unfolded the pillowcase that held the mirror bits, laid the fan in the center, and shook the blade until it was covered with tiny reflective specks. I mounted it on the garage roof like a propeller.

After I put my ladder away, I brought out one of the patio chairs and sat in the bright moonlight of the drive. Almost at once a gentle breeze stirred and the unsteady wheel began to slowly turn. I watched the slow spiral of the mini-cosmos. I thought: That's where we come from, that's where we go. I had a random conversation with my father.

I heard a whisper and turned. Upon a pale curtain in the rear of Daniel's house, I saw the profile of a boy.

Inside, Melissa had fallen asleep on the sofa. I gently removed the white athletic socks she wore and led her to bed.

ᵛᵛᵛ

"My underwear are on fire!" Melissa shouted from the open bedroom window behind me. I was sawing a rusted nut off the chassis.

"Your underwear are always on fire," I said, not turning from my work.

"I'm calling 911."

I grabbed the fire extinguisher on the back porch. Gray smoke snaked up the wall from the outlet behind the dresser where Melissa keeps her lingerie. I switched off the main power and unplugged the curling iron, the lamp, and the thick orange power cord that I'd run out the window to supply the lights and my power tools. The curling iron had done it. The wall was still smoking. I removed the plate cover. Nothing had caught fire. I gave the wood inside a short blast from the fire extinguisher. When I turned, Melissa had risen to her full fifth grade teacher height of ten feet, hands on her hips in that posture that makes discipline not a problem in her classroom.

ᵛᵛᵛ

My imagination blossomed with creative possibilities. I began a more ambitious project. With a torch, I removed the front quarter panels. When I rested them against the house, the idea came to me full-blown: The inside of each fender was smoothly curved and large enough to hold an adult. I stripped the rotted tires from their rims then stacked one rim on another and bolted them together, forming a heavy, secure base. The plan was to convert the teardrop-shaped fenders into high-back chairs. They would be beautiful, futuristic and comfortable—made to last a thousand years.

I assembled the first one and shouted for Melissa to take a look.

"You'll have a better idea once I get it all sanded and painted and the cushions in."

She didn't speak, only tilted her head over one shoulder, stepped back and straightened up.

"This," she said, "has to stop."

❦ ❦ ❦

MY BOSS ASKED ME to drive him and the VAC transition team to the airport. On the drive back, neither McDonald nor I had much to say.

"Where did the plant go?" I asked.

"It was just absorbed, you know, into something else."

We drove without talking.

"The VAC folks," he said, "they don't have Quality Control and Safety officers."

❦ ❦ ❦

PULLING INTO THE DRIVE, I saw that Melissa had left a note on the front door. Thinking she'd soon be home from shopping, I parked the car and quickly gathered my tools. The two teardrop chairs awaited me. I used a grinder to smooth the steel and round the edges, bringing out the shine of the original metal. Special sanding brushes came next. By now it was night, so using my dolly I carted the chairs into the garage. They must have weighed two hundred pounds each. I pulled off my T-shirt and wiped the sweat from my face and chest. After hand sanding the chairs, I sat to catch my breath and appraise my work. They were magnificent, like commander's seats on a spacecraft. Melissa would love these. She should have been home by now, I thought.

I'd discovered that the mirror mounts turned horizontally made perfect wineglass holders. Working to the music of cicadas and tree frogs, I drilled the holes.

The five cans of expensive automotive enamel spray paint I'd bought— two bright yellow, Melissa's favorite color, and two bright blue, my own, along with one can of black—came next. The black paint was for the wineglass holders, the blue for the rim bases, and the yellow for the chairs. I was very careful, applying fine, thin coats of the yellow and blue, allowing the two colors to blend just enough to form a bright green band where the base joined the seat.

Suddenly I felt exhausted. I sat on the cool cement garage floor and wiped my face with my dirty shirt. I checked my watch. It was two in the morning.

I ran to the back door and into the kitchen. Standing in the dining room, I saw the table, formally set: wedding china, wedding silver, and wedding crystal. Anniversary linen napkins and flowers. The candles had melted onto the white embroidered tablecloth where our wedding cake had once stood.

I lifted Melissa from the sofa and helped her upstairs, undressed her, and got her into bed.

When I woke the next morning, she was back on the sofa asleep. When I tried to wake her to say that I was sorry, she gave me an odd, distant look as if she didn't recognize me. She turned away and closed her eyes.

On the dining room table beside where she'd set my plate, I spotted a thin, rectangular package wrapped in old newspaper. I gently pulled the paper away. Inside, in an antique frame, were the title to my father's car and Kevin Asher's scribbled two-word note: "Go figger."

Something about the yellowed newspaper caught my eye. On the front page were two major stories, one about an air show accident in which a plane crashed into a crowd of spectators, and the other about a local man who'd won a lottery.

I thought of the odds and what it could have meant.

On my way out the front door, I saw the note Melissa had left there yesterday. The paper was scented with perfume she knows I like.

❦❦❦

I'D SPENT ALL MORNING working on end-run samples, when a fistfight broke out in the Converting Area. I rushed from my office out onto the catwalk. Below, crowded on the plant floor, I saw the circle of bodies competing for a view. Muscling my way through, I saw my friend Lonnie, who was working out his two weeks' notice, holding a bloody handkerchief against the side of his face.

The two of us spent the afternoon in the emergency room. Lonnie didn't speak, even when I dropped him off at his truck in the parking lot back at the plant.

Before shutting off my computer, I checked email. The memo from Mark McDonald consisted of one sentence: Time to assess your Performance Evaluation Graphs.

✾✾✾

THERE WAS A SECOND note on our front door. This one said, Have Gone Out.

Passing through the empty house, I picked up the framed Eldorado title and continued out the back door. I sat in the shell of the car, in front of what had once been a steering wheel looking at the anniversary gift my wife had prepared for me. My next project plan had been to cut the roof and rear panels into circles, paint them bright colors, and suspend them with cable to make an enormous mobile, those things you see over cribs sometimes, for the playground at Melissa's elementary school. Now, I just wanted rid of the junk.

I reached for my wallet, dug out the picture of my father and the Eldorado, and laid the photo beside the title and Kevin's note. I pondered the combination of title, image, and text.

For a moment, I moved outside myself, becoming an observer of the car's remains and of myself as I sat surrounded by them. "Go figger," I said.

✾✾✾

AT THE HOBBY SHOP, the clerk took my credit card.

"You want that wrapped?" he said, looking down at the telescope I'd bought. "We have some cool birthday wrap for kids."

"No thanks," I said.

✾✾✾

THE FLORIST ASKED HOW many roses I wanted. I joined my hands and made a hoop of my arms. He bowed his head. "Oooh," he said. "Miss it by one day, or more?"

"One," I said.

"I don't have a vase that big."

"Don't want a vase."

"I could tie them together with some heavy, pretty ribbon."

"Don't need ribbon."

He bent his head again. "That bad, huh?"

He returned from the refrigerated vault with a white plastic trash bag filled with red roses. I reached for my wallet as he laid them gently on the counter.

"How would you like the card to read?" he asked.

"No card." I said. "How much?"

"These are yesterday's." He paused, then looked up. "In this heat, by the time you get them home—half price."

I buckled the roses in the passenger seat and angled the air conditioning vents to keep them cool. There was a light tap on my window. The florist held up a smaller bag.

"Here," he said. "You'll need this." I saw tiny, bright specks inside the bag. "Baby's breath," he said.

"Thanks," I said. "What's your name?"

"Vapor," he said.

❦❦❦

DANIEL, WHO IS YOUNGER and stronger than I am, carried the base end of each chair as we wobbled and bobbled our way up the stairs to the bedroom. We set down a chair on each side of the telescope, which I'd centered in front of the window overlooking the Eldorado's remains, then stepped back, both of us panting. Smiling, Daniel pulled a handkerchief from his hip pocket and swiped his black stubble.

"Nice," he said.

❦❦❦

I ARRANGED THE ROSES in Melissa's chair, adding sprays of the tiny white flowers. After positioning and focusing the telescope, I poured two glasses of red wine and set them in the special holders mounted on the chairs. The overpowering scent of roses filled the room. I showered then rested back on the pillows of our bed and watched as dancing dust specks drifted around our trio of spaceship chairs and telescope. I closed my eyes.

You'd never guess it if you saw us now, but when we were young Melissa and I made a striking couple. On our honeymoon cruise, strangers from all over came up to us and asked if Melissa was a movie star or if I was a rock singer. I still wore long hair then; Melissa liked it. A nice thing about being married so young is that you have those memories. You knew her then and can still see her that way forever.

❦❦❦

I WAS SUSPENDED INSIDE a warm, effervescent ocean current, floating weightlessly, when, from somewhere inside my dream, the voice of The Prophets drifted up. I opened my eyes. Through the window, buoyant cosmic particles streamed in on a slanting channel of yellow afternoon sunshine that bathed the chairs, the telescope. Tiny points of light sparkled upon luminous, blood-red petals, and the thick smell of roses filled my insides. At the sound of Melissa's lovely out-of-tune singing, I sat up in our bed.

At the bottom of the stairs, I called her name softly and crept up the hall toward the music. The living room shades were drawn. Melissa—who had tuned in the oldies station—danced across the carpet wearing only a thin sexy gown and white athletic socks. Two sparkling glasses and a full bottle of wine sat on the table. She sang along with KC and the Sunshine Band.

I stepped closer. She looked away. Lifting her arms above her head, she wailed louder and more dissonantly. She turned and glanced up at me, her body freely swaying in lovely motion and countermotion.

As the song faded, she shouted the words to "Get Down Tonight." Her eyes were the color of a blue flame. "Drop 'em," she demanded, spinning and sliding across the carpet away from me.

I fumbled with my trousers. A Beach song from a group called The Band of Oz began. She suddenly reversed direction in a moon walk and skated around me in those white socks. I stepped out of my pants and kicked them across the thick, soft carpet. As she orbited me, I lifted my arms to her. Maintaining her distance, she tilted forward and wiggled her school teacher's index finger, dancing non-stop. "The shorts, they have to go."

I tucked my thumbs inside the boxers.

"I'm taking you to the Land of Oz—so that we can get back home."

She did the steps in double time. I really do like those socks.

"Take me home!" I shouted over the music.

She slid across the carpet to me.

Looking down at my nakedness, she whispered, "And Toto is going with us." Pirouetting, Melissa lowered her index finger to my unimpressive penis.

I would swear that the blue spark jumped from two inches away, a bolt of static electricity that sent my manhood scurrying like a hermit crab.

"That's what you get my little *pretty!*" she shrieked in perfect Wicked Witch. Tearing off toward the hall, she cried, "Ah-ha-ha-ha-ha! Where are the batteries for my broom?"

"You're gonna get it," I shouted looking down at myself. I heard her laughing up the stairs. "You've never had it till you've had it from a flying monkey wearing a bellboy's cap!"

"Hurry," she called. "I'm melllllting."

At our bedroom door I stopped. Laughing still, Melissa sat before the window in the teardrop chair banked by roses. She looked me up and down, closed her eyes and slowly recovered her breath. From a cluster of roses, she held up a small spray of tiny white flowers like an offering. Her eyes filled with tears. Lifting them to mine, she softly smiled.

"Baby's breath," she whispered. She brought the tiny blooms to her cheek. "I don't want to talk now," she said. "Later but not now. Okay?"

"Okay," I said. I sat in the chair beside her. We were silent. On the western horizon the evening sun, an immense flaming ember, descended into night, and from the east the full moon, a levitating snowball, lit up the selfsame night. The sweet scent of roses poured over us. A trace of a smile formed upon Melissa's lips. Below, the El Dorado idled softly. She took my hand. My fingers stroked her warm wrist, and I felt the rush of blood there, the life coursing through her. I closed my eyes. And I knew with infinite certainty that beyond my last breath I'd still want her in my arms.

About the Author

Phillip Gardner is a three-time South Carolina Fiction Project winner and a Piccolo Spoleto Fiction Open winner. His stories have appeared in the *North American Review, New Delta Review, LIT, Interim, The Chattahoochee Review,* and other journals. His stories have been anthologized in *Inheritance: Selections from The South Carolina Fiction Project* (Hub City Writers Project) and *A Shared Voice* (Lamar University Press). He is the author of two short story collections, *Someone To Crawl Back To* and *Somebody Wants Somebody Dead* (Boson Books). He teaches at Francis Marion University.

Acknowledgments

Grateful appreciation to the following, where these stories first appeared:

"Brother" *A Shared Voice: Writers from the Carolinas and Texas* (Lamar University Press)

"Everything I Needed To Know" *LIT*

"Get Drunk and Screw" *North American Review*

"Glory Day" *Louisiana Literature*

"Kids Rule" *Post and Courier* (South Carolina Fiction Project)

"Safe Storage" *REAL: Regarding Arts and Letters*

"That Place Love Built" *Potomac Review*

"There's Someone's Shadow in This One" *Eclipse*

"These Are The Eyes Of Nora Jones" *Euphony Journal*

"Things That Smell Like Food" *Cadillac Cicatrix*

"You Can Laugh If You Want To" *Interim*

"What We Talk About When We Talk About Dean Martin," Jubilee Harvest of Arts Literary Competition

"Winner Take Nothing" *Baltimore Review*

Thanks to my friends who have been generous readers and to my good colleagues. You know who you are. And special thanks to Francis Marion University for its many years of generous support.

www.ingramcontent.com/pod-product-compliance
Lightning Source LLC
Chambersburg PA
CBHW071331250626
47159CB00004B/1560